PRAISE FOR *EXPECTANT*

'From the opening pages, this story left me gasping for breath'
Michael Robotham

'New Zealand's modern Queen of Crime' Val McDermid

'Chillingly intense with a finely honed sense of place ...
Vanda Symon knows Dunedin and brings it vibrantly to life in this
fast-paced thriller' Craig Robertson

'An excellent thriller, *definitely* one of the best of this year. Vanda
Symon is a master of characterisation, plot and dialogue, and with
every book, she exceeds expectations. I loved every moment'
Liz Nugent

'From the ominous and shocking beginning to the heart-pounding
ending, *Expectant* had me in its grasp ... It was great to be back in
Sam's world again ... an every-woman, witty, clever, hilarious,
vulnerable and so extremely relatable ... I'm fully invested in her'
Nikki Crutchley

'I love this series. Sam Shephard is such a wonderful character, full
of determination and bravado, down to earth and as witty as you
could ask for ... Emotional, tense, dramatic and just bloody good
fun to read' Jen Med's Book Reviews

'Full of tension, twists and great characters. A shocking crime
shakes the community, but is this a one-off? Happy to recommend
all Vanda's books to crime-thriller fans' Independent Book Reviews

PRAISE FOR VANDA SYMON

'Fast-moving New Zealand procedural ... the Edinburgh of the
south has never been more deadly' Ian Rankin

'A sassy heroine, fabulous sense of place, and rip-roaring stories
with a twist. Perfect curl-up-on-the-sofa reading' Kate Mosse

'If you like taut, pacy thrillers with a wonderful sense of place, this is the book for you' Liam McIlvanney

'All the thrills of a brilliantly plotted crime novel with some interesting moral questions woven between the words. Fast, furious and intense' Helen Fields

'Edgy, thrilling and terrifyingly realistic' Lisa Hall

'New Zealand's answer to Siobhan Clarke' *The Times*

'It is Symon's copper Sam, self-deprecating and very human, who represents the writer's real achievement' *Guardian*

'An absolute must-have' *Daily Express*

'Vanda Symon's work resembles Janet Evanovich's Stephanie Plum series. She knows how to tell a good story and the NZ setting adds spice' *The Times* Crime Club

'Grabs the reader's attention with a heart-stopping opening and doesn't let go' *Sunday Times*

'A deeply involving novel and a damn good thriller' *NB Magazine*

'Completely gripping' Eve Smith

'Fans of *The Dry* will love Vanda Symon' *Red Magazine*

'Atmospheric, emotional and gripping' *Foreword Reviews*

'Reads like the polished effort of a genre veteran. More, please' *Booklist*

'Another cracking story of life in the police down in Dunedin in New Zealand with our heroine Sam Shephard right in the thick of it' J. L. Nicol

'Real verve and personality ... Excellent storytelling from an author who goes from strength to strength' *Mystery Magazine*

'Powerful, coolly assured, and an absolute belter of a read' LoveReading

ABOUT THE AUTHOR

Vanda Symon is a crime writer from Dunedin, New Zealand, and the President of the New Zealand Society of Authors Te Puni Kaituhi o Aotearoa. The Sam Shephard series, which includes *Overkill*, *The Ringmaster*, *Containment* and *Bound*, hit number one on the New Zealand bestseller list, and has also been shortlisted for the Ngaio Marsh Award. *Overkill* was shortlisted for the CWA John Creasey (New Blood) Dagger. All four books have been ebook bestsellers. Vanda currently lives in Dunedin, with her husband and Louie the cat.

Follow Vanda on Twitter @vandasymon, Instagram @vandasymon, Facebook, @vandasymonauthor or her website, www.vandasymon.com.

Other titles by Vanda Symon available from Orenda Books:
The Sam Shephard Series
Overkill
The Ringmaster
Containment
Bound

Faceless

Expectant

Vanda Symon

ORENDA BOOKS

Orenda Books
16 Carson Road
West Dulwich
London SE21 8HU
www.orendabooks.co.uk

First published in the United Kingdom by Orenda Books 2023

A catalogue record for this book is available from the British Library.

ISBN 978-1-914585-57-9
eISBN 978-1-914585-58-6

Typeset in Garamond by typesetter.org.uk

Printed and bound by CPI Group (UK) Ltd, Croydon CR0 4YY

For sales and distribution, please contact *info@orendabooks.co.uk* or visit
www.orendabooks.co.uk.

To all of the loved ones lost

PROLOGUE

The group swaggered their way down Moray Place, voices loud, giving each other light-hearted grief. They were like any group of teenagers – full of themselves, finding their own fun, out a bit too late on a school night. They came around the bend, heading down-hill towards George Street, but as if on cue, they took a left and ducked down the red-brick Victorian alleyway. The swagger dropped, hoodies were pulled up, and the banter pitch dropped to a soft murmur. The low lighting barely threw shadows as they de-scended the darkened, tunnel-like passage. One of them stopped as he entered, running a hand across the mural, tracing the line of a spindly leg.

'What about here? Everyone will see it.'

The others slowed, turned back to consider the proposal.

Timi shook his head. 'Nah, you can't do that. That's art. We don't shit on other people's art.'

The others turned and moved on. With a shrug, the youth fol-lowed them down towards the open courtyard, still running his fingers along the wall. It was late, and patrons of the hip bar along the side of the lane had toasted their last drinks and gone home. Apart from a couple of cars, the place appeared deserted. All angles and alcoves, the courtyard provided plenty of opportunities out of sight of prying eyes.

'Over here – this one is perfect.'

They stood in front of the wall, a blank canvas awaiting their touch.

'Sweet.'

The quiet was broken by the staccato rattle of ball-bearing peas clicking up and down as spray cans were shaken. They set to, arms sweeping and circling, the sharp tang of solvent and paint cutting the air. They worked in well-practised unison, their moves throwing choreographed shadows in the dim light. They worked quickly – being caught wasn't an option – and the downside of their chosen alleyway was there was only one way in, and one way out. It was high-risk, but it would be worth the reward of having an epic tag here, right in the middle of town.

The *schhhhh* of the spray and shuffling and murmuring of the boys drifted into the night, but then, unnoticed at first, another sound infiltrated, a moaning, low and sporadic.

Timi stopped spraying, tilted his head, straining to listen. There it was again. His heartbeat bounced up. Had someone spotted them? Were they sprung? His head spun around, looking up towards the entrance, but there was no one there. Then he heard it again and realised it wasn't coming from the street, and it didn't sound human. It sounded like an animal, and it was coming from further down the alley. He placed his spray can down on the asphalt and walked cautiously in the direction of the noise.

'Hey, whatcha doing, bro?'

Timi lifted his hand, signalling them to stop.

'I heard something. I think there's a dog or something down there.'

'Well, don't let it get ya. Might bite you, give you the rabies or something.' The sentence was followed by a giggle.

Then he heard the sound again, and there was some quality about it that set every nerve on high alert. It was the sound of suffering, it was the sound of pain, and it was a sound that compelled him forward, urgency overcoming fear. He rounded the corner of a small alcove and stopped dead, his mind grappling to come to terms with what he saw.

The dark stains had to be blood, so much blood. She was lying on her back, both hands clasped around her gaping, oozing belly. The light and shadows must have been playing tricks on his eyes, because he couldn't be sure, but it looked like she'd been sliced in two. His nose was assaulted by a hot, sweet smell that left a metallic tang in the back of his throat.

'Jesus,' he uttered.

Her eyes lifted slowly to meet his, and she let out that primal groan, and everything about the fucked-up sight before him triggered the urge to run.

He stepped backward. 'Guys,' he yelled, 'come here.'

'What is it, bro? A cute puppy dog?' More giggling.

'You got to get here now.'

The panic in Timi's voice must have got them moving, because moments later three figures appeared behind him.

'What's the prob—. Holy fuck.' Hands grabbed at Timi's arms. 'We got to get out of here, bro. We got to get out of here now. We will be in so much shit if they find us here with her. Come on. We have to go.'

Timi staggered backward with the pull, backing away from the woman sprawled before them.

'But we can't just leave her here,' he said, pushing away the hands. 'She needs help.'

'Nothing's going to help her, and if they find us with her, they'll think we did it. Come on, Timi, we gotta go.' Desperation laced his mate's voice, and the others echoed it. 'Come on' and 'Let's get outta here.'

'But what if she dies? And we didn't help. We've got to do something.'

'Jesus, Timi, she's gonna die. No one's gonna survive that, and if the cops find us, they'll think we done it – they always think people like us done it. Don't be a dick. Come on, man.'

'Yeah, move it, Timi.' The others turned and took off, the sounds of their retreating footsteps echoing off the brick walls.

But Timi stood there, staring, torn. He looked over his shoulder after his mates bolting for freedom, then looked back to the woman, to those exhausted, fading eyes. Decision made, he made his move.

He stepped forward and knelt down beside her, angling his body as close as he could get. Fuck, there was so much blood, and he could feel the wetness of it seeping into the fabric of his jeans. He placed one hand over hers, and with the other reached up and gently cupped her face.

'It's okay. I'm here, I'm gonna get you some help,'

She closed her eyes and a big tear rolled down the side of her nose.

'You'll be okay,' he said, softly rubbing his thumb along her cheek, keeping his eyes fixed on her face, resisting the pull to look further down.

'I'm here,' he whispered. 'You're not alone.'

CHAPTER 1

'Are you Timi's parents?' It was a rhetorical question really. The incandescent man before me was the spitting image of the boy, but with about twenty-five years' extra wear and tear. The woman with him looked a seesawing tussle of upset and ropable.

'Where is he? Where is the little shit? I can't believe we've been called down to the police station at this hour.' This was delivered with a fair amount of gusto, and given the fact he was at least a foot taller than me and clearly agitated, it was rather intimidating. 'Wait till I get my hands on him.'

No one was going to be getting their hands on Timi anytime soon. Given the circumstances, we'd taken the exceptional act of letting him use the showers, and found him some clean clothing – although, alas, it was police-custody issue. Our youth-liaison officer was still with him, having accompanied the poor young lad through the process of being photographed, swabbed and examined for forensic evidence, before finally being able to cleanse himself of the woman's blood. He hadn't been formally interviewed yet – that was still to come, and in the light of day – but we knew enough to realise he'd had the kind of night you wouldn't wish upon anyone, let alone a teenage boy.

'Hi, I'm Detective Sam Shephard.' I reached out to shake Thomas Felipo's hand, and as my arm extended his eyes dropped, took in my extremely rotund midriff, and with an almost apologetic look cautiously took my hand. Whoever thought a pregnant belly could so effectively defuse a pissed-off parent. In fact, there had been a number of occasions when my condition had helped calm a situation, which was a good thing, because if it came to beating a hasty retreat, I was now in waddle rather than run mode.

'Come through, let me explain the situation.'

The stark lighting in the family interview room did nothing to soften the expressions of anger that morphed into horror, then disbelief, on the faces of Timi Felipo's parents. It was now 1.00am, and I was quite sure the lighting was doing me no favours either. Sina Felipo sat silent, her hands clasped in her lap as she struggled to absorb the events of the night and what it meant for her son. Her husband for the most part was fixated on why Timi was out in the first place and was barraging me with questions about the tagging. I don't know if it was a deflection thing, but he was completely missing the point about the extraordinary actions of his son, and the profound effect it was likely to have on him. I was tired and borderline hangry, and it took immense patience to calmly redirect his focus away from the fact his teenager had been out vandalising public places with his mates, to the fact that he had committed an act of incredible bravery and humanity.

'Yes, he was down the laneway with a group of his friends tagging, and there is no way I can condone that,' I said, for what felt like the millionth time. 'But what he did was remarkable. When all his friends ran off because they were scared of what they had seen and of being caught and potentially blamed, he chose to stay. He chose to stay with a horrendously injured woman, who he knew was probably going to die, right there and then. He offered her what comfort he could, he made sure she didn't die alone. That is an incredible thing for anyone to do in those circumstances, let alone a sixteen-year-old boy. You should be very proud of him.'

'But he shouldn't have been there in the first place. We brought him up better than that.'

'We thought he was at his friend Oscar's house to study, not out on the streets. He lied to us.' It was the first time Sina had really participated in the conversation, and I felt disappointed that she too chose to take the offended-parent angle.

'True, he was doing something wrong. But when it came to the crunch, he made the courageous choice.'

'So, what will happen to him now?' she asked.

'Well, for a start, the most important thing is that he is supported and looked after. He's had a big shock. He witnessed the result of an awful, vicious crime, and he was alone with a dying person. That is a lot to deal with, so he'll have our counsellors spend time with him and talk him through all that. There was no way he could have prevented her dying, so we have to make sure he knows that in his heart of hearts. That is where it will be really important for you to support him and keep an eye on him.'

'But will he be charged for the tagging?' Thomas asked.

'That I can't say for sure. The circumstances are pretty unique, and the trauma he has suffered will be taken into account, I'm sure. Before all that, though, he'll have to make a statement about tonight, and ultimately, when we do find out who was responsible for this heinous crime, he may have to appear in court to testify. But we'll cross that bridge when we come to it. For now, take him home for some sleep, and bring him back in the morning so we can take his statement.'

I hoped to God they had listened to my words about support, and focussed on how brave their son had been and what an awful experience he'd been through. Although I suspected there would be harsh words about why he was in the alleyway in the first place.

What that boy needed was hugs not hassle.

CHAPTER 2

Dunedin was waking up to the news of the horrendous crime committed on its streets overnight, and I was waking up to the shocking details the media and general public still weren't party to – details we didn't have last night. Courtesy of my expanded girth and imminent popping I always got a chair at the briefings these days, and, man, was I glad of it this morning. Even The Boss, who usually revelled in the drama of standing front and centre, looked sickened by the report being delivered by Detective Malcolm Smith, AKA Smithy.

'The woman who was murdered last night was thirty-one-year-old Aleisha Newman. Her partner has been spoken with, and he is still contacting family, so her name has not been released to the media. What he was able to tell us – and this changes the case completely – is that Ms Newman was thirty-eight weeks pregnant.'

There were some confused looks about the room, but the relevance of that statement hit me immediately, and I felt a wave of cold rush its way down my face. My hands immediately wrapped themselves around my own very pregnant belly as I braced myself for what I knew would be coming next.

Smithy released a large breath and continued. 'Last night, before this information came to hand, and based on a first report from the attending ambulance staff, we thought we were looking at a homicide by stabbing. It is now apparent that the victim died as a result of the massive trauma and blood loss of having her unborn child cut out of her. That child is now missing.'

A collective gasp went around the room, followed by a stunned silence. I couldn't help the swell of tears that sprung into my eyes. A large hand reached over and clamped onto mine. I turned and saw my horror reflected in Paul's eyes.

When I looked back to the front of the room DI Johns was staring in my direction. Usually in team meetings a stare from The Boss, AKA Dick Head Johns, meant I was going to get called out for special attention of the unwanted kind, but this time he gave a tight-lipped, almost apologetic frown and then looked down at the floor.

'We will have more details after the postmortem, but the paediatric and gynaecological specialists at the hospital say the child could still be alive, and until this is proved otherwise, we are going to assume that they are. So, this case is now a murder and a kidnapping.'

CHAPTER 3

The air in the CIB room was sombre to say the least. We had all walked back to the office lost in our thoughts. Mine were turbulent, chopping from anger to disgust to disbelief to horror. My hyperactive imagination could almost feel the slice of steel below my belly, and I couldn't help but wince as my hands, yet again, cupped the precious cargo. I felt a reassuring wriggle within.

'Well, that's about the most horrific thing I've ever heard in my life.' Otto had been around for a long time and had spent considerable time serving overseas, so coming from him that was saying something.

His words broke the ice, and a torrent of comments and exclamations washed around the room. The overwhelming theme was utter disbelief that something so awful could happen in good ole New Zealand, let alone boring Dunners. Dunedin was pretty much Grand Conservative Central. The most exciting things that happened here usually involved drunk students or the ever-present illicit drug scene. This was the kind of abomination that happened in violent, lawless countries, not here. I couldn't get a word in edgeways. Not that I wanted to. I was tired and emotional, and afraid my voice might betray me. The banter stopped as suddenly as it started with the arrival of DI Johns – he who must be obeyed.

'Right, everyone. As you can imagine we are going to be under immense pressure to find whoever did this, and fast. The people of Dunedin are going to be nervous and scared until we get this monster behind bars.' He didn't need to point out the obvious, but never missed an opportunity to make a dramatic speech. 'And it's not just pressure locally. We're already fielding calls from international media outlets. The scrutiny will be intense.'

He paused, as if waiting for comment, or acknowledgement. None came.

'Do you understand?' he asked, real slow. I resisted the urge to eye-roll.

A murmur of obligatory 'yes, sir's' and 'uh-huh's' circulated the room.

'As I said in the station briefing, Detective Smith will be in charge of the operation, and in a moment he will allocate the lead roles.' Now that he was in a small room with the less-impressionable detectives, rather than leading the briefing to the full cast, The Boss spoke with a little less theatre. A little.

'The majority of you will be involved in this case, but Detective Shephard, you will be dealing with current cases that are not so urgent.'

What the...? I had already interviewed a potential witness and set the ball rolling for them for support and follow-up statements. Why the hell was I being excluded now? Dick Head Johns had a history of keeping me away from the coal face in investigations and giving me the shit jobs, but I'd thought we'd all grown up a bit and started moving on from there.

'I'm sorry, sir, I don't understand. I've already been active in the case from the first callout, why am I not able to continue?'

'Well, given that you are only going to be here for another few weeks and are on light duties, your time is best used elsewhere, finishing up cases rather than starting on a new one.' It was semi-reasonable logic, if your idea of logic involved taking a passing glance at a situation and that glance happened to be myopic. I wasn't about to get shelved that easily. And anyway, I was pretty sure he'd be expecting some pushback. I didn't want to disappoint.

'But given the pressure we are under to get this murder solved, as you stated clearly in the briefing, and we're going to be very much in the spotlight, isn't it better to have as many detectives working on the case as possible?'

The rest of the room went conspicuously silent, and I could sense everyone holding their breath to see the reaction to someone questioning The Boss's decisions. It didn't happen often, and when it did, the results weren't always favourable. I don't know whether it was the pregnancy thing, or the lack of sleep thing, or that I'd simply run out of fucks to give when it came to The Boss, but I was in a 'don't just accept it' kind of mood.

The Boss drew in a large breath that made his nostrils flare.

'Detective Shephard, given your imminent departure for maternity leave, there is no point whatsoever you starting on a new case.' His tone was careful but tinged with something else. Condescension? Always. But this time with a pinch of ... what was that? Concern? Before I could figure out the angle, he dropped the clanger. 'I also don't believe, because of your own advanced state of pregnancy, that you would be able to remain objective and emotionally detached from this case.'

The vacuum created by everyone behind me sucking in air almost pulled me backward. I felt a wave of heat rush up my face as my brain absorbed the statement, replaying the words in my head. I couldn't remain objective? What the actual fuck? My eyes flicked over to Paul and took in the startled look on his face. He gave me a slight shake of the head, his eyes widening with warning. When my eyes found their way back to The Boss, Smithy, standing behind Dick Head Johns, was mirroring Paul's micro-message. For once they were in agreement. The Boss bore the expression of someone who fully believed they were right, and were being reasonable.

I inhaled deeply and started to count to ten before I had a crack at showing him just how reasonable I thought he was being. By the time I reached five I'd taken in Smithy's waist-level, hidden hand gestures: *You, me, talk*. I wanted so badly to ask Johns if that meant he was going to stand Paul down from the case too, because he wouldn't be able to be objective, being the father of the offending bump and all. I wanted even more badly to ask if that meant every time a bloke was killed, none of the male detectives would be allowed on the case because they couldn't be objective, because, you know, they all had penises, just like the victim. But at ten I let out the breath I'd been holding, bit my tongue and sucked it up. I was here to win the war, not the battle.

CHAPTER 4

'Don't even start. You don't need to say it.' Smithy got in first before I could unleash the tirade of anger and frustration he knew was coming. He had wandered along to the kitchenette and was in the process of mixing his standard coffee with three sugars. I was a bit of a coffee snob and only drank the barista variety. His particular brew of instant crap was referred to as 'tragic coffee', but only behind his back, of course.

I was just about to say it anyway when Paul appeared around the corner, sliding with Krameresque style and the look of someone about to make a proclamation.

'And don't you start either,' Smithy said, waving his teaspoon.

Paul took pause, noted the waving spoon and turned his attention to me. 'That was a total load of bollocks. Of course you can be objective. In fact, I'd have thought given that' – he pointed to my ample girth – 'you'd be both objective and probably the most motivated person in the room, or at least second-most motivated.'

The vote of confidence made me feel a bit better, but also spurred me on.

'You know he'd never say something like that to one of you guys, and especially not in front of everyone. He just can't help shitting on me, arrogant bastard.'

Smithy eyed the open door, tapped his ear then pointed out to the hallway. He was right. It wasn't exactly private. I lowered my voice, leaning forward to make sure I was heard.

'He's a misogynistic—'

'Yeah, yeah, enough of that. Not denying it.' Smithy still had his teaspoon in hand and was waving it around like a conductor. 'And we all know he can't help himself, but don't make it worse than it is. You know how he gets when he's under pressure.'

Did we what.

'But he was wrong. I should be a part of this investigation. I already have been.' I thought back to the blood-covered young man I'd counselled earlier. God, I hoped his parents had taken what I said on board. Poor kid. The thought also reminded me how flaming tired I was. I failed to stifle the yawn. Some non-tragic coffee might be in order.

The yawn had been noted though. 'You really should head home and get some rest. You've been up half the night.'

Paul may have been well meaning, but after The Boss's declaration earlier I'd had quite enough of men making assumptions on my welfare. He looked a little confused at the withering look I gave him.

'Look, Sam, don't you worry about The Boss,' Smithy said. 'He's put me in charge of the case, and we need everyone on board. Frankly, we don't have the staff and the luxury of being selective, and I'm damned if I'll leave you on the sideline for this. You'll have a role, just give me a bit of time to figure it out. It may have to be on the periphery though.'

'To keep off his radar?' I asked.

'That's one thing,' he said. 'But also, he is absolutely adamant you won't be able to be in contact with the victim's family.'

I chucked him a baffled look.

'With you finishing up soon, he doesn't want them getting used to having you working with them and building up that rapport, and then next thing you're gone. And he does have a point there.'

Somehow I didn't think The Boss's motives were that noble.

'That's one stance I won't be able to fudge for you. But if you stop and think about it, it would be a bit tough on them to deal with someone about to have a baby of their own, considering who they've just lost, and that their baby is still missing.'

The mere thought of their loss gave me a sick and sinking feeling in my stomach. I hadn't really thought about that. He did have point. For a big-unit bloke with a perpetually grumpy demeanour, Smithy could be thoughtful at times. It made up for some of my other misgivings about him. At least the case was in good hands.

CHAPTER 5

'Sam, wake up. Sam...'

I startled awake with a big gasp of breath, and a twitch that near threw me off the bed. 'Shit, what?'

'You were moaning and yelling out in your sleep.'

'Ugh, I was?' I moved my arm out from under me and winced as the pins and needles from sleeping on it weird hit with a vengeance. I checked the time on my watch – 3.35pm – and then deposited the back of the hand on my forehead.

'Well, you were sort of yelling. You were doing that muffled shouty thing that sounds like you have a pair of socks stuffed in your mouth.'

I smacked my tongue onto the roof of my mouth. It tasted like the said socks had spent a couple of days wrapped around wet feet stuffed in tramping boots. It wasn't ideal. A remnant wave of the dream Maggie had just rescued me from washed through my mind, and the dread and repulsion it evoked made my eyes well with tears. I squeezed them shut.

'Hey, you okay?' I felt her hand rubbing my shoulder. I was but I wasn't. Maggie was my flatmate, and my rock. Calling her my best friend didn't even come close to summing up what she meant to me. It wasn't often in the world you found people who just got you. She got me.

'Ugh, tough case at work, no sleep, rampant hormones, impending popping, you about to bugger off and leave me, and the worst case of parrot mouth known to mankind, but other than that, I'm fine.'

'So same old, same old, then?'

'Yup.' I managed a smile. I tried to push myself up into a sitting position, but courtesy of my rather changed centre of gravity I had to do a few rocks to get some momentum going. Finally got there. 'I think tea is in order.'

'No argument from me.'

We wandered out to the kitchen, and Maggie set about filling the kettle and finding the requisite packet of Toffee Pops biscuits. I stared out the window, trying to replace the tumultuous images in my head with something more calming. The backyard of our house was dense with trees, which as well as providing a sense of peace and solitude, attracted a multitude of native birds. The energetic flitting of a couple of wax-eyes feeding off the bright-yellow flowers of the kōwhai tree provided a welcome antidote to the deep-seated unease from my dreams. Torie the cat sat on the window ledge doing that odd jaw-clacking thing cats do when potential fodder is in their sights. Fortunately for the birds she was on this side of the glass.

'I've caught a few snippets on the news about the woman found down the alley off Moray Place. I'm guessing that's the case you're re-ferring to. It sounds pretty horrific.'

Maggie slid me over a mug, and I wrapped my hands around its warmth.

'It's the stuff of nightmares.'

She smiled while raiding the biscuit packet. 'Well that much is obvious. Who the hell could commit an atrocity like that – and why?'

Why indeed? So far my brain had imagined everything from a des-perate need to be a parent, to black-market baby snatchers to alien abductions. The last idea only went to prove how tired and distraught I was by the whole thing. I looked down at the rather large bump sitting on my lap. This case was shit timing.

Maggie noticed the direction of my gaze. 'Do you think you're up to being part of the investigation?'

If anyone else had asked that question of me I would have shouted them down with the indignance of someone who had an axe to grind and a mind of where to bury it. But because it came from Maggie, I had pause to honestly consider the question. Was I up to it? Could I be objective? There had been plenty of occasions in my professional career when I had needed to set aside my personal views and demons in order to get on with the job. Sometimes that had been successful, on others, spectacularly not. But even in those instances where I had followed my heart rather than my head, my instincts – or some would say my impulsiveness, inability to follow the prescribed rules and general pig-headedness – had provided the breakthrough that was needed, even if it came at a personal cost.

I knew there was no way in hell I would be able to keep emotion out of this investigation, but this wasn't a case where being emotionally compromised would prevent me from fulfilling my duties. I wasn't captaining the bridge of the Starship Enterprise, for heaven's sake. I was trying to find justice for a family in mourning, and, more importantly, justice for a murdered woman, her and her children's futures stolen. In a way, my unique perspective was a strength. I too was expectant, waiting to bring life into the world. I felt vulnerable, repulsed ... and something else. What was it? As I cradled my hands around my belly I realised what I felt was anger. Deep-seated anger. Rage that someone could have committed such an atrocity against someone else – someone so vulnerable. It was that anger that would sustain me through this. It was that anger that would focus my mind, channel my critical thinking. I would find justice for Aleisha Newman. This felt personal.

CHAPTER 6

The morning briefing had been a case of lots on the go but no break-throughs. Not that anyone in their right mind had expected a miracle overnight – other than the media of course; miracles were good click bait and made it easier to sell papers. The entire front page of the *Otago Daily Times* had been dedicated to the case, along with the tabloi-desque headline 'Mother Killer Still At Large.' It wasn't helpful. The quarter-page photograph beneath the headline showed a windswept family on the esplanade at St Clair Beach on a clear, sunny day. They were in front of the shark bell. My mind was trying to find some strange significance in that. Justin Newman stood, arm around his wife's shoulders, wisps of Aleisha Newman's long, dark hair swept across the face of the cherubic girl she was holding in her arms – the cherubic girl holding on to her floral bucket sunhat, trying to keep it on her head. They all wore the grins of people who were having a stellar day. Ac-cording to the caption beneath the picture, the girl's name was Charlotte. My heart went out to that wee girl, to the mother she would grow up not knowing, to the family that had been shattered.

The team had sprung into action, canvassing as far and wide as they could with their basic preliminary investigations. Businesses in the immediate vicinity of the alleyway had been called on. Most were retail stores so weren't open at the time the crime took place, but they were checked to see if they had security-camera footage that had cap-tured anything that could be of assistance. Trouble was, Dunedinites were a trusting lot, so most security footage was of blind spots in the shop and the till area, to spot staff ripping off their bosses. Okay, so maybe they were not that trusting. Coverage of the store entrance was also popular. Unfortunately, most didn't offer a wider view that included the street. Likewise, the security surveillance of the bou-tique bars down the alleyway was minimal, generally consisting of the inside of the premises and one external camera trained onto the door. Also not very helpful.

The Rialto movie theatre complex was just across the road, and that would be visited later this morning, as soon as it opened. The last movie had finished at 10.45pm on Monday night, so we were putting the call out to anyone at that screening, in case they noticed anything odd, or saw people acting strangely as they returned to their cars – anything that stood out around the alleyway entrance.

Dunners wasn't awash with outdoor security cameras like many other cities around the world. Other than down at the university and in studentville, it was only really the nearby Octagon in the city centre that had surveillance, mostly because it was Grand Bar Central at night and the police needed to keep an eye on the drunks.

The overwhelming undercurrent at the meeting had been the sense – and burden – of a ticking clock. Somewhere out there was a newborn, stolen from its mother's womb. Everyone was still getting to grips with the sheer horror of that thought, and even the most seasoned among us were struggling with it. The usual frisson of excitement over a new investigation was noticeably absent.

I refreshed the feed for the online *Otago Daily Times* on my phone and noted the new headline 'Police Appealing to Public over Newborn.' I clicked on it and scrolled quickly through the text, Police were looking for any sign of the newborn baby of the victim of Monday night's horrific murder ... Police were asking people to call if they noticed anyone with an unexpected newborn ... Police said people could call 0800 Crime Stoppers if they wanted to remain anonymous...

0800 Dob in a Murdering Bastard more like. Well, we needed all the help we could get, and the public could be great sources of information. We were bound to get some calls about families who'd suddenly acquired a baby, and I already felt sorry for those who'd been called on to foster at short notice, or whose desire to adopt had finally, and suddenly, been realised. It would take the shine off the occasion if they were being looked at sideways courtesy of some sick bastard's unfathomable actions.

My allocated task du jour was to read up on recent incidents involving baby snatching. I knew I was tossed this one because it was a desk job, and therefore safe for the pregnant woman – keeping the resident arsehole happy. And even though I knew everyone was looking out for my interests, it didn't stop me from resenting it a bit.

The office felt very empty, as everyone else was out in the big, wide world doing what seemed like more hands-on and productive work. The lack of people energy in the room made the task feel even more grim and lonely, but, nevertheless, I settled down to do the bizzo.

I was aware there had been a couple of examples of baby abductions in Dunedin in recent years. Smithy had given me the heads-up on them. He was a born and bred Dunedinite, and although not assigned to those particular cases at the time, he remembered the furore they caused. I was only a recent arrival to the city, so they hadn't lodged in my memory. The case that did loom large in my consciousness though, was the alleged baby-trafficking exploits of Minnie Dean, who was legend in these parts, and not for good reasons. But considering that all went down in the late 1800s, I didn't think she'd be on the current list of suspects. Hers was a bloody sad case all around, really, and she had the dubious honour of being the only woman ever to be hanged in New Zealand. After the demise of some of her charges – and carelessly burying the bodies in her back yard – she was found guilty of infanticide. She was hanged in the Invercargill jail in 1895. Being a Southland girl, I was brought up on threats of being sent to Minnie to be 'looked after' if I misbehaved, which, being young and impressionable at the time, resulted in plenty of nightmares. Gee, thanks for that, Mum.

I decided to cast the net wider than Dunedin. Christchurch was only five hours' drive up the road, which was nothing to us southerners. We wouldn't bat an eyelid at hopping in the car and driving four hours along the twisty, turning, scenic road to Queenstown to get a pie or an ice cream, then heading back home. Me and my mates had done it a couple of times – it was almost a rite of passage, and the dungier the car the better.

I thought about the keywords to search for in the police database, and also in the general search engines. There were the obvious ones: baby abduction, kidnapping, snatching, assaults on pregnant women. But there were also the broader-picture subjects: baby trafficking, disputes over paternity, custody, Hague Convention cases. I stared out the window, trying to come up with scenarios where conflict might arise – not just at the extreme end, with violence, as this case certainly was, but also at the contention and argument end of the scale. I jotted 'surrogacy' down on my list, and 'stored sperm', even though it felt very left field. But there had been examples in the media of partners wanting to use the frozen sperm of their deceased loved-one to try and conceive a child, not always to the joy of the deceased's family. It opened up a number of interesting ethical and moral dilemmas that the sensationalists latched on to pretty quickly. Even if wildly unlikely, in my experience the process of contemplating the outliers and low-odds cases often helped you focus in on the right path, or ignited the spark of an idea that led you to the truth of what had really happened. Sometimes you just had to trust your process.

Of course, none of this addressed the motive behind something as up close and personal as carving a baby out of a woman, and that motive had to be the key to everything in this case. It was also something I felt a little ill-equipped to deal with at present. My emotional range was yo-yoing between intense gratitude that I seemed to be having a hale and happy pregnancy, to guilt that I was having a hale and happy pregnancy. Chuck in outright paranoia and fear that something awful might happen to me and this precious cargo, and I was a jittery bundle of anxiety. I gave a little shudder and my hands dropped to their default positions – top and bottom around my belly.

I spent some time reading through the results of my search – various depressing cases and situations. One headline in particular stood out. Yes, there had been a baby abducted from a maternity ward in Timaru hospital just shy of three years ago. Timas was a small port city only two and a half hours up the road from here, and was more renowned for its boguns and boy racers than its rich cultural scene and tourism charms. It certainly wasn't a place I'd be lining up to live in anytime soon. I jotted that down for follow-up and continued scrolling through the search results. There were a number of historical abductions that I ruled out for now – they were quite specific, involving relationship breakdowns and custody disputes. Again they left me feeling saddened and repulsed. It must have been awful for everyone involved, and it appalled me that children became a gambit or bargaining chip in adults' toxic relationships. The cases were complex and no one won, particularly in the Hague Convention cases, where a parent had secreted the child out of the country, to the devastation of the other party.

The Timaru case was the only straight-out abduction, where the victim and family was unknown and unrelated to the perpetrator. The family unfortunately happened to have a baby in the wrong town and at the wrong time. It all ended happily, with bubs returned safe and sound, but it had certainly taken the gloss off their happy occasion, and would likely have stoked a life-time paranoia around their child's safety. I think in this instance it would be very hard not to become helicopter parents, and for that poor child not to be cotton-wooled and over-guarded for the rest of their natural.

My bladder was telling me it was time to go for a walk to the facilities, and my stomach was telling me it was time to go eat. One of the perks of being pregnant was that no one questioned when you decided it was time to take a break, particularly if there was food involved. Not that there was anyone around to question it. I had an hour before it was time to catch up with the team. They'd had the morning out doing the interesting stuff while I'd been wedded to the computer. At least it hadn't been a colossal waste of time. I'd come up with some interesting things to follow up and scoped some background information on past cases. But the whole business had left me with an empty feeling, and a gloomy outlook that went against my usual faith in humanity. What was in order was an infusion of cheer.

I needed some company to go with the food.

CHAPTER 7

It didn't take much convincing to get Paul to meet me at Kiki Beware for a quick bite before the team meeting. My hormones were telling me I needed carbs, and bitter experience told me that I argued with by body at my peril. It was the chip butty or go home. I'd been fantasising about hot fries and gravy stuffed in a bun all morning.

'You really going to order that atrocity?' My culinary tastes weren't appreciated by everyone.

'This coming from a man who thinks peas belong in mac 'n' cheese?'

The guy behind the counter gave a snort.

After ordering the drinks and carbs, I manoeuvred myself between two of the barstools bolted to the floor in front of the counter in order to wave the magic plastic over the contactless machine. What did we do before PayWave? Deed done, I went to back out, but to my dismay found myself quite firmly wedged in place. Whose dumb idea was it to stick the bar stools right in front of where people had to pay? Whoever it was, I was sending some serious ill-will vibes their way.

'Fuck.'

'Fuck?' said Paul.

'Fuck, I'm stuck.' I was starting to sound like a character in a rhyming children's picture book – the sweary edition.

There was another snort from counter guy, which was matched by the one that came from behind me. Snorts in stereo. Yay.

'You could at least pretend to be sympathetic,' I said as I braced a hand on the brown vinyl top of each stool and attempted to hoist myself up a bit to dislodge my belly. That action only succeeded in provoking straight-out laughter. Before I could retort back, two arms appeared from behind me and wrapped themselves around my chest, and I felt myself being gently lifted up and out of my predicament.

'Jesus, Sam, you're a goon,' Paul said, still laughing. 'I don't know any other person on the planet who could get themselves into some of the scrapes you do, woman. I should start keeping a diary.' He placed my feet back on the ground, spun me round and planted a kiss smack in the middle of my forehead. It was impossible to stay miffed with that kind of adoration.

'It's a gift,' I said, and had a quiet chuckle too. Dignity be damned.

We parked ourselves at one of the high tables, which involved an undignified scramble to get up onto the seat, and I pretended not to notice the smiles from the other patrons. Thank God no one had whipped out their phone to record my moment of glory.

'How did you get on with the online searches?'

'Good,' I said, 'as far as potential trains of thought and avenues of pursuit. It was all a bit depressing though.'

'How so?'

'Well, all of the scenarios I was looking up were the result of desperation of some form or another. People snatching babies because they couldn't have one of their own, or because they'd lost a child and their grief was so profound it was having a huge effect on their mental health and they were beyond making rational decisions. Even when looking at the less extreme ends of offending, the majority of it was driven by distress rather than malice.'

'Well this case is pretty much the most distressing one I've come across in my life. I don't know about you, but I'm finding it disturbing, and we haven't really got started.'

'Yeah, I hear you.'

Counter guy came over and slid a lemon tea onto the table for me and a long black coffee for Paul. The lemon tea was famous in Dunedin and was a tasty if token nod to reducing my caffeine intake.

'There's one thing I thought I should flag, and I'll bring it up in the team meeting later. One of the historical cases I was looking at, the woman concerned had actually planned the kidnapping so far in advance that she'd faked a pregnancy, so no one would bat an eyelid when she arrived with a newborn. She was from Dunedin but travelled up to Timaru to snatch a baby.'

Paul tapped his lip. 'That is next-level planning.'

'Yeah, family and friends would be celebrating with you, little knowing that their gain of a new little bundle of love was some other poor family's loss.'

'And kidnapping from out of town was smart, because when kinfolk read it in the news they wouldn't make the connection.'

'There was lot of planning involved and a huge risk of being caught, which of course she was. It's amazing what the need for a child will make people do. Some will try and adopt, some put themselves into debt trying multiple rounds of fertility treatment, and I don't want to imagine the emotional toll of that. And some, like this woman, go for the steal.' Having a child had not been on my agenda at all at this stage in my life, but fate, luck and, as my mother so coarsely put it, taking seriously something poked at me in jest, had taken the matter out of my hands. Out of our hands.

'I'm also guessing that if they went to that much trouble, the planning also involved looking for victims with shared traits – you know, ethnic background, hair colouring, that kind of thing?'

Paul made a damn good point.

'I hadn't thought about that side of it, but it makes sense. I'll dive a little deeper into that.' I took a sip of the tea – it lived up to the hype. 'What I'm getting at though, is we shouldn't make the assumption that a baby will pop up out of the blue, although God knows I hope this one pops up, safe and sound.'

'Ditto.'

Paul gave me that look – the intense one that made you hold your breath so you could keep looking back. It usually meant he was going to say something serious, or suggest a shag. I was guessing, given the location, it was the former.

'Am I being silly if I'm feeling, well, a bit guilty – at you ... at us being so happy to be expecting this little person into our lives, when there's this other family out there who have been torn apart?'

I gave a long exhale. People say you should be on guard for red flags in relationships, but they neglect to consider the opposite – looking out for the green flags; the, lordy, this one is a keeper, flags. With all his bluff and bravado and reputation for being a bit of a lad, few people understood what a caring and empathic guy Paul was. He concealed it well.

'Nope, not silly at all.' He'd just articulated a feeling that had been churning away in the recesses of my mind, but that I hadn't quite been able to nail down. 'I'm with you there. I think this case is going to be challenging in a myriad of ways. So let's just make a promise to each other right here and now to keep talking about it if we're feeling uncomfortable, or thinking that it might overwhelm us. No secrets – no bottling it up, huh?'

Paul reached out his hand, little finger extended.

'Pinkie promise?' he asked.

I reciprocated and linked mine in his. 'Pinkie promise.'

CHAPTER 8

The station phone desk and the 0800 Crime Stoppers line had been pretty busy since the public appeal for information. Dunedin's residents' abhorrence of the crime's nature had prompted a number to phone in and report suspicious people and newborns. Not that a newborn could act suspicious – but the presence of a newborn might be.

Detective Constable Sonia Richardson had just returned from following up on one of these calls. Judging by the way she tossed her bag onto her desk, I guessed it hadn't gone well.

'Not quite the lead you had hoped for?'

'Nope.'

I waited for her to continue and realised she was boiling with what looked like rage. I had never seen her get to even a rolling simmer before, so something must have seriously gaffed her axe.

'Going to tell me what happened.'

'I might need a moment.'

She plonked down into the chair and proceeded to log into her laptop with a ferocity that had me fearing for the life of the keys.

'What did the poor computer ever do to you?' I asked.

She gave me her best brow-furrowed scowl and leaned back in the chair with an exaggerated humph.

'There are some seriously arseholish people out there.'

'You've only just noticed that?'

'Oh, I'd noticed alright, but I mean like properly fuckish fuckers.'

My eyebrows almost hit my hairline. I wasn't sure if I'd ever heard her say the F-word, let alone the F-word squared.

She must have clocked the look on my face, because she promptly apologised.

'Look, I've just spent half an hour talking down a hysterical woman, who had clearly recently given birth, and her horrified husband, trying to reassure them that no we weren't going to take their baby off them. Some piece of shit had called in and said that they knew they must have murdered the woman and stolen the missing baby because the couple weren't expecting, and then suddenly, there they were out and about with a baby. Instant family.'

'That would not have been fun.'

'Nope. And when I asked her why someone would make a report like that, she reckoned it was probably her ex, who had never accepted that it was over and years later still tried to make her life a living hell.'

'Surely no one would be that shit,' I said, knowing full well that, actually, yes, people could be.

'Well, then you'd be wrong. The caller hadn't given their name or contact details, and did it anonymously through Crime Stoppers, so there's no way to trace it back. But I'm going to be paying him a visit later this week for a little chat, because if he was responsible then...' She unscrewed the lid of her drink bottle with particular vigour.

'That is some next-level shittiness.'

'Yup. Just destroy what should be one of the happiest moments in a couple's life with your own self-serving pettiness. It defies all common decency.'

'So what could we charge him with?'

'Besides monumental fuckerism?'

'Besides that.'

'Well, his behaviour sounded like it had been the next best thing to stalking.'

'It could be a starting point – and wasting police time.'

'Yeah, well we'd better come up with something, because I'm buggered if I'm going to let this one lie. That fucker needs a reality check.'

CHAPTER 9

This was one of those phone calls that made me feel dirty and sickened even to think about.

One of the aspects we couldn't ignore was the possibility, no matter how remote, that this mother had been butchered, and this baby had been taken, to satisfy the warped appetites of the truly depraved. It was awful to admit it, but there was an element of society that got off on watching the pain and abuse of others, including of the youngest of infants. The internet provided a platform and an international market for the denigration and abuse of children. Anything inhuman you could imagine, these bastards enacted worse.

You had to be a special kind of person to work in the Online Child Exploitation Unit. But despite the amazing work they did exposing paedophile networks and the rewards they must have felt when rescuing victims and prosecuting the guilty, I could never do their job. It would be soul-destroying. I had an immense respect for those who did respond to that call to duty. There had to be some pretty heavy-duty support in place to keep them mentally and emotionally safe, working in that space.

Unfortunately it wasn't the first time I had the occasion to speak with Simon.

'I am pleased to say nothing's come to the surface on the online forums we monitor. Because it's been all over the news, it would be the kind of sensationalist material that would draw them like moths to a flame. There hasn't even been a flicker.'

That was a relief to hear. But it was early days.

'I imagine whoever posted something like that could demand top price if it was so high profile?'

'Yes, it makes it very attractive to the punters.'

Click bait of the most perverse kind.

'We've only been talking in terms of potential abuse of the baby. But what of the whole crime itself? I mean, is there a market for people watching the whole shebang? The murder, the removal of the baby, and anything after that?' I couldn't even bring myself to say the words.

'I hate to say it, but yes, there is. You see it all the time – reports of people watching live streams of things like massacres and murders. Unfortunately there is a niche that caters for every taste.'

'There are some sick people in the world.'

'No debate from me there.'

'So there have been no whispers of the murder being posted anywhere online?'

'To be honest, I haven't looked into that scenario, but I will. From what you've described though, it would be highly unlikely. Remember, these people are thinking about the filming – the cinematography, for want of a better word – that's what they make their money from. In past crimes of a similar ilk, victims have been kidnapped and taken to somewhere where the perpetrators can record securely, and where they get a reasonable-quality picture. And where they won't get caught. It's well planned.'

'I guess a rush job in a dark alley wouldn't fit the business model.'

'No. And it's one fucked-up business model.'

It was a relief that nothing had surfaced so far. It was a line of investigation I could tick off the list.

'All of that's kind of encouraging, actually. I know it's a real long shot, but as you know we have to consider all possibilities.'

'Look, happy to chat anytime. I'll follow up on the big-scene scenario, and if I hear any whispers I'll be in touch.'

'Thanks for all your help, and I mean this in the nicest possible way, but I hope to never have to speak with you again.'

He laughed. 'The feeling's mutual.'

CHAPTER 10

'Right, everyone, gather round.' DI Johns strode into the CIB room and took up position, centre-stage by the windows, clapping his hands together twice in the manner of Mrs King, my standard-one primary-school teacher. My internal monologue started its automatic playlist of colourful adjectives for slagging him off, but checked up short when I caught the look on his face. The frown was very real, not his usual 'well rehearsed for the audience' version, and my heart sank. Whatever was coming, it wasn't going to be good. My mind catapulted straight to worst-case scenario – Jesus, I hoped they hadn't found the baby dead. Even the thought of that word induced a visceral repulsion in me. For once in my life I was keen to hear what The Boss had to say. Smithy, Paul and Otto were in the room, and they too picked up on the urgency in his tone and wasted no time in obeying the gather-round command.

'There's been an unexpected development.' True to usual form though, he left the pause hanging a moment too long. 'We have received a ransom demand for the baby.'

There was a variety of 'ohs' and a 'really?' from around the room, one of them from me. My train of thought on motive for this crime had revolved around people wanting the baby for keepsies, not for profit. I'd never considered a ransom demand was even a possibility, so part of me was surprised, but a huge part of me was relieved. A ransom demand meant the baby was alive. People didn't generally demand ransoms for corpses. It offered a first glimpse of hope.

'Did they contact the family?' Paul asked.

'No, the demand came through the Crime Stoppers hotline. It's just been picked up, so we need to formulate a plan on how to tackle this, and quickly.'

'What was the demand?' I asked.

'One million in cash.'

That seemed a very parochial amount, lacking in imagination, but I guessed it was an easy round number for someone to come up with. You never saw a ransom demand for something like nine hundred and sixty-four thousand, two hundred and eighty-eight dollars and thirty cents. And in cash? But then it wasn't like you could request electronic banking and handily leave your bank account number for the deposit without a guaranteed visit from the police, unless you conveniently had a Swiss bank account. I was fairly confident most New Zealanders didn't. And I had no idea how the family would be able to front up with a million bucks in a hurry.

'For when?' Smithy this time.

'Tomorrow.' The Boss put his hands on his hips and paced back and forth across the front of the room. 'Of course, because the demand was made through the hotline there is no way to trace it or to respond. They didn't leave a number to negotiate through.'

The great thing about Crime Stoppers was that it was run by an intermediary in such a way that anonymity was guaranteed. That gave people the confidence to report things that they might otherwise not, for fear of the repercussions. The downside was it was untraceable. If they had rung the Police 105 line or their local station, we could get in touch and say, hey, in the real world there was no way in hell anyone could rustle up that kind of money. And if they were smart they would have used a mobile phone with an unregistered pre-pay SIM card. No one would be stupid enough to use their endless-data, home-and-internet-plan number, although some crims did suffer from basic stupidity, so stranger things had happened. Whichever it was, at least there could have been a conversation.

Smithy must have been thinking along my mind. 'How on earth do they think we can contact them to sort out a drop, if there's going to be one?'

'They said they would call again in the morning to give details on where to leave it.'

'Another slight problem,' Paul said. 'I'm pretty sure there's no way there would be a million dollars in cash sitting in the vaults of every bank in Dunedin combined. Even if they did try to pay the ransom, it would be impossible to get that kind of cash in a day.' He was right. Our recent holiday across the ditch to Melbourne to see his folks had proven that even getting a paltry amount in foreign currency was challenging, let alone a small fortune in notes. Hardly anyone used cash anymore – the financial world spun on a digital axis.

'I can't recall there ever having been a ransom demand like this in Dunedin before,' Smithy said, and he'd been around a while. 'Is there a nationwide police policy on it – like the "don't negotiate with ter-rorists" thing?'

'The police default is don't pay a ransom, but ultimately it is the call of the party involved,' DI Johns replied. He had started dragging his fingers through his hair. The case appeared to have got under The Boss's rhinoceros-thick hide as much as it had under ours. Made me wonder if he was human after all. 'We can only advise them, but it's Aleisha Newman's family who will have to make the final call. They haven't been informed of the situation as yet. I'll be paying them a visit this afternoon. In the meantime, we all need to come up with a way to track this bastard down. If the family decide to try and pay the ransom in a bid to secure the safety of the baby, then we need to come up with a way to use it as a trap – without putting the child at risk.'

That was going to be a challenge. I'd seen enough high-octane Hollywood movies to know that it could all end in catastrophe.

'One last thing: this stays in this room. We don't want the media getting a sniff of it and blowing our chance to track down the perpe-trator. That would be a disaster.' His eyes fell on me. I don't know why in hell he thought I'd go blabbing to the press, but every time a coconut he gave me the side-eye, no one else. 'Once we have formu-lated our plan and the time is right, we'll make a statement. But for now, we zip it.'

CHAPTER 11

Bubs had decided to dance on my bladder, so I'd had to skip out to visit the facilities and avoid creating a water feature in the office. I'd got sidetracked on my way back by a conversation with Laurie, one of the admin staff. She had been regaling me with her three child-birth experiences, none of which imbued me with great confidence for the adventure ahead. I know the mothers on staff were only trying to reassure me, and those that had what I considered were frankly traumatic deliveries involving long labours, agony, rips, tears and stitches in unmentionable places, or having the baby delivered via the sun roof, vowed that you forgot all the bad stuff when you got to hold your new arrival in your arms and gaze lovingly at them. So far I wasn't feeling it.

The Boss was back from his visit to Aleisha Newman's family, and they had indicated there was no way in hell they could raise ten thousand bucks let alone a million, short of one hell of a crowd-funding campaign. What they had asked though, was could they pretend to pay the ransom, use some real and some fake money or something, and find a way to bring their baby home? It was under-standable. If you were desperate with worry you'd see this as your only chance. Of course, the risks were immense, and I could hear the discussion continuing from halfway down the hallway. The volume indicated things were a tad more animated than when I had left the CIB room, with voices trying to climb over the top of each other.

'There is no way we can risk leaving the money in such a crowded situation. Anyone could pick up the bag and take off with it.' The Boss's voice wasn't hard to pick out, and as usual when trying to debate a point, he used volume over finesse.

'Well, we haven't exactly got a choice, have we? He left a message and no number, so it's not like we were able to have a nice little chat at the time and talk him out of it.'

Judging by the turn in the conversation, something had come to light in the time I'd been away. I walked into the room and saw four faces standing around my desk. Only two had been doing the talking in the time I'd been in earshot. They all glanced up at me and stopped. One looked pleased to see me, two looked ambivalent, and one looked unimpressed.

'What?' I said, feeling suddenly very much the centre of attention. I looked down to check I didn't have a toilet paper souvenir hanging from anywhere it shouldn't.

'You looked like you were about to proclaim something,' Smithy said.

'I did?'

'Yes.'

'Well, I wasn't, but can you tell me what's going on?'

'We've just been informed the ransom person has left another message – on the station phone line this time instead of using Crime Stoppers. They've instructed us that the money be left in a backpack at 8.45 in the morning at the farmers' market.' Paul delivered the news with an eyebrow 'hi' and a smile.

'The farmers' market?' I said. 'That's a bit random – and bit of a longer time frame.'

The farmers' market was a Saturday morning institution, held next to the iconic Dunedin Railway Station in the not-so-iconic carpark. Every man and his dog came along to the market to buy anything from fresh fruit and vegetables to breads, cheeses and meats, to local grog, and to that all-important coffee. It was as much a social event as it was a local produce showcase, with lots of people using it as a weekly catch-up spot with their friends. It was crowded, chaotic, and also pretty central, being a few blocks away from the city centre. I suppose as a place to pick up an exorbitant amount of money and have a few different directions for escape, it wasn't awful, but it was small, quite enclosed and basically not great. Also, by pushing out the drop date, they were giving us plenty of time to put surveillance and contingencies in place. I thought ransom-guy could do better.

'Anywhere specific there?'

'Down the northern end, by the "green electrical cabinet thing" – his words. That's near where the platform ends. There's often some seating around there, and a few vendors.'

'But anyone could pick it up and take off with it. You know what people are like – if it's not tied down they'll nick it, especially a bag.'

'That is precisely the point I was trying to make.' Oddly it didn't make me feel grateful to have The Boss agree with me.

'Actually, I think in Dunedin, people are too honest, and someone is more likely to pick the bag up and hand it in to the market office.' Paul had a fair point there. It also brought another idea to mind.

'How bulky and hefty is a million bucks?' I asked. 'Even if it was in hundred-dollar notes, would it fit in a backpack?'

Judging by the shrugs around the table no one had ever had the opportunity to test it out. There were no lotto winners in the room – well, confessed ones. And if they had won the big one and were still working here, they were idiots.

'I guess it depends on the denomination,' said Paul. 'It would be easy enough to look up.'

'I'll Google it. Hang on a tick.' Smithy directed his attention to his nearby computer. The tick took a bit longer than he thought due to his archaeological method of typing – dig around for the key until you find it. He was also one of those people who typed very loud.

'Actually, it's not too bad. A note is around a gram, so a mill in hundies would be around ten KG.'

'Well, that's less than I thought it would be,' said Paul.

I did the maths in my head. 'They didn't state what notes they wanted it in, so we could do it in five-dollar notes and they'd have a hell of a problem running off with two hundred KGs' worth.'

'Or coins.' Paul chipped in. We all had a chuckle at that one.

'But seriously, setting up surveillance at the market and covering the roading around there would be a little challenging. The only high vantage point is the station building itself. Everything else around there is single or double-storeyed.' The Boss brought it back to the task at hand. 'How many roads exit from that point?'

'Anzac Avenue, both directions. St Andrew Street in front and behind the station.'

'Leith Street and Harrow Street shoot off nearby. And that funny little through street to the one-way south.'

'They could also scoot through the industrial area behind to the harbour and boat access.'

I was starting to imagine one of those crazy James Bondish chase scenes involving parkour, bicycles, cars and jet skis.

'Don't forget the railway lines themselves,' Sonia piped in.

'Pardon?' The Boss seemed to only just have noticed her.

'The railway lines, they pass through behind everything. He could take off alongside them, or even on one of those vehicles, you can get those jeep-like things that can run on the rails as well as roads. If they had access to one of them you could head north a way before changing vehicles – confuse your pursuers.'

'No one would think of that,' The Boss said.

'She did,' I piped in. Sonia could be quiet, but she had some unusual ways of thinking, which in my mind made her a real strength in the team. But some others viewed her as weird. Unfortunately one of those was The Boss, so she only scored slightly higher than me in his popularity ratings. The cynic in me did wonder if that was because we both had vaginas.

'It's unlikely.'

And that was how imagination and innovative ideas were stifled.

I changed the topic slightly. 'So what did the message say exactly?' I asked.

'We can just play it if you want to hear it – they isolated an audio clip,' Smithy said. 'The caller ID was for a non-registered pre-pay number, so not useful – although we can at least contact them back now and possibly get a trace.' Smithy clicked on a few files on the computer, and then lo and behold, a very Kiwi-accented, male, mid-pitched and slightly shaky voice came across the speakers.

'We have the baby. If you want her back safely leave the one million in a black backpack behind the green electrical cabinet thing down the end of the farmers' market at 8.45am. If anyone tries to stop the pick-up or interferes in any way, you will never see her again. If the pick-up gets arrested, we will kill her.'

'Christ in a hand cart,' I said.

'Yeah, it's a pretty blunt threat,' said Paul.

'Yes, it is,' I said. 'But it's not that.'

'What is it then?'

'Play it again.'

Smithy duly clicked the play button, and the not-so-dulcet tones replayed across the room. I shook my head as it confirmed my suspicions.

'Bloody idiot. You're not going to believe this, guys, but I'm pretty sure I recognise that voice.'

CHAPTER 12

Waiting sucked. Naturally, I wasn't allowed to go along with the armed officers and the heavies to pay a visit to the suspect's house. For one thing, my current shape and the available dimensions of body armour were mutually exclusive. For another, no one was going to let me assume that kind of risk, even if the armour had been available. So I had to wait. Patience wasn't one of my strong points, and despite knowing that Paul could handle himself in any situation, I still felt a jumble of nerves. Unlike my usual sunny, optimistic self, I was catastrophising the situation, playing endless worst-case scenarios in my head. Of course, none of these scenarios were focused where they should have been – on the welfare of the baby. No, they were a lot more self-indulgent. My thoughts couldn't help but venture into 'what if something happened to Paul?' territory. How many times had you seen the tragic and tear-jerking stories in the news about young widows, pregnant or with newborns, whose partners had been killed in the line of duty? Images of women in black flooded my brain, veils concealing tear-stained faces, hands clasping those of loved ones or little children while bravely standing grave-side, watching as the flag was folded and presented to them with military precision, the devastated widow accepting its solemn weight. I imagined having to endure the agony of watching the coffin lowered into the ground. My eyes looked down to the large, wriggly lump between me and my toes. I didn't want to imagine a life where I was doing this alone. I couldn't. We needed him.

My anxiety levels had almost reached the 'I might have to have a puke' tipping point, when said man marched into the room, a scowl plastered across his face and foul mood radiating like an Imperial Death Star force field. Despite the scowl, I launched myself at him for a hug – professionalism be damned. As was common sense, I realised, as I hit the solidity of his BAS vest. Despite clunking against his body armour, I must have diffused his mood a bit, as he wrapped his arms around me and gave me a tight squeeze, crushing me even harder against the chest plate. The small squeak I let out made him realise the error of his ways, and he quickly released me.

'How about I get this damned thing off and we try that again.'

I stood back and watched as he un-zipped, un-velcroed and manoeuvred the bulky thing off his shoulders.

'So, are you going to tell me what happened?'

He let the vest drop to the ground with a *thunk*.

'Stupid, stupid, idiot.'

The way he looked at the vest made me suspect he would quite like to have thrown it, or at the very least kicked it.

'Are you referring to yourself or...'

'Stupid dickhead, weasel-faced idiot fuckwit.'

That was my usual description of The Boss, so I required a bit more clarification.

'Which one?' The Earth almost tilted from his eye-roll.

'Your fucking mate.'

'Oh, he ain't no mate of mine.'

'You know what I mean.'

'I take it things didn't go well.'

'It depends on what you define as well. No one was harmed, so that went well.'

'I feel a but coming.'

'But...'

He let that hang longer than strictly necessary.

I gave the little winding-hand signal to hurry him along.

'But we didn't quite achieve the objective.'

There was only one objective that was important, besides the no one getting hurt thing.

'So, where's the baby?'

He stood there, looking at me, steel-faced.

'There wasn't any baby.'

'What do you mean there wasn't any baby?'

'Didn't have it, never had it. The stupid bastard had seen all the hoo-ha in the media, and in whatever chemically induced haze of stupidity he was operating under, he decided here was a way to make a quick buck, so thought he'd try and screw the family out of a ransom.'

'Sorry, so you're telling me he didn't have the baby, but decided to extort money anyway?'

'Yup.'

'Shit, what a stupid bloody idiot.'

'Shit indeed.'

CHAPTER 13

'For fuck's sake, Marty, what the hell were you thinking?'

The crew had left me to deal with Martin McAndrew – AKA 'The Fly' to the police, due to him being a low-irritant pest who always seemed to hang around, regularly got himself into shit but was generally fairly harmless. Unfortunately for him the pile of shit he had gotten himself into this time was of epic proportions, and even the most creative social worker and legal-aid team were unlikely to keep him from spending some time under state hospitality. He looked uncomfortable enough under the hospitality of the station's cells. I stood in there with him, a concern for my safety nodded at by the presence of a rather burly constable glowering a few metres away. Not that I felt threatened in any way by this dopey specimen. If anything, he should have been afraid of me, because even the most unperceptive of human beings would have been able to tell just how pissed off I was right now.

'Look, Detective Sam, I didn't think it would blow up this big. Honestly I didn't.'

We had had enough dealings over the years that we were practically on a first-name basis, and up until this point I had kind of tolerated him because of his usefulness as an informant. But unfortunately for him, all amassed pity points had been redeemed.

'I don't think you thought at all.' It also meant I felt free to be very blunt.

He looked abashed and suddenly became very concerned about the state of his fingernails, which to be honest had enough gunge under them you could probably crop some potatoes. I winced as he dug a chunk out and flicked it to the floor.

'You do realise the seriousness of this, don't you?'

'Well, I do now,' he mumbled. He was a study in abject misery, not helped by his bloodshot eyes, what looked like three-day stubble, and shoulders permanently drawn up around his ears.

'You're looking at being charged with blackmail and threatening to kill. That's jail time, Marty, serious jail time. You fucked up big time.'

His shoulders drew up and in even more. The green high-necked jumper he was wearing made him look like a turtle trying to pull its head in.

'And it's not just because you tried to deceive everyone by demanding a ransom as a quick way to get a buck.'

I banged my hand against the wall and made him flinch. The shooting pain up my arm was worth it.

'You do realise your actions have now put that baby at serious risk? Not only have you completely wasted our time on your ridiculous wild-goose chase, whatever the kidnappers had in mind has probably been scuppered by your actions – your selfish, stupid, opportunistic actions.'

As my voice rose, he cringed further into the corner of the wall.

'And if anything bad happens to that wee girl because of what you have done, anything at all, by God I am going to rain down on you like radio-fucking-active hail, you got that?'

Even the constable's eyebrows raised.

I fired the last volley.

'You should be bloody ashamed of yourself.'

CHAPTER 14

After dealing with the stupid piece of shit that was Marty, I needed to do something on this case that at least felt like constructive activity. The postmortem results had come in, and after reading them I wanted to talk them though. Fortunately for me I had a bit of history with the local pathologist. Not in a romantic kind of a way – more in a sisterly kind of a way, despite his best efforts to make it otherwise. Alistair, who liked to be called Alistair and never Al, was in the same class as my brothers at Southland Boys' High School. We had the pleasure of his company on the farm over many a school holiday, as his over-achieving parents seemed to value their work more than their kid, so he was offloaded on our family more often than not. I liked to think that we had a positive influence on him, and that, courtesy of the love shown by the Shephards, he showed less of his latent psychopathic tendencies than he may have if under the loving care of his parents. Then again, it did mean he spent time around my mother, so it could have swung either way.

I picked up the phone and hit his cell number.

'Sam,' came the familiar drawl. 'What can I do you for – I'm assuming you want something. It's the only time you call. You know a man could get a complex about things like that.'

He had me pegged.

'You know me too well, what can I say?'

'Yes to a date would always be nice.' Bless him, he still tried.

'Sorry, but I think the ship has well and truly sailed on that one.'

'Yes, let me extend my congratulations to you both yet again. When are you due to pop?'

'Theoretically, around three weeks, but the way I'm feeling at the moment I hoping earlier, because if this thing keeps growing it's going to explode out of my chest like an alien.'

'Ooh, if it does that can I be the one to do the autopsy? That would be fascinating.'

The thought of Alistair trawling around in my deceased innards was a bit off-putting, no matter how fascinating he'd find it.

'You're a sick puppy, you know that?'

'Yes, thank you very much. I can attribute that to you and your family's fine influence.'

'Touché.' He had a point.

'Ah, those were the days. How is the old battle-axe by the way?'

'Mum's mum.'

'Enough said.' I could hear the smile in his voice. 'I assume you're calling about our unfortunate recent arrival.'

'Yeah,' I said. Even after a few days of getting used to the case I still had a visceral reaction whenever I thought of what she must have gone through. I had to breathe away the shudders.

'Was there anything specific you wanted to know?'

'Not really. I was just wanting a general run-through and...' How did I phrase this carefully? '...anything you thought was amiss, besides the obvious.' I knew Alistair well enough to know he actively sought out the unusual – the outlier things. Sure, it was part of his job to be systematic and thorough, pay attention to detail, but he was very good at looking that step beyond, at solving the puzzle, which was one of the reasons I respected him so much as a pathologist. Maybe it started on the farm when he seemed to get too much enjoyment poking around the insides of smelly dead things. It wasn't just a job to him, it was a calling.

'Cause of death was acute blood loss and shock from being cut open. The cuts themselves were clean; there was no dragging, so performed with a very sharp implement – a knife or perhaps even a scalpel – but they weren't what I would call proficient, and they were large.'

'They?' I asked. 'There was more than one?'

'Yes. In a normal caesarean section there will be an abdominal cut first, to get through the muscles etc, and then when the uterus is exposed, the cut through the uterus. Normally these would be just enough to fit a baby's head and body through. In this case the cuts were much, much larger, twice the size a surgeon would make, and, like I said, messy. Also, the uterine cuts were more hesitant, like they were trying to make sure they didn't cut through and wound the foetus.'

'So we can pretty much rule out an obstetrician as the perpetrator.'

'Unless they were a rubbish one and a bit of a butcher.'

The thought of all this was making me fervently hope Bubs here decided to exit my womb courtesy of the opening nature provided. My hand had automatically started to rub my belly. The kid responded with an obliging kick.

'Along those lines, they had also managed to nick the bladder, so yes, very confident it wasn't done by a surgeon.'

Not even a back-alley surgeon. Whoever did this performed under extraordinarily crude circumstances, without the luxury of a sterile environment, operating table and lighting, with an anaesthetist on hand. It begged my next question.

'No one would sit still or silent for that kind of treatment if awake. Surely she would have had to have been unconscious at the time?'

'She had a blunt-force trauma wound to the back of her head, which externally looks quite severe, and resulted in a fractured skull and internal bleeding. Looking at the shape of it, to me it looks consistent with an impact from, for example, the edge of kerbing or a ledge of some kind, rather than a weapon, and would likely have rendered her unconscious. We've taken bloods for a toxicology screening in case she was given some sort of sedative or anaesthesia to ensure she stayed unconscious throughout, or was under the influence of any drugs or alcohol. I wouldn't expect the results back for a couple of weeks.' Knowing full well the list of no-nos a pregnant woman constantly had rammed down her throat by health professionals, family, friends, and even the occasional stranger, who seemed to think they had a right to put in their two-cents' worth, I doubted there would be alcohol or illicit drugs in her system. But, hey, you never knew. The most illicit thing from the no-nos list I'd indulged in was a cold chicken sandwich, and my mother had even told me off for that.

'And she didn't have any signs of defensive wounds, or evidence she'd tried to fight someone off?' I asked.

'No, nothing like that. Nothing under her fingernails, and apart from the major trauma to the back of her head, and of course the make-shift caesarean section, she had no other sign of injury.'

'So you think she was pushed, or tripped over something and fell backward.' I was going to have to look at the site reports and see if there was blood and tissue evidence on any of the angular edges around where she was found.

'Well, I can't speculate on the circumstances, but certainly she struck her head, going backward with enough force to do some serious damage.'

I thought about what he said about toxicology reports.

'You didn't find a site of injection?'

'She had evidence of recent needle puncture to her median cubital vein, but that could have been due to a routine blood test. We will follow up with her medical records to see if any had been taken in the previous few days.'

I remembered his earlier comment about the person being cautious not to cut the baby.

'Is there any way to know if, when they were cutting through the uterus, they did accidentally cut the baby?'

'No way to tell. We took blood samples from a number of sites in case there was evidence left by the perpetrator, but to be honest, given the immense amount of blood lost by the victim, that is needle-in-haystack territory. Also, at this point we don't know the blood type of the baby. Again, we will check the victim's records for any ante-natal investigations. If she had amniocentesis or any other tests, that could help us there. Oh, and in addition to the baby, they took the placenta.'

'Pardon?' I asked.

'Yup, they took the whole kit and caboodle.'

'Why the hell would someone do that?'

'Good question. Maybe they were in a hurry.'

Maybe indeed. I guess if you'd just sliced open a woman in a back alley in the middle of the night to snatch her probably crying baby, you wouldn't be sticking around to tidy up the mess.

CHAPTER 15

The reception I got from the Felipos could not have been in starker contrast to the last time we met. Granted it was a civilised time in the afternoon rather than a very uncivilised 1.00am in the morning, and likewise we were in the comfort of their home rather than the unwelcoming halls of Dunedin Central Police Station.

On the drive over here I'd marvelled at how Dunedin busted out the spring fever. The cherry blossoms were in full flower, the last of the season's magnolia blooms still clung onto branches, and carpets of daffodils and spring flowers blanketed the roadsides, parks and gardens. Of course, this being Dunedin, it could turn winterish at the drop of a hat. Today the daffs were waving their cheery heads in the sun. The next thing they could be poking through a blanket of spring-time snow, that other random feature of Dunedin's southern latitude and proximity to Antarctic blasts. I mentally did a hat tip to the Daffodil Man, as I did every year when the city got to enjoy the fruits of the two million bulbs donated by local millionaire and philanthropist, Les Cleveland. Glad I didn't have to plant them though.

Walking up to their home I had admired the display of spring flowers cheerfully erupting all around their garden, providing fresh bursts of yellow and white beneath the reds and purples of rhododendrons and azaleas. Like many houses in Mornington it was a multilevel brick number, arranged to maximise space within the contours of their hilly section. The lawns look recently mowed, and someone had kept on top of the weeds, which were proliferating at this time of year. Our garden had a bumper crop. After climbing the stairs to the front door, I had noted the porch filled with carefully paired shoes and gumboots. I pressed the doorbell, heard the *bing bong* from within the depths of the house and then proceeded to deal with my footwear.

Sina must have been waiting nearby, because within seconds the door opened and she was standing there, gloriously cheerful, dressed in a vivid, orange, floral puletasi.

'No, no,' she said. 'Please, leave your shoes on.' I had been trying to lean down over my belly to reach them. If advanced pregnancy had taught me anything, it was Velcro had its place, and I would never dis shoes featuring the fastening ever again. Or Crocs for that matter. Although Crocs and socks was a step too far.

She led me down the hallway, through the kitchen and into a sunny and warm lounge beyond. A large woven-flax mat covered a large proportion of the very busy, red-patterned Axminster carpet, and was surrounded by a mismatched array of comfortable-looking sofas. A veneer coffee table that came straight out of the seventies graced the centre of the room and sported a vase holding a bouquet of happily imperfect daffodils, which looked cut from the garden. There was an eclectic mix of ornaments and books on the shelves, along with mementos from the Islands, but it was all carefully arranged and house proud. Family portraits graced the walls, beautiful faces smiling down on the room. Some had shell necklaces hanging around the frame, and others gloriously garish fake-flower leis. It reminded me an awful lot of our family room at home on the farm, with the exception of the mat and the leis, and also the substantial portrait of Jesus that took pride of place in the centre of the wall.

'I'll go get Timi for you. Would you like a tea?'

I was reaching the mid-afternoon sleepies time of day, and tea sounded wonderful. 'Yes please, medium strength with milk would be great.'

I sank down into the corner of a sofa and contemplated the information I'd gleaned during the day. It didn't feel like much, and research by computer didn't spin my wheels. Talking with people was a much more effective way of finding not only the solid evidence that made the foundation of an investigation, but also those little gems that could put a stalled case back on the right track. I was hoping that would be the case here. When I'd last questioned Timi he was still overwhelmed by what he'd seen and done. Hopefully a little time and space would have helped him to recollect other aspects of that night.

'Pass the detective a biscuit, Timi,' Sina said as she placed the mugs of tea onto woven coasters atop the coffee table and sat down in the armchair opposite. I'd hoped I'd get to speak with Timi alone, but, small consolation, at least it was just his mum sitting in, as Felipo Senior was at work.

'Would you like a biscuit, miss?' Timi asked as he proffered a plate of shortbread.

'Take a couple,' Sina said, 'You've got more than one mouth to feed there.'

There was no argument from me and I popped two onto the saucer.

'You sit next to the detective, Timi.'

The boy looked slightly embarrassed, but none the less plonked down onto the sofa next to me. It was only half past three so he hadn't had time to change out of his school uniform. It was good that he was back in the classroom. The routine of day-to-day life was hopefully helping him to process the trauma he'd been through. I felt a twinge of guilt that I was about to try and bring it all back.

'How are you feeling about everything now, Timi?' I asked.

He shrugged in that awkward and extended way only teenage boys seemed to manage. 'I guess I'm feeling better. I just still feel really sad for the lady, and her family, you know. Especially when I found out about the baby. That's really bad.'

'Yeah, everyone is doing their best to try and find the baby. Hopefully whoever did this is looking after her, keeping her safe.'

'Do you really think that? They haven't hurt the baby?' he asked. He was twirling the shortbread biscuit in his hand round and round with his fingers, like one of those fidget gadgets that were all the rage not so long ago.

'I honestly think the baby is safe somewhere. I don't think they would have gone to all of that trouble, done the awful thing they had done, to not keep the baby safe. And that is one of the reasons I'm here again to talk with you. We have to find the person who murdered that woman, and we have to find the baby and return her to her family. They need justice, and she needs to be with her loved ones.'

Timi nodded, still spinning the shortbread. I noted the rather large crumbs detaching themselves and falling down to the floor. I glanced over at his mum, her eyes followed where mine had come from, and when they returned to mine she merely gave a tight smile and a small shrug of the shoulders. I was grateful she let it lie.

'You've had a few days to think things over, and I'm sure you've re-played everything in your head time and time again. But looking back, is there anything that comes to mind that you didn't tell us on the night? Anything else that seemed out of place or odd? Were there any people that you recall being around near the alleyway?' It was too many questions at once, but hopefully they would start the ball rolling'

'No, not really. There definitely wasn't anyone else down the al-leyway except her.' He took a wee gulp, and I could see his eyes start to fill. 'There were a couple of cars parked down there. That's why we didn't see her at first, because she was down and around the corner, in that bit off the side where the bird picture is.' I had no recollection of a bird picture anywhere down there, even though I'd been down that alleyway before to go to the Pequeño Bar, and I'd looked at the scene photos. I was going to have to go down and check it out in person, get a feel for the scene, but it wasn't something I was looking forward to. The place was forever tainted now.

'And one of those cars was a big car, an SUV, so it really blocked the alley so you couldn't see down that bit. The only reason I found her was because I heard her, you know, groaning.' He was beginning to punctuate words with sniffs.

'You okay, Timi?' his mum asked gently. Sina appeared to have gotten over her initial upset that her son had been out tagging and vandalising property in the middle of the night. Time and hindsight had put things in perspective.

'Yeah, I'm good, Mum,' he said. He flicked the tips of his fingers, causing a wee cascade of crumbs to shower the woven mat. 'I don't know that I can help much more than that.'

The big SUV he talked about must have been the victim's car. According to the reports she had a white Kia Sportage that had been located at the scene. It was a favourite SUV of the school-run mums so there were plenty of them doing family duty in Dunedin. Aleisha had worked as a manager at the nearby Etrusco restaurant and had use of a carpark down the alleyway, but she had finished up for maternity leave two weeks earlier. Her husband had said she was out at a book group that evening, so was baffled as to why she had been back in the vicinity of work. She hadn't mentioned to him, or the group, that she was going to pop in to see anyone or pick something up on the way home. And the restaurant had closed up by 9.00pm that night anyway. So why on earth was she there?

'Going back to Monday night, when you were walking down Moray Place towards the alleyway, did you notice any other people about?'

'There were a few people around, you know. I guess coming out from the bars around, mostly guys. There were lots of cars though, all the carparks were full.' That made sense as there'd been a seventies tribute band in concert on at the town hall that night that didn't finish until after 11.00pm.

'No one out with a baby pram?' It was a long shot, and I felt slightly foolish asking it. You'd look pretty obvious out at that hour of the night when most people would have babies tucked up in their beds, except for the poor parents who had the ones that didn't do sleeping. I hoped to God my one did sleeping.

'No, it was late.'

'So what time would that have been again?'

'That was around half-ten, I suppose, when we went back to the alley.'

My ears pricked up at his wording.

'What do you mean by "when we went back to the alley?" Had you been there earlier?'

'Yeah. We'd been hanging out around out the front of the library for a bit, in the plaza there with the whirligig sculpture thing, cos the first time we went to check out the alleyway we couldn't go down.'

This was new.

'Why couldn't you go down there then?'

'Too risky,' he said. 'There were lights on in that little bar as you go down the tunnel, so too much of a chance someone might see us, so we kept on walking down the street and found somewhere to hang out for a bit.'

'Could you see who was in the bar?'

'Nah, you can't see that much of it from the street, and we didn't want to be obvious, so didn't turn around and take a look. When we came back later, they had all packed up and gone home. The lights were off.'

'How much later?'

'Half an hour, I guess.'

'And when you went back and everything was closed, there were still some cars down there?'

'Yeah, that's right. There was the white SUV, and another smaller, dark-coloured car in the courtyard. I don't know about any in that carpark under the building, it was too creepy in there so we didn't check.'

So if the bar had still been open, there would have been a few people around who may have gone further down the alleyway if they were parked there, especially if there were no spaces on the street. I wondered where the staff parked? Indigo Room wasn't usually open on a Monday, so they must have had a private function on. It was another of those atmospheric, quirky little restaurant bars that Dunedin did so well. I'd seen it described as a Bohemian space, and I'd enjoyed an evening or two in there before. One of its features was the distinctive views out of the windows that lined the sloping alleyway. You didn't really pay any attention to cars going up or down the tunnel-like covered entrance passage, but people walking always caught your eye. It was a bit like that pretending to go downstairs gag, but in reverse. You couldn't help but track people progressing from full body view to feet because the last window in the row was pretty much at shoe level. If the killer had walked out with a freshly minted baby while the bar was open they might have been noticed, but if they had been parked down there it would have been easier for them to drive out of there without turning a head. Cars were handily soundproof too.

But it still seemed so incredibly risky, if you were planning a crime, to have a location with only one escape route and such a high chance of being seen. Going back to the bar patrons and staff was something worth pursuing, and reviewing traffic movement again on any security cameras in the vicinity. Timi's information potentially narrowed the time frame for searching cars. Even if the number was high – Moray Place was busy – there could be a chance that there was a vehicle registered to someone with a connection to the victim. We could get lucky, and at the moment we'd take every bit of luck we could get.

CHAPTER 16

Café visits were going to become a lot more of a logistical challenge in the very near future, so I was making the most of their services while I could. Maggie had a convenient break between lectures so didn't need much convincing when I texted her to suggest a quick cuppa. This time it was at RDC, one of those quirky little places accessed from a carpark or down a dodgy-looking brick corridor off George Street that you didn't know was there unless you knew it was there. Its courtyard and eclectic cave-like interior made it a bit of a sanctuary from the semi-bright lights of the city. It was a fave of mine because it took the usual notion of a cinnamon scroll – one of my café staples – and tipped it on its head by making it a cardamom scroll. Genius. It also had one of the largest collections of VHS movies I'd seen in Dunedin. They played on one of the smallest TV-video players known to mankind. Today Sarah, Ludo and her rag-tag friends were trying to negotiate the labyrinth in search of baby Toby. Considering the current situation, the timing seemed perfect. Although, for me it was a case of mixed feelings about the villain. Ahhhhh, Jareth.

I tore my eyes away from the pint-sized screen and returned my attention to the business at hand.

'You were really quite sure this baby was a girl, weren't you?'

Maggie smiled as she bit into a butter-slathered chunk of her perennial favourite, the cheese scone. It had been toasted in the sandwich press, and the delectable smell of all that caramelised cheese was making me drool.

'Not a doubt in my mind,' she said. At least she had the decency to chew and swallow before replying. 'Was happy to wager the house on it.'

'You don't own the house.'

She shrugged. 'Minor technicality.'

'But seriously, how did you know. I mean, really know? It wasn't just a lucky guess?' The girl-or-boy thing was a fifty-fifty chance, so anyone could make a lucky guess, but Maggie's luck ran at one-hundred-percent accurate as far as I was aware, which even with my fairly average understanding of maths I realised was statistically im-probable.

'I just do.'

'Well, that's not much of an answer,' I said. 'It's up there with "just because".'

'You're not going to let this go, are you?'

'Nope.'

'Any particular reason? Are you planning on employing me down at the station as a baby-gender screening device?'

The thought had crossed my mind. 'Well, you'd be a cheaper than some of the other tests. All we'd need to do was feed you a scone and a coffee every now and again. And you'd be a lot friendlier.'

She tapped on the table, clacking her nails, which were painted orange today.

'Firstly, my rates would go up, and secondly, it doesn't quite work like that. I have to know the woman, have a connection with her. Can't turn it on and off on demand.'

Typical – up the pay rate.

'We could probably stump up a wine and chippies salary,' I said. 'Although with the current budget, it could be a stretch. Pity your ability isn't on tap though. And you still haven't said how you know. Come on, I'm curious.'

Maggie let out a sigh, like the question was the biggest imposition in the world. The cheese scone had now gone south, and she reached over for what remained of her large flat white to wash it down. 'Well, if we're going to thrash this one out, let me start with the knowing you were pregnant thing.'

Cool, I was going to get double bang for my buck. I leaned back in the chair and reached for the last quarter of my cardamom scroll before Maggs tried to claim it. Someone had to finish it, and it was going to be me. She looked at it heading to my mouth, gave a little frown, then clearly realised it wasn't safe standing between a pregnant woman and her tucker.

'Realising you were in the family way, that was like a visceral, physical thing. It's the same with everyone. I'll look at a woman, and it's like I really see them, they come into this amazing sharp clarity and the world blurs out around them, and then it's like ... well a tilt-shift is the best way to describe it. It feels like the entire Earth tilts beneath me, in a vertigo kind of a way.' She looked up at the ceiling, as if finding the right words, then looked back at me intently. 'And it's a two-way street. It's as if the baby is reaching out and moving Papatūānuku, Mother Earth, to let me know they are there. They want to be seen. When your girl reached out, it was really strong, the tilt. We felt each other, connected. And she felt like a girl. Boys feel different.'

'You know, Maggs, for a scientist, you can be freakily airy-fairy.'

'Who ever said that science and being attuned to nature had to be mutually exclusive?'

It was a good point.

'That's true. Down on the farm Dad always talked about having a feel for the land, and that his love for it was lodged under his skin, deep in his bones. He knew when something wasn't right, when an animal was ailing, or the soil was lacking in something. It was a feeling in his gut, both instinct and experience. I even watched him do dowsing – you know, that water-divining thing with the forked stick – and always thought it was a load of tosh until they drilled down for a bore and sure enough, there was the water. I guess that's the same kind of a thing.'

'Yeah, like it or not we are connected to this earth in so many ways. Although, I think more people are starting to realise that it's a facet of life we ignore at our peril. And I think if people took more pleasure in and notice of nature they'd be a damn sight happier.'

She paused for a bit to check her coffee cup, looking crushed that it was empty.

'Your dad was such a cool man. He would have been so proud and excited for you, you know that?' She gave me a rueful smile.

'Yeah, I know.'

The thought of Dad and what he was going to miss out on brought a lump to my throat, and Magg's face swam out of focus. She reached across and gave my hand a squeeze. His loss still felt so raw. There wasn't a day passed when I didn't wish I could hear his really bad jokes one more time, eat his signature super-crunchy, borderline burnt apple crumble, or share a conspiratorial eye-roll with him behind Mum's back. I wished with all my heart he could have been here to meet his granddaughter.

'He would have spoiled this little girl rotten,' I said.

'He sure would have. He'd have loved her to pieces. But don't you worry. She'll get plenty of spoiling. I am going to be that kind of aunty. The kind that will spoil her worse than rotten, the one that will teach her all the bad tricks and how to wind up her parents, provide her with a repertoire of smart-arse comebacks fit for any occasion. And I promise to guide her in making totally outrageous fashion statements.'

I could just imagine. It made me wish I'd had that kind of an aunty to grow up with.

'It's what I'm counting on,' I said with a laugh. 'That way when she turns into an opinionated and stroppy young woman, my mum can blame you.'

CHAPTER 17

My catch-up with Maggie had left me feeling a damn sight chirpier and had rekindled my usual optimism about the world. Alas, the benefits quickly evaporated when I got back to work and some of the team reported on what they'd been working on.

The citizens of Dunedin had embraced the call-out for information and had responded with unbridled enthusiasm. Having an anonymous hotline was both a blessing and a curse. In this instance it was resulting in a lot of running around and following up, with not much reward. People had phoned in with 'critical information' that ranged from the crack-pot to the downright malicious. And of course there were the 'why haven't you caught them yet', 'why haven't you found her yet', 'you suck' brigade. The reach was not limited to Dunedin – reports of suddenly appearing offspring were popping up in towns and cities across the country. It wasn't quite mass hysteria yet, but I could see how it could easily get there.

On the crack-pot end, someone who must have been smoking way too much of something trippy had reported that their rural neighbour was baby-farming at scale, to supply an international black market for babies, and had even built proper facilities to do it. They were convinced they were making their millions from it. When Otto had paid a visit to the pretty flash facilities, he found that yes, there was baby-farming going on – of the puppy variety, and not to supply international black markets, but Kiwi's insatiable demand for Labradoodles. At least that waste of time had a cutesy factor.

On the not-surprised end of the scale, as predicted, there was a Dunedin family that had been blessed with an out-of-the-blue adoption in the most scrutinised week of the year. Back in my Mataura days, a friend and her husband were on the waiting list to adopt. They had been trying to conceive for years, but after several failed rounds of fertility treatments and lost pregnancies had decided that trying for adoption was the least heart-breaking way to go. I always thought they would make amazing parents, but they had to prove it to the powers that be, which was fair enough – you wouldn't want to place a baby in a completely inappropriate and unsafe environment. But the checks and screening process they had to go through was pretty intense, including me being interviewed as a referee, and some of it was outright intrusive. It was worth it in the end, because we got to toast their acceptance as prospects. Essie and Jack had been warned a baby could arrive at short notice, and, boy oh boy, they meant short notice. She got the phone call from Oranga Tamariki while at work in the pharmacy in Gore and had literally two hours before a new addition to the family would be delivered to their door. It was a hell of a mad scramble, but a joyous and slightly shocked one. Best day of their lives. I imagined some well-meaning neighbours of the newly insta-family in Dunedin, not being in the know, had taken the good-citizen approach and reported the sudden appearance of a newborn. I hoped it hadn't tainted what should otherwise have been a time of celebration.

What got to me most, though, was people dobbing in their neighbours because they hadn't even realised there was a new member of the family on the way. How on earth did they not notice? And how on earth did we become so disconnected from each other? Neighbourhoods just weren't what they used to be. It was as if, in this crazy, busy world, people weren't even taking the time to get to know the people they lived smack next door to. Back when I was young, you couldn't do anything without the neighbours prying or keeping an eye out. Everyone in the area quietly made sure we all kept safe. All us kids herded together, and we could be out all day adventuring around the countryside, and get home and Mum could give us a report on where we'd been and pretty much what we'd been up to, courtesy of the spies-and-eyes network. Back in my youth neighbours lent each other stuff, swapped excess veggies from the garden and used to bring around a casserole when a new baby arrived – not phone the police.

CHAPTER 18

Under normal circumstances, if you got caught scrolling – doom or otherwise – through your social media while at work you'd get the side-eye, or the tut-tuts, or if it was The Boss, the thermo-nuclear telling-off. Most of us tried to check it on the sly though, under the noses of, but hopefully not noticed by, our colleagues – seeing if anyone had liked our latest post, how many hearts we got for the cat being cute destroying a toilet roll, or if we had struck the proverbial jackpot and someone had commented on our splendid baking effort. What amused me the most was the blokes around here surreptitiously holding their phones just under the edge of the desk, trying to look down with their eyes and not move their heads. They weren't fooling anyone.

Today, though, I had a mandate to scroll through social-media feeds – hell, I was being paid to do so. It never ceased to amaze me what people shared on the web. Aleisha Newman's Facebook, Instagram and Twitter accounts were all still active. No one in her family had posted a statement about her untimely and awful demise. As much as it would be painful, confirming the worst would actually be a good thing to do, not least to stop all her friends and acquaintances second-guessing about their Aleisha. It was understandable though, given the circumstances, and I guessed they had bigger things to worry about.

Her Facebook page had moderate security settings so I couldn't see everything, but her Insta and Twitter had complete public access. Aleisha had been what I'd consider a modest sharer as far as volume was concerned, but her content was loaded with her personal life. Her Instagram in particular was packed with photos portraying what looked like a fun and loving family. Family frolicking at the beach, family goofing off in the whale's mouth at Marlow Park, family in the butterfly house at the museum, family pretending to sleep in a pile on a sofa. The last post before her death had me reaching for the tissues. The reel showed her, Justin and Charlotte dancing and cavorting around what looked like their lounge room, all pointing to Aleisha's very expectant belly, to the strains of 'The Final Countdown'. That one required a wee walk and a few moments to compose myself.

There was an abundance of colourful and exuberant pictures of Charlotte. Charlotte feeding the ducks at the Botanic Garden. Charlotte trying to eat an ice cream that looked bigger than her head, and in the process spreading most of it across her very earnest-looking face and her pink unicorn T-shirt. Charlotte standing perched in her mum's high heels, wearing nothing but a smile, nappy, string of beads and a floppy hat. I did wonder how Charlotte the teenager or adult would feel about all and sundry having seen her in various states of silliness, messiness and nakedness. I guess it was the cynicism that came with the job and with dealing with the more predatory elements of society that made me cringe every time I saw a friend post naked or semi-naked photos of their kids online. I'd seen too much of the depravity out there to excuse their naivety.

Paul and I had already had the discussion about how we were going to tackle that conundrum. In a world where we were used to seeing everyone's most personal moments and the day-to-day play of their lives, how did you share enough to keep friends and family satisfied, but keep yourself and your loved ones safe? We'd decided on the 'no identifiable photos of the kid until they were old enough to understand and give their consent' approach. I didn't know how well that would go down in our family, as my siblings were definitely in the over-sharing camp, but hopefully they wouldn't notice among the avalanche of other family feeds. Actually, second thoughts: avoiding the issue wasn't going to work. I would have to have grow some kahunas and have *that* conversation with my mother. She always took great delight in splashing photos of her grandchildren all over Facebook. I'd look forward to that talk like a hole in the head.

Searching through the snapshots of Aleisha Newman's life had left me feeling sickened and saddened at the loss of what looked like such a vibrant and loving woman. As I continued scrolling through her Instagram photos, it occurred to me that the one advantage of our every moment being posted for the world to see, was that she'd left an extensive record of herself. She existed. She was. There weren't that many photos of me around. My younger years were in the days before the explosion of the internet and digital photography. Taking pictures and getting them developed and printed was an expensive faff back in the day, and being the youngest child, the novelty of taking lots of pictures of the kids had worn off by the time I arrived on the scene. There were plenty of Mike and Steve, but not so many of me.

I wasn't sure how far back I'd look. There was nothing in any of her feeds so far that triggered my internal alert settings, but I continued down a few more rows. By this stage in the moonwalk backward through time we were getting to pictures of Charlotte as a baby. In fact a few more swipes down there was a picture of her as a newborn, swaddled in cheerful green hospital linen in her transparent plastic bassinet. Something about the picture perturbed me so I clicked on it to make it fill my screen. You had to admit most newborns looked pretty squidgy, and Charlotte was no exception, but it was cute squidgy. Apart from the hospital-issue linen, she wore what looked like a dusky-pink, fine merino wool hat with a little knot tied in the top. Keeping watch over her slumbers, tucked in the corner of the bassinet was a golden-fluffed teddy bear wearing a tiny tartan waistcoat. I wondered if he was still on guard duty on her bed today. My childhood guardian, Mrs Mary Bear, was still a companion, even if she did look a little the worse for wear.

At last the cause of my unease came into focus, staring me in the face. It was a prime example of people letting their emotions overcome their brains and not thinking about what else they might be sharing with the world along with those cute photos of their newly arrived pride and joy. In full sight, attached at the head of the bassinet, was Charlotte's hospital information card, complete with her name, parents' names, midwife, date of birth and National Health Index number.

Dumb, dumb, dumb, plain dumb.

It was identity theft just waiting to happen.

CHAPTER 19

In the past I had always admired the spindly, owl-like bird mural at the entrance to the alleyway. It perked up the area, gave it some intrigue. Dunedin was blessed with some incredible street art, including a lot hidden down the recesses and odd thoroughfares of the inner city. It was well worth the effort to hunt them down. Today the bird's long scaly legs and hooked beak felt sinister, the look it was giving its rat companion in the palm of its hand predatory.

Having talked with Timi, I felt the need to finally come and check out the scene of the crime with my own eyes. Police photographs were all well and good, but there was something about being there in the flesh, experiencing the sounds, the smells, feeling the temperature, the mood of a place ... Part of me had been putting it off though. The thought of getting that physically close to where the woman had been murdered – a young woman not unlike me – gave me the heebie-jeebies. But it needed doing. Work was finished for the day so I decided to set aside my misgivings and take a detour on the way home.

The alleyway had been re-opened to the public for the benefit of the two bars whose premises hid down there, although I didn't think its recent notoriety would be good for business. Then again, there were always the morbidly curious – those that got a kick out of being in close proximity to a murder scene. Hell, in some cities in the world murder tourism was a thriving business. Jack the Ripper was a name that came to mind, but as soon as it did I tried to shove it straight back where it came from. Too close to this case for comfort. There was also the possibility that this murderer was the special kind of sicko who liked to observe others marvelling at their handy work, needed that kind of perverse glorification, so a part of me considered the value of continuing to monitor the surveillance video footage or even set up better coverage, in case the killer came back for a little visit. It was something to raise with the team.

Last time I'd been down this particular Victorian alleyway it was for a boozy night out with the girls to celebrate Maggie's birthday. That was back in the days I could enjoy a boozy night out, before I had a passenger on board. On that occasion I'd tottered down on spindly heels, half cut, on the arms of my gal pals, concentrating hard on not going arse over kite. This time I waddled down stone-cold sober, in sensible shoes, still concentrating on not slipping, which was made all the more challenging by the fact I couldn't see my feet. It was a steep incline to what was a less than aesthetically pleasing destination at the best of times. Today's glum, overcast skies did nothing to alleviate the sense of foreboding. Goosebumps erupted on my skin, and not just from the drop in air temperature as I descended from the street. The ceiling of the tunnel had an unusual stepped structure that accommodated multiple levels of the building above and what looked like the angled underside of a set of stairs.

Once down the dark tunnel section I emerged into the red-brick surrounds of the open courtyard. I wandered a little further down the slope and once at the centre turned around and looked back up towards the street. Cars whizzed past the entranceway as they made their way around Moray Place, pausing when the traffic backed up due to the lights at the intersection with Princes Street. The occasional pedestrian walked past, but none looked down this way. Despite the street itself being busy, it felt like a sequestered world down here, the sound of traffic muffled all the more as I worked my way around the edges of the courtyard area. There were half a dozen cars parked here now it was opened up to the public again. The only remaining crime-scene tape was further around, in the area where Aleisha Newman had been found.

There was something fascinating about the steadfastness of the industrial architecture, its snaking coils of pipes and ducts. It was hard to tell how many buildings backed onto this enclosed yard with its odd angles and overlaps. There was only one way in and out, unless you had access to one of the buildings, and although it felt isolated and out of sight of the street, without a secondary escape route it seemed a very risky place to undertake even a petty crime like tagging, let alone something as monumental as murder.

My eyes took in the black, gaping yaw of the entrance to the private underground carpark on my left. Even in daylight it was creepy. No wonder Timi and his friends had avoided it. My gaze then moved around, clockwise, to the wall that Timi and his friends had decided to upgrade. The boys had succeeded in tracing out the basic outline of their moniker before they were interrupted by other, more deadly events. I stepped up close to the wall, getting a sense of their proximity to it, imagined the sound of their hissing cans, and overlaid it with the kind of noise someone stricken, someone fighting for life, would make. Like a wounded animal, was how Timi had described it – low, primal. My shudder was entirely involuntary. It transformed into a tightening under my belly that took my breath away, buckled my knees and forced me to reach out, hand steadying me against the cold, smooth brick. It passed almost as soon as it came. Bloody Braxton Hicks contractions. My body was practising for its big moment, so I was getting quite a few of those now. If that was a little taster of things to come, I wasn't looking forward to the main course.

Once I had regained my composure I walked further along the wall to the corner. From this vantage point I could see in multiple directions. To my left was an off-shoot of the alleyway, lined with that modern accessory no respectable alleyway seemed to be without – a regiment of wheelie bins, and also some blue plastic barrels that I guessed contained waste oil from the surrounding restaurant's vats, or were for organising refuse of some kind. Directly across from me was the entrance to the Pequeño Lounge Bar, the quaint and boutique establishment that was a favourite of mine. The white painted-brick exterior offset the glossy black of the doors that enclosed a rich and warm interior that reminded me of those speak-easy bars from prohibition days. The effect was smart and oddly welcoming within these grungy surrounds. Just down from the bar was the other, smaller bird mural Timi had been talking about, the one that marked the entrance to the out-of-sight recess where he had found the tragic source of the noises. But you didn't need detective skills to figure out where the murder had taken place – a bank of floral tributes adorned the ground.

I worked my way around to the area still surrounded by crime-scene tape. The forensic crew had done their work, but we still wanted the area cordoned off. An opportunity for final examinations, and also a mark of respect for the woman who had lost her life there. Several of the bunches of flowers placed around the perimeter had cards, and there were two small teddy bears standing guard. They were looking a little the worse for the weather. I squatted down and worked my way along, reading the messages within each card. I also took a shot of each with my phone camera. You never knew what could be useful.

From my down-low angle I also scanned around, seeing what was visible and what wasn't. The angle was such that the tunnel way and Moray Place were obscured. I noted the spray-painted corner outlines of Aleisha's vehicle, which had served as an additional visual barrier between the crime scene and entrance to the street.

The door to the Pequeño was clearly visible from this corner but would have been partially obscured by the vehicle. It was interesting that the crime had taken place on a Monday night, the one day of the week the Pequeño was closed. Coincidence or design? Somehow I suspected the latter. No one in their right mind would chance being discovered in the middle of what was essentially a surgical procedure by some merrily drunk patron staggering out of the bar door. Not that anyone who would perform such an act could be considered in their right mind. I hauled myself to my feet, pausing halfway for the savage headrush to pass.

I lifted the tape and walked a little further down the side shoot so I had an unimpeded view of the scene. Basement-level windows and a door faced out onto the area. Red fire-escape stairs zig-zagged their way down from the top storey to the ground. Other than outdoor heat-pump units, there didn't appear to be any obvious electrical fittings in this area – lights, security cameras. Breathing in deeply all I could smell was the hint of damp, mossy brick. It screamed lonely. Finally I turned my attention to the ground. Ground that had until very recently been soaked in blood. My mind threw up the mental image of Timi, kneeling there next to Aleisha, desperate, and I had to turn and walk off the wave of chill and emotion that threatened to engulf me. I walked down past the wheelie bins, concentrating on the red solidity of the wall, rather than the tragic scene at my back. Writing caught my attention, and I paused before a curious message, traced my fingertips along someone's poetry, scrawled out one white word per brick:

> *Many solemn nights*
> > *Blonde moon, we stand and marvel*
> *Sleeping our noons away*

A hedonistic haiku? Had a few beers or whiskeys brought out someone's inner philosopher? With its intimate scale yet earnest out-pouring it was a far cry from the grand gesture that Timi and his friends were set on creating. What message were *they* trying to express? I hadn't paid attention to the actual wording of their tag. Most of the bold, graphic tags I had seen on the sides of railway carriages and on unsuspecting walls were all about identity – this is who we are, take note, world. I was guessing Timi and his crew's would be the same. Curious now, but also actively avoiding a return to the emotional trap that was the crime scene, I walked back around the corner to where the boys had started their work. It was impossible to make out any pattern from right in front, so I backed up as far as the mouth of the tunnel. The experts always said it was better to appreciate art from the centre of the room.

One of the first things I contemplated was their choice of place to tag. The paintable surface was a tapered segment between the slope of the hill the building was on and the straight line of the first row of windows above it. It was low to the ground, and there wasn't that much space. I guessed it was chosen because these kids were young, and none of them were that tall. They didn't have to dangle precariously and risk life and limb, and didn't have to bring along something to climb up on. It made life simple.

Even standing from a distance the extremely stylised letters were difficult to string together. The first was definitely a B, and there was another B further along. There were two Os. My inner crossword geek was able to fill in the rest.

BloodBroz.

Blood brothers.

Cute. I knew they weren't literally brothers, but I wondered if they were related in some way? Cousins? Was the blood literal, or figurative, expressive of a common bond?

I frowned. Something in my consciousness told me this was important. I'd learned over the years to trust my radar.

A common bond?

In the time I had been playing desk jockey, searching for anything in common between the region's few related incidents of baby snatching and ... well, however you'd describe the current events, I hadn't looked into familial relationships. Were victim and perpetrator related in any way? Blood brothers. Blood sisters in this case. And why would that matter?

I did one last scan of the courtyard, then turned around and gladly started to ascend the tunnel. Coming down here may have stirred up some emotion that was a bit too close to home, but it felt like the scene had been trying to tell me something, and I now had another angle to look into. Who knew if it would lead anywhere, but it least it felt like I was doing something.

Coming here had been more confronting than I had thought. It was hard to fathom the indescribable horror that Aleisha Newman went through that night. My hands reached underneath my own, gravid belly, and I prayed she was unconscious in the moment she was cut open. I fervently hoped that her baby was out there somewhere, safe and sound, and I thanked God that in those final moments she hadn't been alone. That someone had cared enough to stay.

CHAPTER 20

'Hand over the garlic bread, and no one will get hurt.'

Both Maggie and Paul slowly raised their hands, being careful to make no sudden movements, and I slid the long wooden board holding the last remaining pieces towards me. Mealtimes had descended to a competition for the crust ends.

I enjoyed watching the interaction between Maggie and Paul as they continued the banter by trying to claim the last of the salad and lasagne. It was enjoyment tinged with a wistfulness, because with the arrival of Bubs life was going to change dramatically for this extended family unit of three. It would become a different unit of three. Maggie was due to make the big shift out next week to embark on her own new adventures in cohabitationland with Rudy, her longtime beau. He was returning from an extended archaeological stint digging up Roman ruins in his homeland of France, to more permanent digs here. I was thrilled for them both as they were one of the coolest couples I knew, but it still felt like a wrench and their coolness didn't make accepting the change any easier. It would be the end of an era. Maggie and I had been through a lot together, to put it mildly.

After they'd settled on the distribution of the food, Paul resumed the conversation we'd been having about the case. One of the pitfalls of a two-detective family was that work never stayed at work, and shop talk was inevitable. Maggie was well used to this and understood the cone of silence and privilege. What was discussed at the dinner table, or the sofas with a cup of tea, stayed at the dinner table, or on the sofas, even after the cup of tea was drunk. We welcomed her discretion – and her opinions, as she often provided a different and useful perspective to that of two investigators too absorbed in the case.

'So the big question, really, is what was she doing down that particular alleyway in the first place?' I said. 'Most women have enough common sense and instinct for self-preservation not to be alone late at night in an isolated spot.'

'Ummm, you've been guilty of that on a number of occasions, as I recall.'

'What he said,' Maggie chipped in.

I made a token defence. 'Yeah, but that's different. I was on the job, and I'm police.'

'And you really think that made it any safer?' Paul had done that one eyebrow going up thing, which was annoying. I'd tried practising it in the mirror and all that happened was they both raised and I looked surprised rather than bemused.

'Ahhh, point taken.'

'Anyway, we know the alleyway was familiar territory for her.'

'How so?' Maggie asked.

'She'd worked at Etrusco before heading off on maternity leave and had access to a parking space down there.'

'Ahhh, Etrusco, one of my favourite eateries.'

'Maggie, everywhere is your favourite eatery,' Paul quipped. He wasn't wrong.

'So why was she there late at night when she wasn't even working anymore?' Maggie asked.

'That is the million-dollar question,' Paul said, finger beating in time with each word. 'Her husband didn't know why. She'd been out at her, as he put it, "boozy book group" that evening. They'd put on a special supper in her honour as a pre-baby last hurrah. She'd left around nine-thirtyish, but for whatever reason she hadn't gone straight home.'

'And she had no reason to pop into her old workplace on the way?' Maggie asked.

'No. He said she had gone back in to work a couple of times recently, but both times earlier in the day when the place was open. He'd thought it was to get a few last things in order and for some final handover tasks, but other than that he was baffled as to why she was there.'

'So she hadn't mentioned meeting up with anyone?'

'Not that he could remember. He'd started to get concerned when she wasn't home by ten. Had texted her but had no reply.'

By then she was possibly in no position to be able to reply. My shoulders gave their customary shudder. Maggie noticed and gave my leg a little pat.

'So let's throw in some left-field reasons why she was there,' Maggie said. 'Perhaps she wanted to stop at the mini-mart on the corner to get milk on the way home and had used the carpark.'

'At that hour you'd just park outside the shop,' Paul said.

'There was a concert on at the town hall, remember,' I said, 'there weren't any spaces on the street.'

'True. Might not be such a dumb suggestion.'

'She decided to gate crash the last of the concert,' said Maggie.

'That one is a dumb suggestion,' said Paul.

'Well, you were asking for left field.'

'Yeah, but not on the other side of the county.'

'The Indigo Room had a private function on that night. Perhaps it was something to do with that? Giving someone a ride home?' I said.

'Yeah, but if that was the case she would probably have mentioned it to her husband, or the people at the book group,' Paul said.

'Maybe, maybe not. I'm sure Sam doesn't mention every last little thing she is up to to you,' Maggie said.

'Good point, and I'm grateful, because I'm sure there are plenty of things it would be better not to know.'

'You're right there. I know this is not pleasant to ask,' I said. 'But was there any suggestion that she had been having an affair? Could she have been meeting someone else? Another man?'

'Or woman?'

'Ooof, that's not the sort of question you could ask her grieving husband at this exact moment in time,' Maggie said.

'Yeah, that would be a little insensitive, even for you, Sam, but I am sure you wouldn't be the first person on the team to wonder.' Paul reached over and grabbed the repurposed gin bottle to top up his water glass. 'The thought had crossed my mind.'

'Otto's the one going through her phone calls and text messages, isn't he?' I asked.

'That would be correct,' Paul said. I tapped the side of my glass in a little yes please gesture and he obliged.

'Might have to have a chat with him tomorrow and see what has come to light.'

'If there was anything illuminating, I'm sure he would have already let us all know.' Paul looked chuffed with his own joke.

'Yeah, from what I've heard he's pretty switched on.' Maggie looked pretty smug too.

'Well, he's a bright cookie.'

'You could say his work was enlightening.'

I groaned.

The puns were painful, but man, I was going to miss this.

CHAPTER 21

Sleep was starting to become a bit of a luxury. Trying to get comfortable when your hips felt like they were trying to split in two wasn't fun, and trying to turn over in bed involved a heave and a twist that would have made an Olympic gymnast proud. The thud from my landing felt like it could have registered on the Richter scale, but, incredibly, it never seemed to wake Paul. That man could sleep through anything. Bastard. I suppose in a way it was nature's cunning plan to get me used to sleep deprivation before Bubs arrived.

The downside of all this was I was a bundle of yawns and coffee cravings by the time I got to work. It also meant that poor Otto must have been doubting how scintillating his conversation was when he kept being presented with a view of my tonsils.

Fortunately for me he was taking it with his usual good humour and would pause until I'd done with trying to crack my jaw.

'Do you want me to go make you a coffee?' he asked.

'Thanks, but no, I'll go out and get a proper one later.'

'What's wrong with the stuff in the kitchen?'

'Besides the fact the tin always seems to be empty on the odd occasion I've been desperate enough to attempt it? And have you seen how much sugar Smithy has to put into it to make it drinkable?'

'Fair point.'

I turned my attention back to the task at hand, which was asking about the contents of Aleisha Newman's cell phone.

'So there was nothing in her text messages that raised red flags for you?'

'No. Just the usual chit-chat with family and friends, the occasional automated reminder text, and promotional things from stores.'

God, I hated those. No matter how important the shoe shop

thought it was, I didn't need to know they were having a sale right now. It always felt so intrusive.

'No arrangements with anyone to meet on the Monday night?'

'No, nothing in her texts or her email. Her calendar only shows the book group meeting we already know about, nothing else.'

'Well, it's disappointing that she hadn't put the meeting with her murderer in her diary.'

'Shame,' Otto said, in that way only the South African accent could manage.

'Shame indeed. Would have simplified matters greatly.'

If you were going to arrange to meet someone with ill intent in mind, texts and email were a bit too easy for the authorities to follow up on. A clear paper trail – in a digital kind of a way. Phone calls, on the other hand, were easier to disguise. Sure, they could be traced back to a number, but other than the two people involved, no one would know what they had been talking about, unless one of them had been recording it, which wasn't standard for most of us.

'Nothing odd on her recent contacts list?'

'Depends what you class as odd.'

'Oh?' My curiosity piqued. 'There was something there?'

'Yeah, nah, just messing with your head.'

My laugh morphed into a yawn. Otto had a subtle way of trolling you.

'Am I asking too many questions?' I asked.

'Well, it feels a bit like an interrogation. You sure you don't want to take over my job?' It was offered with just a hint of sarcasm, but I knew, with Otto, the sarcasm was tinged with good humour. He was one of the few men around here who I always knew where I stood with. I could be straight up with him without worrying about offending a fragile ego.

'Sorry,' I said, 'I'm just feeling a bit side-lined, and you know what I'm like, I always have to know what's going on.'

'It's one of your charms,' he said. 'How about I save myself the agony and send you a list of the texts and calls.'

'Thank you.' I thought a moment about other ways of getting in touch. 'Did they have a landline?' Not everyone had one nowadays. We'd got rid of ours because the only people ringing it were the scammers. We no longer felt like paying for the privilege of having someone trying to part us with our money.

'Yes, and I'll send you that too.'

'Twitter, Messenger and WhatsApp?'

'Now you're pushing it.'

CHAPTER 22

The slight flicker from the fluorescent tubes added an otherworldliness to the already tense scenario playing out before me. The woman on the right seemed folded in on herself like some form of human origami. Opposite her DI Johns glowered, fists balled, plonked on the table in front of him. Seated next to him was Detective Malcolm Smith, arms folded across his chest. Whoever thought that it was appropriate to have two high-powered and physically imposing men interviewing this poor woman needed to be shot, or at least marched off to undertake some cultural and social-responsiveness training. The power imbalance was ridiculous and was manifest by the woman's cowering body language. I could not understand for the life of me why they didn't have Sonia Richardson in there instead. Well, actually, I did, and unfortunately it had nothing to do with her abilities, and more to do with the fact she didn't possess a rod and tackle. I could feel the woman's discomfort through the screen as I watched the recording of the interview from the relative discomfort of my desk in the CIB office. Why hadn't she had an advocate of some kind with her? Because at that point she hadn't been under arrest.

I leaned in closer to the computer to hear better, but then laughed – I was wearing headphones. A couple of taps on the keyboard fixed the issue.

Lena Cameron had been invited in for a 'conversation' after an anonymous call to the public help line. According to the tip-off there had been a new arrival in the house in recent days, and the caller had their suspicions. The reason Lena had attracted so much attention was because, unfortunately for her, she was a name we were familiar with. My earlier research into previous baby-snatching had flagged the case of a twenty-two-year-old woman who had been found guilty of brazenly walking into the maternity unit at Timaru and walking out with five-hour-old Imogen Wells, lifted out of her cot while her mother slept, exhausted after the rigours of giving birth. The baby had been quickly tracked down, and was completely unharmed, but the family was already traumatised. Needless to say, Timaru Hospital had drastically increased their security since the incident. Three years later Lena was looking a little the worse for wear but was still recognisable as the young woman who had stood in the dock, charged with kidnapping, and been made to undergo psychiatric assessment.

'Where did you get the baby from, Lena?'

'Isobella is my baby. She's mine.'

'We've looked into the hospital records, and there's no record of you having given birth. Yet here you are, with a baby, and we all know that's happened before.' The Boss's tone was accusatory to say the least. 'Did you try it again, Lena? Did it become too much and you had to take another baby?'

'No, that was a long time ago, and I was very sick at the time. I was sick in the head, I know that. It was an awful thing to do, and I understand what I put her family through, but I'm better now and I would never do that to anyone ever again. Isobella is my daughter. You've got to believe me.'

'Then how do you explain the fact that there's no record of her birth?'

'I had her at home. I didn't even go to the hospital. She was a home birth. You can ask—'

'Is that so?'

He didn't even give her a chance to finish her sentence, and the way he said it, with such enmity, made me wonder if he just plain hated women. Actually, I was pretty confident of the answer to that thought.

'And who can verify that you gave birth at home? Was your husband there? Family?'

In the absence of any such witnesses, I was pretty damn sure any doctor worth their salt could verify if a woman had just given birth. But clearly in Dick Head Johns' rush to get her down to the station and try and nail a quick result, a basic consultation with the police doctor hadn't happened. He was out to appease the public and the media. At the expense of the woman in front of him. It would appear that The Boss had not even entertained the idea that she might be telling the truth. I wished Smithy would take the initiative and steer the questions in a more considered and less confrontational direction, but he just sat there expressionless, like an oversized baked potato.

'I don't have a husband,' she whispered.

'Then where is your supposed child's father?' Again the spat-out question was weighted with accusation.

'Isobella's father isn't here right now.' Her eyes were downcast and she picked at the side of her thumbnail.

'Well, that's convenient, don't you think? And where would he be, then?'

I didn't think it was possible for someone to shrink into themselves more.

'I don't know.' Barely audible.

'What do you mean you don't know? Has he stepped out to the pub, off with his friends to celebrate?'

'I haven't seen him for months. He skipped out when he found out I was pregnant. He buggered off, refused to believe the baby was his, didn't want it.'

Oh, that poor woman. I couldn't even imagine how it would feel to be in that position, feel that vulnerable, that rejected.

There was slightly too long a silence, which verged into the awkward.

'And was it his?'

Jesus, I couldn't believe he actually asked that question. Insensitive bastard. I started to seriously consider going down to his office and offering a little advice on how to conduct an interview with a vulnerable person – make him think twice before opening his mouth with that kind of bullshit in the future. To hell with the consequences.

'Of course she's his. He was the only man I'd been with in years. And he left me.' The tears were rolling down her face now. Smithy finally did something other than sit like a spud and passed her a box of tissues.

'But you had the baby anyway?'

And I'd thought he had scraped the bottom of the inappropriate-questions barrel. Whether or not she chose to have the baby was her decision and none of his fucking business.

Lena looked up at this point, clearly aghast at the question.

'Of course I had her, why wouldn't I have this precious gift from God? She is everything I have ever wanted.'

'Wanted enough to steal from somebody else? To kill for?'

'No, hell, no. I'm not some monster. How many times do I have to tell you, Isobella is my baby. You can ask my mother, you can ask my friends, you can ask...'

At this point I could hear what sounded like raised voices in the background, getting closer to their interview room. The Boss and Smithy's heads swung around in the direction of the door just in time to see it fly open and a red-haired and what looked like matching-tempered woman storm into the room, very closely followed by a flustered constable.

The Boss leapt to his feet, chair tipping backward in the scramble, Smithy somewhat slower to stand.

'Lena,' the woman said, and strode over to her, placing her arm around Lena's shoulders, giving her a squeeze.

'Miriam,' Lena cried, and twisted around, burying her head into the woman's waist.

'Who the hell are you, and what are you doing in here?' The Boss roared. 'Constable, what is this?'

'Sorry, sir, I couldn't stop her,' the young man said. He looked all of eighteen, and I didn't recognise him, so he had to be very new to the job. He looked mortified and frankly scared by The Boss's reaction. But he also looked like someone who had enough sense not to get between a riled-up woman and her mission.

'I am Miriam Hardcastle, and I am Lena's midwife. And I want to know why the fuck you have this woman in here for questioning when she has just given birth two fucking days ago. Of course she didn't do that awful thing to that woman and kidnap the baby, you fuckwits, and if you'd just bothered to check you would have known that. But no, you drag her down here and take her baby off her, and put her through all this trauma, making ridiculous accusations.'

The men in the room had frozen, The Boss's mouth half open.

'Get up Lena, we're getting out of here.'

Lena stumbled up to her feet, still latched on to her rescuer. Miriam Hardcastle pointed her finger dead at The Boss and delivered a waggle that left no question as to how disgusted she was.

'And I can personally vouch that, yes, Isobella came out of Lena's fucking vagina, you muppets, and if she is not returned to us in the next five fucking minutes, I am going to be reporting you to the Human Rights Commission and the fucking prime minister, if necessary, and ringing every newspaper known to man. You will pay for this, you understand me?'

And with that she steered Lena in the direction of the door and left a room of gobsmacked men in her wake.

I found myself rising to my feet and actually applauding.

She was fucking magnificent.

CHAPTER 23

Even an hour later I was still chuckling at the grand entrance and rescue performed by Miriam Hardcastle. I couldn't resist the urge to rewind and replay the expressions on The Boss's and Smithy's faces. If only I knew how to make a GIF.

I'd gone back to the two more recent abductions that had happened in Dunedin. Thankfully, in both cases the babies had been found, safe and sound, and both people responsible had been successfully prosecuted. Given that the guilty parties were still in jail, contemplating the foolishness of their actions, I didn't think they were likely involved in the current situation. But it was still good to revisit them and see how the investigation had unfurled, follow the trail of breadcrumbs that had led to their arrest.

The first case was astonishing really. On a winter's morning in July, two years ago, Anne-Marie Metcalff had walked into the main entrance of Dunedin Hospital wearing jeans and sneakers, a standard-issue, oversized, black puffer jacket, and a dark-green beanie. She'd walked through the foyer, past the cafés and main enquiries desk, and taken an elevator to the second floor and the Queen Mary Maternity Centre. There she had coolly walked down the corridor until she had come to the room occupied by Stephanie Graham and her day-old daughter, Katie. Unfortunately for all concerned, Stephanie was otherwise occupied in the bathroom at the time. Anne-Marie had exited the room with a much fuller, zipped-up puffer jacket and had calmly walked out of the hospital to the car she had parked in the five-minute parking space out front, then driven off into the sunrise. Stephanie had exited the bathroom to every mother's worst nightmare.

It had taken a full week before the trail of crumbs had led to Anne-Marie's home in South Dunedin. A week in which the Dunedin public had been howling for answers as to how someone could walk into the supposedly safe environment of a hospital and take a baby; a week in which it became abundantly clear how desperately under-staffed the maternity centre was at the time. A week that was probably the longest of the Graham family's life.

At the trial, under cross-examination, Anne-Marie's partner, Jimmy, was asked why he hadn't questioned her arriving home with a newborn, why he hadn't reported it, done something about it? He had replied that she had really wanted a baby. They hadn't been able to conceive, so when she'd said she was going to go get one for them, and then arrived home with a bundle of joy, he was happy and didn't question it any further. That, more than anything else in the case, I found impossible to comprehend.

The second case was something you'd think could only happen in the movies. Brendon Edgar had popped down to the local corner dairy to get some milk and bread. He'd taken three-week-old Tiffany along in the car in the hope that that after half an hour of epic crying the ride would send her off to sleep, and give him and his frazzled partner some longed-for relief. The ploy had worked, as by the time he'd reached the dairy, via a fairly indirect route, the wee poppet had finally nodded off. Given the circumstances, he was loathe to wake her up just for the minute he'd be in the shop, so he took a chance and left her snoozing in her car seat in the back. Unfortunately for him, that minute was all it took for nineteen-year-old Clint Suther-land to steal the vehicle. Clint thought he was getting a Mazda Demio. What he was rather un-nerved to discover fifteen minutes later was he had scored a Mazda Demio with a bonus Tiffany Edgar. His panicked response had been to dump the car, complete with now screaming Tiffany Edgar, by the Marlow Park playground and dis-appear on foot into the relative anonymity of the streets of St Kilda. It didn't take other parents making use of the park long to investigate the source the noise, and much to the relief of all concerned, the child was reunited with her parents pretty quickly. I didn't even want to imagine the guilt that Brendon Edgar must have felt that day, and I vowed that I would never, under any circumstances, leave this poppet in the car alone. I was also pretty certain that if, when released, Clint decided to resume his former profession, he'd be checking the back seats from now on.

One of the hit-you-in-the-face things that connected all of the past cases and the Aleisha Newman one, was the baby concerned was a girl. The four cases were completely unrelated, but it did get me to thinking about what other things they had in common, so I could apply them as general filters when looking at the Newman case.

What were the patterns here? I asked myself. Although I had a disparate collection of material spread across my desk, there had to be some commonality, something I was missing.

Well, there was commonality in the obvious things. All of the babies were healthy, of good weight and robust. There was only one that had needed a little time under lights for jaundice, and that took care of itself quickly. They were all newborns, with the oldest being only two weeks. That meant looking into what was particularly special about newborn babies, other than them being gorgeous little bundles of joy. Were there any special characteristics only a newborn held? Yes, some babies came out looking overcooked and older than they were, or larger than the average, but on the whole, newborns had quite a distinct look. That whole squidged-in nose thing, and the way they seemed to have a 'Who turned on the lights? What the heck is this place? When will I be fed next?' expression.

What assumptions was I making that were pulling my focus in the wrong direction? The word 'assumption' make me smile. Dad's catch phrase ran through my head: 'When you assume you make an ass out of u and me.' It was good to be able to replay his voice in my head and it bring a smile rather than tears. That milestone was only a recent development, and still somewhat tenuous. In the spirit of the old boy, I went analogue and pulled an A4 piece of paper out of the drawer and reached for a marker pen.

I wrote *THE BABIES* at the top of the page in careful block letters.

My pen wavered above the page. What was the grandest assumption I was making so far?

So far I had only considered that a man would have the wherewithal to cut open a woman to take her unborn child. Could a woman do that? Would a woman do that? Of course, the answer had to be yes. Women had committed astounding atrocities over the course of history. Violence and horror were not the domain of men alone.

I wrote a big *MAN?* and then *WOMAN?* on the page.

What else was I assuming?

I had only thought of the murder in terms of someone doing it for their own direct benefit. What if it wasn't for them? What if they were in fact taking babies or getting something from babies to order?

Personal benefit and *For a third party* went down.

There would have to be a hell of a lot of dollars involved for someone to kill and carry the risk of being caught if it was babies for order. But then, history was full of accounts of people killing to supply a demand for everything from cadavers for medical dissection to organs for the transplant market – we'd all heard the urban myths about people getting blind drunk and waking up minus a kidney. The lust for money could make people go to extraordinary lengths.

What about the focus? Was this actually about the babies? What about the parents? Was there something special or distinctive about either of them?

The Mums and *The Dads* occupied the space in the middle of the page.

I thought back to Paul's comments about someone taking care to match for physical characteristics such as ethnicity. How far would someone go to make a baby fit in, look the part? Would people hunt for blondies, or red-heads? Someone tall?

While I was at it a thought popped into my head. And I wrote the words *planned* and *unplanned* – referring to the crime, rather than the pregnancy.

The fact that the object used to remove the baby was extremely sharp suggested that there was a degree of planning involved. Most people didn't just happen to carry around a finely honed knife or surgical scalpel. When in civilian mode I carried one of those little Leatherman multitools in my bag, because you never knew when you might need a little set of pliers or a pocket knife. Being an ex-girl guide the 'be prepared' motto was firmly embedded in my brain, but I didn't think I'd be able to inflict that much damage with its four-centimetre blade.

My eyes drifted up to the clock on the wall. Not that I needed a clock to tell me it was lunchtime, my stomach had been doing its very best to remind me of its approach. One of the features of this pregnancy was an obsession with food. I was looking forward to the day when my life didn't revolve around the next meal.

I was worse than a Labrador.

CHAPTER 24

'I mean, how hard would it be to fake a pregnancy? I know it would be difficult, and certainly implies a large degree of forward planning...' Paul paused to sidle an efficiently twirled spoonful of spaghetti carbonara into his mouth. We'd decided that a proper lunch was in order to shut me up, so had popped into the Italian in the nearby mall. There was a token salad sitting in a bowl in the centre of the table. Thus far it was ignored.

'It would definitely be a taking the long-game approach,' I said as I tried to match his pasta wrangling – bolognaise in my instance. It was being uncooperative.

'When you think about it, it would be such a gamble. If people found you out before the baby's arrival, they'd think you were a total nut job.' He managed to eat his forkful without wearing it. I wasn't quite as successful. In the process of twirling, a flick of sauce landed smack in the middle of my chest. This was why I never wore white.

'Yes, I imagine there would be some mental-health evaluation, and a bit of attention from the police. Faking a pregnancy implies that you were either going to be acquiring a baby, one way or another, or were deceiving people for some gain, whatever that might be – money being the frontrunner.'

'Money can be quite the motivator.' He stabbed some salad onto his fork and waggled it in my general direction to make sure I'd noticed. 'From a practical perspective though, what would you have to do? There's the obvious – expanding your girth over time.'

'Which begs the question of who you were trying to deceive? I mean, if it was me pretending to be up the duff, you'd cotton on pretty quickly.'

'You're right there. I'd figure out that your squidgy bits were fake squidgy as soon as I got your kit off.'

'Unless I decided the playground was closed as soon as I was pregnant.' Paul laughed at that one. I'd been one of those women who, aside from that unsettled period of morning sickness, had been rather partial to a preggers shag. Although that had waned somewhat now I was at the ready-to-pop stage.

'If that were sadly the case,' he said, 'if you suddenly came over all modest so you could hide it, I'd still know something wasn't right from cuddling you. You'd feel all wrong.'

'Basically anyone they were intimate with would know, which implies collusion. They'd have to be planning this together.' I heard my midwife's 'eat healthy' echoing in my head and reached for the salad. 'Which again begs the question, who would you be trying to fool? You might get away with duping friends and relatives, unless they were the huggy-huggy type.'

'You could fool employers.'

'I suppose.' I popped some of the token green stuff into my mouth. It didn't resist capture as much as the spaghetti had. 'Actually, simulating the physical side of pregnancy would be the most complicated part, because when it comes to the pregnancy care or the birth, you're not legally required to have a midwife, or any medical assistance. You can completely go it alone if you are healthy and confident enough to do so. If you'd managed to convince everyone with your carefully planned expanding waistline, then you could just lie about going for check-ups, appointments, scans, that kind of thing.'

'Yeah, but family would want to see the ultrasound. Mine did.'

'True.' They'd been quite insistent. 'But it would be easy enough to find a picture of one online and do a copy and paste. You could slap it all over your social media: hey, look what's coming, people. Keep everyone happy.'

'They'd still badger you about the gender. God knows our lot have asked us to the point of nagging. And unless you'd planned far enough ahead to know who your victim was going to be, and knew whether it was a girl or a boy, then you'd be a bit hobbled there. And what's with that whole gender reveal party thing. I really don't get that.'

He wasn't the only one.

'Just an excuse for a party and a cute video clip for your Insta, I guess. I take it you're not feeling mortally disappointed that we didn't have one.'

'Yeah, nah. Never in a million,' he said.

'So if you were faking a pregnancy you could just lie like we did about the gender, and tell people that you were taking the old-school approach and were looking forward to a surprise on the day.' Maggie was the only person in the know when it came to our impending wee girl. We'd decided everyone else could wait.

'Trouble with lying is you've got to remember what you said and to who. And then there's the questions people would probably ask. Like, oh, who's your midwife? Especially your girlfriends – they seem to care about stuff like that.'

Did they? I thought about it a second. 'Yeah, they do. They want to know every last detail.'

'And don't forget Dunedin is pretty much a small town. Everyone knows everyone, so if you name-dropped a midwife, someone would be bound to say, oh, I know her, tell her I said hi, or, that's funny, because she's our midwife too. And then if they asked or commented to the midwife, questions might be asked, and you'd be sprung.'

'Well, no, I don't actually think that would be an issue.'

'Why not?'

'Patient confidentiality. No midwife would comment about another woman they were attending. They're far too professional for that,' I said. 'And most people nowadays are familiar with the importance of confidentiality, so they would know not to ask in the first place.'

'That's a good point. Still, it all feels a very risky proposition. Wouldn't it be easier to explain a sudden new baby as, hey, we've been on the adoption list for ages, and woohoo, a baby came up and we had seven hours warning, or something like that? Like your friends in Gore who had that happen. Crikey, imagine having that mad scramble to acquire all the stuff you need.'

'Friends and neighbours rallied around with most things.'

'I still can't believe how much stuff a baby needs.'

'Tell me about it.' The room that was to be the baby's, when we got our shit together, was chock to the gunwales with baby paraphernalia. Hopefully it would all fit in there properly when we finally got to arranging and assembling things. It certainly wasn't going to be one of those showcase *House and Garden* nurseries, all colour co-ordinated and chic, with cutesy accessories. We didn't have the time or inclination for that.

'Logistically pretending an adoption would be easier, but you could still arouse suspicion if a baby had suddenly been reported missing at the same time, and with all the government family services involved in adoptions it would only take a phone call or two and you'd be found out.'

'Yeah, you're right.'

'Either way, you'd have to be pretty motivated to put yourself through the stress of it.'

'It's bad enough when you're doing it the natural way.'

'Ain't that the truth.'

CHAPTER 25

Jogging was out of the question – neither my belly, nor my bladder for that matter, were up to it. But that didn't stop me from undertaking the brisk-walk alternative. I'd finished up for the day, but Paul would still be occupied for the next few hours, so it was a good opportunity to stretch my legs and contemplate the mass of information swirling around in my brain. It wasn't a 'Dunner stunner' day – quite the opposite, with the city clagged in by a persistent mist of the type that hung somewhere between damp and drizzle. The kind of mist that would have made our early Scottish settlers take one look and think, aye, this'll do – just like home. The only thing that would have sold it better would have been driving horizontal rain. Despite the chill, the benefits of fresh air and the semi-great outdoors had outweighed the allure of the sofa, tea and Netflix.

The rhythm of footfall, whether at run speed or waddle mode, had always been my go-to soother. That mesmeric cadence had both a calming and focussing effect. When I was in the thick of a perplexing case, epiphany had often come when out pounding the pavement. It was as if tuning out the noise of my over-active mind gave my subconscious the opportunity to process the vast amounts of input, move the pieces around like one of those puzzle games, where you slid a square around one at a time until the complete image came into view. There had been no great revelations on this walk, though, but the exercise had helped shake off some of the restlessness I had been feeling, and taking in the verdant green of the trees along Queen's Drive was refreshing.

I paused to listen for any traffic approaching along the twisty road before nipping across to the base of the steps up to Preston Crescent. They were steep little suckers and had an oddly deep tread, so I took them slow and careful, given that I couldn't see my feet and the last thing I needed was to trip over and fall flat on my face. I stopped at the top to catch my breath and looked across to the playground. Oddly enough, given the gorgeous weather, it was still as empty as it had been when I came down past it half an hour ago. Actually, that wasn't entirely correct. There was a dog over by the swings with its nose investigating a cardboard box that hadn't been there earlier. Whatever was in the box must have been interesting because the golden retriever looked to be licking it. I hope it tasted good. Curiosity got the better of me, so I set off up the rise towards it. The dog spotted me and immediately came bounding over, in a 'hi how are you?' kind of a way, dancing in front of me before running back to the box. He repeated this twice more, with the addition of a whining noise, and then the penny dropped and I got his 'follow me' message loud and clear. His sense of urgency spurred me into a jog.

The contents of the box came into view.

'Fuck.'

It took a moment to believe what I was seeing, but the significance was not lost on me.

'Good boy,' I said to the dog as I patted him on the head. 'That's a good boy.' It took a bit of shuffling to get him out of the way so I could turn my attention to the contents of the box.

Her cheek felt beautifully warm as laid my hand against it, and it was with an immense sense of relief that I saw the little face crinkle up.

'Hey there, baby girl. We've been looking for you. It's going to be all alright.' Whoever had left her here had at least wrapped her up warm, with what looked like multiple layers of blankets. They were damp, though, and one thing was certain – I had to get her somewhere warm and dry, and fast. Our house in Rosebery Street was only a few blocks away, so I hoisted up the box, held it the best I could, propped on top of my belly, and high-tailed it in the direction of home. The dog decided to escort us, and I didn't make any attempt to stop it.

The moment I got into the house, after having to convince the retriever he wasn't getting an invitation indoors, I set the box down on the floor in the middle of the lounge, stripped off my wet parka, then carefully lifted the precious bundle out of her makeshift carrier and placed her on the rug. I pulled my cell phone out of my pocket, pulled up my contacts, hit Paul's number and whacked it on speaker phone.

Answer, answer, answer. It seemed to ring forever before he picked up.

'Why, hello there,' he said, putting on his alluring voice.

Charm wasn't what I was after.

'No time to chit-chat,' I said, as I gently peeled away the first layer of wet blanket. 'I'm home, and I need you to call an ambulance.' As soon as the words came out of my mouth I realised I should have framed that better.

'What's happened,' he said, the tone of his voice immediately jumping to alarm. 'Are you okay? What's going on?'

'Not for me, I'm fine, I'm fine. But I've found the baby. I've got the baby here.'

There was a puzzled pause.

'What do you mean you've found the baby?'

'Aleisha and Justin Newman's baby. I've got her. She was dumped in a cardboard box down at that playground round the corner at the bottom of Preston Crescent and Harcourt Street. She was wet, so I've brought her home. I think she's okay, but we need to get an ambulance here, and you need to get home.'

The wrap underneath was also damp, so I removed it as well. Big eyes were looking up at me.

'Holy shit. You sure it's her?'

'No, it's probably just another baby abandoned in a cardboard box at a park.'

Jesus.

'Sorry, sorry. Dumb question. You've just thrown me, that's all.'

He wasn't the only one feeling rattled.

'I'll get off here and call the ambulance, and I'll be on my way.

Where exactly at the park did you find the box? I'll get someone up there to cordon it off.'

I didn't think there would be any potential evidence where I found her, what with the wet, and the dog, but he was right, it was correct procedure.

'Coming up from Queens Drive it was directly in front of the forward left-hand leg of the swings.'

'Okay, I'll get someone on to it. Take care. See you soon. And well done, there are going to be a shit load of relieved people.'

Paul's question about evidence prompted me to lift the discarded blankets off the floor and pop them back into the box. As if on cue, Torie appeared out of nowhere and was showing a bit too much interest in the carton. It took a few nudges to get her to give up on it as a prospect for a nap.

I turned my attention back to this wee, precious girl. Thank heavens, under those wet two layers her clothing was dry and she felt warm. The front edge of her hand-knitted hat was wet, so I carefully edged it off her head to reveal a substantial amount of dark baby fuzz.

'You've got quite the do there, young lady, but we might have to do something about the hat hair.' I lifted her up, careful to support her neck, and rested her on my shoulder, then began the complicated manoeuvre of getting to my feet. She smelled delicious – that warm, new baby smell, with a hint of shampoo. Whoever had taken her had bathed and looked after her, and I guessed from the fact she was awake and not squawking, had fed her recently too.

I took her up the stairs and into the room that was going to be the nursery for our soon-to-be arrival. Holding a baby and looking at the piles of paraphernalia and mess made me realise we really had to get our act together and sort it out sooner rather than later. But, for once I was also glad of my procrastination, as the bits I was looking for were sitting on top of the guest bed in there. Mum had been on a knit-a-thon from the moment she found out I was pregnant, so there was a selection of hats, booties and cardies from pastels to brights in a range of sizes from teeny-weeny to tiny. There was also a stack of wraps we'd bought. I shoved aside a pile of unread parenting books, grabbed a fleecy pale-yellow one and managed to single-handedly shake it out flat onto the bed. Once arranged I placed the precious wee bundle down onto it. Looking through the beanies I chose a pastel-green hat from Mum's pile and gently placed it on her head before wrapping the blanket around her, snuggly and warm. She looked like a little baby burrito. I didn't know that she was too impressed with her new hat and being rebundled, as her little face began to crumple and with the drop of a lip came the first chirps of a half-hearted cry. I knew from years of being around my nieces and nephews that the best thing was to get on the move so I picked her back up, popped her on my shoulder and carefully made my way back downstairs to wait for the cavalry. The bloody cat had taken up residence in the box.

The little chirps from the burrito started to build into an aria. After all this wee poppet had been through, with her godawful entry into the world, and then being dumped outdoors in the cold and damp, hearing her wee protests was music to my ears. I don't know that I'd ever been more happy to hear a baby's cry.

CHAPTER 26

The mood shift in the station was palpable. News of the baby's discovery had spread like wildfire and a borderline euphoria had swept the staff.

I'd been allowed to travel with the baby in the ambulance to the hospital and had accompanied her through her once-over from the paediatrician. The verdict was that she was indeed a hale and hearty newborn. She was well hydrated, which meant she'd been fed. She'd been bathed, and there were no obvious signs of injury or abuse. The stump of her umbilical cord had dried and was looking good. They had taken precautionary x-rays, but nothing was amiss. Dr Harris described her as a miracle baby, and, Lord knows, we all needed a miracle in this case.

The elation of her discovery was quickly diminished, courtesy of Dick Head Johns. I was gutted, and frankly outraged, that I was not allowed to be there for the reunion with her family. You'd think it obvious I should be present, considering I found her and all, but apparently not. Dick Head Johns had felt it important that as the most senior officer on the case he be the one to represent the police as the medical staff introduced her to her family. In other words, he was going to make the most of a photo op and hog the limelight. I shouldn't have been surprised, but it did gall me. He'd also taken great pains to replay the 'we can't have a very pregnant officer working with the family under these circumstances' card. Arsehole.

Whereas The Boss had fobbed me off, when everyone else at the station realised it was me who had made the discovery, there was a steady stream of people coming through the office, 'just passing by and while I'm here...', clamouring to get the full story. Regaling the first couple of people had been cathartic, but the novelty quickly wore off. Now the temptation was to run away and hide.

My radar was therefore on high alert, and when I heard yet another set of footsteps coming down the hallway, I wondered how I could slide under the desk without doing myself and the kid a mischief.

'Well, that has certainly cheered every one up.'

Thank God it was the voice I longed to hear. Paul strode into the room and wrapped me in a big hug. 'How you doing? You okay?' He gave me a kiss on the forehead. 'And I've been meaning to ask you – what was the story with the dog?'

I laughed at the barrage of questions.

'He kicked up quite the stink when you guys left in the ambulance, did not like that at all.' He released me from the bear hug and plonked himself down in a chair.

'Let's just say he turned out to be our baby girl's canine guardian angel, and he took his responsibilities very seriously.' I made a mental note to track down where Muttley lived and drop off a suitable reward. I was pretty sure his humans would be tickled pink to know the role their pooch had in reuniting the baby girl with her family.

'Gotta love doggie loyalty. But really, how you doing?' Paul had been around me long enough to know I was pretty good at putting on the all-is-well front when it damn well wasn't.

'Pretty good, I guess. It just feels such a relief to find her. In the midst of such utter awfulness, it makes it a smidgeon less awful.' That was a partial truth, and also a bit of a lie. Despite everyone else's euphoria, there was a part of me that couldn't stop obsessing on the thought that I had got to hold her, stroke her hair, feel her warmth when her mother probably never even saw that beautiful little face. Maybe it was just the hormones talking, or maybe this single-mindedness was part of my ever-growing determination to get the bastard that did this.

'I know what you mean,' he said. 'In the middle of everything that's happened it feels like a beacon of light for the family to cling to.'

'What about you?' I asked. 'How are you going?'

Quid pro quo and all.

'Yeah, I'm okay.' He fidgeted with his hands for a bit, and I could see he was trying to formulate his words. 'I guess the big thing for me with all of this is it's really driven home what I have to lose, you know, if anything happened to you' – he reached out and placed his hand on the side of my belly – 'or this one.'

'Jesus, Paul,' I said, as I placed my hand on his and gave it a squeeze. 'You're not going all soft on me, are you?'

CHAPTER 27

'Shephard, my office, now.'

I had been tracking the sound of the tell-tale footfalls as they approached the squad room and had been fervently hoping they would just pass on by. But no. Was it fatalism or paranoia that had me expecting a summons?

Sonia and Otto looked up, startled, from their work, checked the expression on The Boss's face, then promptly became fascinated with their computer screens. DI Johns didn't bother to wait for a response and continued his march down the corridor.

'Any clues as to what that's about?' I asked. Usually when I got summonsed to the Grand Poo Bah's room it meant I was in trouble. But considering the events of today I was in most people's good books, so I couldn't for the life of me think of anything I'd done to piss him off. His face indicated something had gotten his goat, though.

'Beats me,' Otto said. 'Maybe he wants to thank you in person.'

Sonia actually snorted. She too had experienced the extra-special treatment only The Boss could give. Probably because she also possessed a vagina.

'Sure, that'll be it.' I hauled myself to my feet, grimaced at them and headed out the door, a mix of curiosity and dread swirling in my gut. You'd think by now I'd be used to dealing with the unreasonable attention The Boss felt obliged to give me, but it still elicited my flight-or-fight response. Unfortunately for my career, it was mostly fight. 'Wish me luck.'

'Luck.' In stereo.

I walked up the stairs, paused in front of his office, adjusted the sit of my jacket, tugged the sleeves down, then knocked on the door with what I hope sounded like confidence.

'Come.'

The thought 'officious twat' immediately jumped into my head, and I had to remind myself that I should give him the benefit of the doubt and not assume our impending chat would be unpleasant.

'Sit.'

I also reminded myself I was tired and that could sometimes make me a little over-reactive. I lowered myself into the chair and took the 'when in doubt, get in first and ask a question' approach.

'How were the Newman family?' I asked. It seemed to catch him off guard.

'They were very happy to have the baby back safe and sound, obviously,' he said. 'It was a very touching reunion.' Great for some that they could be there. As if reading my mind, he felt obliged to justify his actions once again. 'I'm sorry I couldn't allow you to be present for it. The family have been through so much trauma already, I couldn't have you triggering any further distress for them, given your condition.' Condition. Only The Boss could manage to make my pregnancy sound like a disease rather than a blessing.

'I thought, given that I found the baby, they would have wanted to meet me, despite my condition.'

'That is what we need to talk about. You are a detective now, and as a more experienced officer I expected much higher levels of professionalism from you.'

I did not possess a poker face, so my confusion must have been patently evident. Alas, neither did he and the smug pleasure he got from the statement was obvious.

'I'm sorry, what do you mean?'

'Today you heavily contaminated a scene and potential evidence that could have assisted in this murder investigation.'

My mind was still in go-slow mode. 'Pardon?'

'Do I have to spell it out for you? For a start, you removed the baby from the playground. We don't know the exact position she was in, and any traces left by the person who left her there were well and truly obliterated by you.' He leaned forward across his desk. 'And then, to make matters worse, you again compromised any evidence by removing items from her that may have helped us to identify the kidnapper and murderer.'

What the hell was I hearing? The fucker had actually found a way to turn me discovering a kidnapped baby into a bad thing. This was low, even by his standards. There was no way in hell I was going to take this one on the chin. I took a very deep breath before choosing my words, and leaned forward in the chair.

'You do realise this is a newborn baby we are talking about?' I said in what I thought was a very calm voice. 'A newborn baby that was wet and cold, and exposed to the elements. I had no idea how long she had been there. Could have been minutes, could have been hours. But we are talking about an infant, a vulnerable, living human being, not an item of evidence.' An edge of sarcasm may have crept in at this point. 'An infant that could have been suffering from hypothermia, could have been injured. So yes, I did the only thing any sane person would do. I took her from that wet, exposed playground, and I brought her somewhere safe, and I got her warm and dry.'

My finger index finger had risen and was waggling dangerously close to The Boss's face.

'Those were my first priorities, not the preservation of evidence, not worrying about whether or not there might be some blade of grass bent the wrong way at the park, or a footprint. My priority was her wellbeing, not worrying that there might be a fibre or a hair embedded in a blanket. My priority was keeping that tiny, vulnerable baby fucking-well alive.'

Any attempt at keeping my voice calm and even had gone out the window by now, and rant mode was engaged. At some stage I had even risen to my feet.

'You watch your language, Detective, and don't you dare stand there and lecture me about priorities. You might think your actions were justified, or heroic, but the first thing you should have done was call for back-up, secure the scene and wait for the help to arrive. In acting the way you did you blew any chance of us getting a lead on who had her.'

By this point I had given up any pretence of trying to be reasonable.

'You are fucking kidding me, right? Are you telling me that in your mind it was more important to preserve the scene and risk the baby's health and chances of survival? I certainly hope that's not what you are insinuating, because that would make you utterly lacking in compassion and less than human.' I could see the creep of red up his face, and I didn't know whether it was rage or shame, and frankly I didn't care. I was on a roll and had thrown all caution to the wind.

'And as for there being no potential leads now, that is a load of utter rubbish. Every single item she was wearing and wrapped in, hell even the cardboard box, is a potential source of information, and you know it. So don't you dare try and pin your lack of having a firm lead in this investigation on me. I'm buggered if you are going to throw me under the bus. I did the right thing – the only thing that should have been done – and I would do it again in an instant, and if you don't like it, then that is your problem.' And with that, before he had a chance to spit out any words between all of that sucking of oxygen he was doing, I turned and stormed out of the door.

'Detective,' came the roar behind me, but I ignored it and stomped my way back to the CIB room.

Fuck him.

CHAPTER 28

'That bastard,' I said as I stormed my way into the CIB room. I desperately needed to hit something, or throw something, but given the lack of a suitable projectile, I gave the rubbish bin a hearty kick instead. Apart from making a sadly hollow noise as it bounced against the leg of my desk and giving my colleagues whiplash, it wasn't at all satisfying.

'Paul not empty the dishwasher again?' Smithy said, a wry look on his face.

'Oh funny,' I replied, and thwumped down into my chair. 'The Boss just chewed me up for contaminating evidence because I did the outrageous thing of putting the welfare of the baby first.'

'Well, there could have been trace.' Then he saw the look on my face. 'Kidding, stop with the dagger look.' He pretended to shield his eyes. Having someone as craggy-faced and dour as Smithy trying to put on a feigned terror act couldn't help but make me smile.

'It's a fine line you're walking there.'

'Thought I'd crossed it for a second,' he said. 'And how did you take his comments?' Smithy had been my mentor and guide during my first years on the detective ladder. He'd been patient and understanding of my refusal to take undue crap and my inability not to say what I thought. It had meant he'd had to smooth the waters on more than one occasion.

'I may have made a bit of a faux pas. I got a bit shouty and stormed out, so I imagine that's going to come back to bite me.' In fact, I was frankly surprised that DI Johns hadn't appeared down here already, armed with a DCM. Mind you, even if he did, a Don't Come Monday wasn't as effective against someone who had already submitted a Not Coming the next Monday, and following six months for that matter. The former wouldn't look too flash on my records though.

'Did you do sweary-shouty Sam or just shouty-shouty Sam?'

'Sweary-shouty.'

'Oh,' he said. Oh indeed. 'Would quite liked to have seen that.'

'What would you have done?' I asked. 'You know, in that situation. Would you have whisked the baby off somewhere safe and dry?'

'Of course I would have, as would anyone else with an ounce on sense. I wouldn't get too hung up on him bawling you out about it. Besides, he was probably feeling a bit grumpy to begin with.'

'Why?' I asked, suspicion aroused by the smirk on his face.

'Because he just found out that despite his best manoeuvring to keep you away from Aleisha Newman's family, they have specifically asked to meet with you, to thank the person who found their baby.'

'They have?' My eyes went a bit swimmy, and I had to blink it away.

'They have indeed.'

Suddenly the day seemed a little bit brighter. I couldn't help but bust out in a big grin. 'Well that would have right royally pissed him off.'

'Somewhat.' He had a gift for the understatement.

I thought about the ramifications of that – the good and the bad.

'I guess that means he'll be busy trying to dream up the shittest job he can to punish me.'

'You'd have to presume so. He's very grown-up like that.'

'Bring it on.'

In this instance, it was worth it.

CHAPTER 29

They named her Hope. I got the impression that some of the men in the squad room thought the name was a little overly sentimental, but in my mind it was perfect. God knows that family needed every ounce of strength and comfort to cling to, and if a name that looked to the future rather than an horrific past could do that, all power to them. That wee girl would also need a helping hand when she became old enough to understand the terrible circumstances of her birth. To me the name Hope was a gift of optimism and love.

Every item of clothing baby Hope had been wearing, with the exclusion of Mum's knitted hat, had been sealed up and sent off for testing at ESR up in Christchurch. Unfortunately, we didn't have the facilities for that level of forensic examination here in Dunedin, otherwise by this stage in proceedings I may have had the actual objects in my hands to examine, rather than relying on high-resolution photos. I guessed the pics were better than nothing.

The job allocated to me by The Boss was, by his standards, pretty mild on the shit-o-meter. The items would be getting the forensic scrutiny up north, but here my task was to see if there were any clues as to where they were bought and then potentially trail them back to the purchaser. It was a long shot, so the likelihood of a successful lead was slim to none. He was setting me up to fail, which of course made me determined to make sure I didn't.

The police photographer had done a great job of providing a detailed set of pictures for each item. There were full-view shots, close-ups on any tags and branding, weave and patterning, any stains and flaws. The only thing missing was smell-o-vision, thankfully.

The inventory list was pretty comprehensive:

Cardboard carton – sour cream and chives Heartland potato chips, eight packs.

Huggies nappy in newborn size – clearly used.

A white, cotton, crutch-domed, short-sleeved bodysuit. Simple Is Best brand.

A pastel-green, cotton, Simple Is Best brand, long-sleeved, footless stretch and grow.

A pale-yellow, acrylic yarn, button-up cardigan with white love hearts all over it. Baby Berry brand.

Cotton cell wrap in a natural colour, Simple Is Best brand.

Polar fleece wrap, with gold, silver and grey stars and moons on a pale background. No tags.

Hand-knitted hat and matching knitted booties.

With the bring-your-own bags and pack-your-own groceries policy at a number of supermarkets there were numerous places someone would be able to pick up a cardboard chippies carton. There was often a 'help yourself to an empty box' area in the foyer – I'd raided them myself on occasion when shifting flat or needing a decent-sized box for an op-shop run. The box was kind of a snug fit for a well-wrapped baby, but it did the job. I guessed that would prevent any movement and keep them a bit warmer. There was absolutely no point in spending time looking at supermarket security footage to spot someone grabbing an empty chips carton. It could have been picked up anytime in the last year, and from anywhere. That was beyond needle-in-a-haystack territory. Mind you, I wouldn't put it past The Boss to make me sit and do precisely that.

The bodysuit, stretch and grow and cotton cell blanket were all Simple Is Best brand – one of those basics house brands that was the mainstay of The Big Red Shed chain store. They were produced in their gazillions – cheap as chips and high-turnover items. I know because we had some of them in the layette we'd bought for Bubs, the kind of items that if the poo-nami was too disgusting you wouldn't feel too bad about binning.

The nappy was a Huggies brand. Available at any supermarket, Four Square or convenience store. Again, there was no way of tracing it. The only thing it could contribute to the general profile of the killer / kidnapper was that Huggies were priced at the higher end of the nappy market. Still, you couldn't make assumptions of the socio-economic status of the perpetrator based on one shitty nappy.

The cardigan had come from Postie Plus, so again, was at the budget end of the market, from a high turnover retailer, and could have been purchased in the Dunedin store or online. An online sale would include a delivery address, so if push came to shove it was a potential avenue to try. But it could just have likely been purchased in a store, so it was a very long shot.

The polar fleece wrap with its stars and moons was really pretty, and I felt a slight twinge of blanket envy. It didn't have any identifying brand labels, which was disappointing, so I wondered if it was hand-made. It had a perfect blanket-stitch edging that could have been done on a domestic sewing machine. Even the most basic models had that stitch. I made a note to myself to check out the Spotlight or Lincraft websites to see if the fabric was listed. Otherwise a visit to them might be in order – Oh dear, how sad. I spotted with a little embarrassment the presence of some long, white cat hairs on the polar fleece. I had apologised in advance to the forensic team and warned them that Her Majesty had not been able to resist a box and a blankie.

Lastly, I turned my attention to the hand-knitted items – the little hat and the booties. They weren't the sort of items that most people had hanging around the house in case they accidentally, or otherwise, found themselves with a baby. The fact that the perpetrators had hand-crafted items implied a number of possibilities. Firstly, that they already had children who had used them, or had them at the ready for a new arrival. Secondly, hand knits were usually made with love by relatives or friends in anticipation of an addition to the family. This gave me a sense of disquiet and again begged the question, why had baby Hope been so brutally taken in the first place? How far in advance had this been planned? Were others – friends, family – a party to it? Or had they been duped, led to believe there was going to be a legitimate arrival at this time? I guessed it would all come out in the wash – hand wash in this instance.

I looked at the pictures of the beautiful workmanship on the knitted items and smiled to myself. Dick Head Johns had put me on this task because he knew it would be a hiding to nothing, something I would fail at, and then he could crow about my shortcomings as an investigator. But, on the contrary, there was a very real possibility of a useful lead because I had something he didn't count on. I had a secret weapon.

CHAPTER 30

I pressed the number for my secret weapon, and mentally girded myself for the conversation. Unfortunately, this secret weapon could also be a bit of a double-edged sword.

'Hello?'

'Hi, Mum, it's Sam.'

'Oh, Sam, lovely to hear from you. Hang on a moment, I'll just turn off the kettle.'

I waited a moment, listening to the click as she flicked up the switch, silencing the simmering hum in the background.

'I'm back,' she declared, before launching straight in, no customary hi's or how are you's.

'So have you finished up at work yet? You know it's not good for you to carry on so late in your pregnancy. You need to get some rest and get your strength up for what's ahead. In my day we didn't work right to the last minute like you young people do nowadays. It's not healthy for you, or the baby.'

At some point I knew she had to draw a breath and I might get a word in.

'Your sister-in-law was sensible and took two months off before Harriet was born.'

I liked the way she not only managed to compare me to Saint Sheryl, her beloved daughter-in-law, AKA 'she who could do no wrong', but with the accent on the words 'sister-in-law' also managed to get a subtle dig in about the fact Paul and I weren't married, something she did not approve of. I actually really liked Sheryl, but in Mum's eyes her attributes had grown to mythic proportions.

'I don't think you appreciate how tiring it is to give birth to a baby, and then have to deal with the newborn.'

I was surprised she hadn't brought up her disapproval of my chosen profession yet, compared to Sheryl's godly nurse status.

'Believe me, you'll regret not having a proper break.' She took a pause to breathe, so I grabbed my opportunity.

'I've only got a week left at work, which will give me a good couple of weeks before the baby is due.'

'Oh, Sam, that's not enough. What if the baby comes early? Then you will have had no time to yourself.'

'That's not likely to happen. My midwife said the vast majority of first babies end up overdue, so—'

'Yes, but your job isn't safe either. There are all sorts of stresses and dangers that could bring baby on. It's not like Sheryl's situation in nursing, where she was in a normal, stable environment. And they took her off night shifts early on in the piece. No, you're out there with all of those criminals, and, you know, it's not just about you anymore, you've got that baby to think of. You shouldn't be putting it at risk.'

I was beginning to regret activating the secret weapon. She was going full guilt-trip on me. I had to somehow turn the conversation around, away from the usual expected pings and recriminations, and get to the main reason I rang her, other than getting lashings of her peculiar form of love.

'Speaking of babies, I need to ask you a bit of a favour.'

Mum was one of these women who liked to feel needed so that she could then be martyrish about any help she gave. I felt no shame in appealing to this. Anyway, after her onslaught, I felt quite justified in deflecting her attention by pandering to her ego.

'You know you can ask me anything.' I almost snorted. 'What do you need?'

'I need your knitting expertise,' I said. That would pique her interest.

'Oh? Do you need some more knitting done for you?' No I didn't, well, yes I did, because you could never have too much, but that wasn't the purpose of the call.

'You know the big case we're working on?'

'The murder and kidnap one, where they just found the baby?'

'Yes, that's the one.'

'I saw it on the news – that poor man carrying her out of the hospital to take her home. It was very upsetting, but I'm so happy she's safe.'

We all were.

'You know how an off-duty police officer found her?'

'Yes, they mentioned that.'

'That officer was me.'

'Oh, really? That was you? But he didn't say it was you – that man who spoke on the news, the man in charge.'

'Detective Inspector Johns, yes, my boss.'

'Why didn't he say it was you?'

I'd watched the news segment, and The Boss had mentioned that a staffer found the baby, but true to form, had turned it around so it looked like the find was a result of his hard work in leading the investigation, rather than blind luck that I happened to have been walking past that particular playground in the rain and had stopped to investigate. I didn't have the energy to go there with Mum, so I got to the point.

'Did you notice the hat she was wearing?' I asked.

'I saw she had a knitted one on. It was very cute.'

'Well, it was very cute because you made it.'

I heard a sharp intake of breath. 'Sam, did you give away the things I knitted especially for you and my grandchild?'

Bugger. I should have anticipated she'd turn that into a negative. My bad.

'Look, Mum, when I found her she was wet and cold, and desperately needed something warm and dry. Your hat was there and it was perfect. You have to admit, it was exceptional circumstances. And I couldn't really ask for it back afterwards, could I? That would have just looked mean. Think of it as a gift to the wee girl from you. It's a pretty special hat for them now.'

I could just about hear the whirr of the cogs as she thought this over, no doubt trying to find a way to turn my argument back against me, but even her abilities would be stretched to counter that reasoning.

'Well, I guess that is rather nice, then,' she said, slowly, making the concession. 'You know, I thought it looked familiar, but it never occurred to me in a million years that it would be one I'd made, and that you'd passed it on to someone else.'

Ping.

I sighed. 'Well, there is something you could do that might help us solve the case – find some justice for baby Hope's family.'

'I don't see how I could be of any help. I'm not even in Dunedin, and I'm no detective.'

'No, but you have knowledge that could be useful. When I found her, she had on a lovely hand-knitted hat and some booties that were really quite distinctive. It was a cabled pattern and variegated wool. Do you still belong to that big knitting group on Facebook?'

'Yes, of course I do. I like keeping up with what everyone else is making.' I imagined she posted pictures of her work on the page – well, I hoped she did, because she was a very beautiful and skilled knitter, her work was near perfection. She had tried to teach me, which was excruciating for us both, and I could do the basics, but I left the complicated stuff up to the pro.

'It could really help the investigation if we could find out who knitted that set. I was wondering if you could do a bit of enquiring to your group for me. It's a bit of a long shot, but it might help lead us to who was responsible for all of this. You'd have to be discreet, no one can know it's about the case.'

'Well, how am I supposed to do that?'

'I was thinking you could post a photo of the set on the group page and ask if anyone knew anything about it.'

'Pifft, well that wouldn't work,' she said straight away. 'That would just make people wonder why? Get all suspicious.'

I knew there would be resistance from her, but I had to keep trying. But before I could put in an amended plea, she carried on:

'What I'd have to do is pop up the picture and say something like, "I saw these at a craft stall and really like the pattern and the wool. My daughter's having a baby soon and I'd love to knit some for her. Can anyone help me out?" That would work better. I'd be sure to get some suggestions, and someone might even pipe up and say they had knitted that pattern in that wool, then you could just look at the profile of the person and see if they were from around Dunedin, or if they weren't, if they'd been posting pictures of things they were knitting and bragging about for an upcoming baby or grandchild. People get very excited about grandchildren. You can just check through their friends list and see if there's anyone from there, and Bob's your uncle.'

Well, that was a bit of a surprise, and I had to give Mum full credit for coming up with a pretty solid plan. It also made me wonder how experienced she was at cyberstalking people on Facebook. For a self-confessed technophobe she was doing pretty well on the ins and outs of that platform.

'How about you email me that picture, and I'll get it on there straight away?' She sounded positively excited by the prospect. There was nothing Mum liked more than a puzzle, or a challenge.

This had actually gone better than expected.

CHAPTER 31

For some reason I felt ridiculously nervous as I approached the porch of the modest-looking red-brick bungalow in Caversham and climbed the steps. A few steadying breaths were needed before I reached out and pressed the doorbell. While I waited for someone to come to the door I took in the surroundings. A well-worn coir-and-rubber 'welcome' mat greeted visitors. There was also a cheerful burst of colour courtesy of a decorative wire frame attached to the wall bearing a rectangular planter full of crimson geraniums. A large jade plant in a terracotta pot sat directly beneath it. The tree must have been pretty old as it had a thick, sturdy trunk and spread to the size of a Swiss ball. It would take a few decades before my baby-sized version at home reached anything like those proportions, if I didn't manage to kill it first.

The sound of approaching footsteps caught my attention so I quickly straightened up the top stretched over my belly, and pulled the sides of my jacket in as close as they could get to meeting. The door opened, and I was met by a warm smile attached to a bearded face in its thirties. Some of my apprehension dissipated.

'You must be Detective Shephard?' he said, reaching out his hand.

I took it and felt his firm, but not too firm, grasp.

'Please, call me Sam,' I said as I shook it.

'Come in, come in. I'm Justin.' He paused for a moment, taking me in and shaking his head in a chuffed kind of a way. 'I am so pleased you could come.'

I stepped into the entrance way and noted the tidy arrangement of shoes by the door, so leaned over to undo mine.

'No, don't you worry about that,' he said. 'It's a bit challenging to find your feet when you're that round. When are you due?' he asked.

A wave of relief hit, now the potential elephant in the room had

been addressed. My being so heavily pregnant wasn't adversely affect-
ing Justin Newman – well, not that it showed.

'Just over three weeks to go, in fact. This week coming is my last
one at work.'

'Well, I'm sure you'll be looking forward to that.'

He led me through into a cosy lounge strewn with a variety of toys
and one of those little ride-on, scoot-along plastic cars. The domestic
scene, complete with toddler, hit me with a jolt. Life had to go on
for this family, and that life involved another little person too. It must
have been bloody hard.

'This is my mother-in-law, Helen, and this is Charlotte. Say hi to
Detective Sam, Charlotte.' I gave her a little wave. 'It was Sam that
found your baby sister.'

There was no doubting that Helen was Aleisha's mother. She was
a beautifully mature version of the daughter I'd seen in the family
photographs. The blonde, curly-haired junior version hid behind her
nana's knees and gave me a tentative smile rather than a greeting. I'd
take it.

'You all take a seat, and I'll go put the kettle on.' Justin headed
through the back of the room, nudging a stuffed giraffe toy out of
the way with his foot as he went.

'And of course, you've met Hope,' Helen said, nuzzling the baby
blissfully clapped out on her nana's shoulder.

'Yes, we've had the pleasure.' I noted the beautiful white crochet
shawl she was wrapped in this time and wondered if it was Helen's
handiwork. 'Thank you for inviting me around. I really appreciate it.
And, look, I'm so sorry for your loss and all that you've been through.'

In the wake of what they'd suffered, my words felt so inadequate.

'Thank you. It's been a very tough time.' That would have to be the
understatement of the century. Helen edged towards one of the sofas,
then carefully lowered herself down, baby on her shoulder and cling-
on attached to her leg. 'It's not something I would ever want anyone
to go through. But it does feel more bearable now we have this
precious little one back where she belongs.'

Justin arrived in the room with a tray holding three mugs of tea and a plate with some Tim Tams. Second best things to Toffee Pops.

He passed me a mug, then paused a moment before blurting out, 'I didn't even think to ask you how you have it. I hope with milk is okay.'

'Standard mix is perfect, thank you.'

Charlotte finally ventured out from the safety of Nana's legs, lured by the temptation of chocolate biscuits. A girl after my own heart.

'How are you all getting on?' I asked. It seemed like a lame question, but it gave a good invitation for them to vent, ask questions or be stoic, in that good, old Kiwi fashion that seldom did anyone any favours.

Justin went for honesty. 'Not that great, really. I still can't quite believe all this has happened, that Ali's gone. Thank heaven I've got Helen here, otherwise I don't know what I'd do. Between us we're muddling through and trying to remember what to do with a baby. I think we've done okay so far, but it's blimmin' hard.'

Of course, on top of grieving for his wife, let alone dealing with the horror of how she died, they had the practical realities and demands of a newborn to cope with, as well as a toddler who would be missing her mum but was too young to understand why she wasn't here. I didn't think there would be much sleep going on in this household, for anyone.

'If there's anything I can do to help...' I offered. Wasn't sure exactly what I could do in the practical sense, short of delivering a casserole or two.

'You've already done the best thing possible, finding this one and getting her to safety. We can't thank you enough for that.' Helen punctuated her sentence with another kiss to Hope's ruddy cheek.

'Well, I was in the right place at the right time. I'm just so relieved she's home safe with you now. It wasn't just me, though. Did they tell you she had a doggy protector before I got there?'

'Yes, that was quite funny. Dogs are very clever animals and so sensitive. Her guardian angels were certainly watching over her that day,' Justin said. 'I hope he got a good reward.'

'Yes, he sure did,' I said. 'We tracked down his owners and made sure he got lots of special treats.'

We all took a moment to sip our tea and munch on a biscuit.

'Can I ask you a question?' Justin said.

'Of course. What do you want to know?'

'We haven't really heard much about how the case is going. Whether they have any idea who did this ... any ideas at all. It's been almost a week now, surely they must have some suspects. Can you tell us anything?'

That wasn't a simple question to answer. I wasn't sure how honest to be with them. Sometimes people just wanted reassurance that everyone was out doing their best, and that the police had some solid leads to go on. Truth was, we didn't have anything concrete at this stage. Real life wasn't like the police programmes on television where they could follow an instant tantalising lead, use their amazing technology to test the DNA on the tiniest of scraps of evidence, and, hey presto, have the results back in an annoyingly long ten minutes, complete with the perpetrator's name, address and current location – at a fast-food outlet. The occasions where it was cut and dried in a matter of days were the exceptions rather than the norm. Most of the time it came down to hard work and patience.

I went for the unvarnished-truth approach.

'At this stage I'm sorry to say we don't have any solid leads. Everything we found Hope with is being forensically examined for any evidence, and I'm following up with some other ideas about the clothes she was in. The security footage we've seen so far from the area around where Aleisha was found hasn't come up with anything useful, but there is still more to go through. Our witnesses, the boys who found her, didn't report anything that can help us, so at this stage there are no obvious suspects. But that being said, we have got everyone we can working on the case – a top team of really great investigators. We are being methodical and systematic, and please be assured every one of us is utterly determined to find who did this to her and bring them to justice.'

Justin stared into his tea before returning his gaze. 'Thank you for being up front,' he said. 'We couldn't really get any answer out of anyone else. I think they were just trying to make us feel better by not telling us anything, if that makes sense.' It kind of did.

Courtesy of The Boss's machinations I hadn't been able to get near to the family until now, and I didn't know if I'd get the opportunity again, so I took full advantage of my time.

'One of our main considerations, and something that will affect the direction of the investigation is why anyone would do this to Aleisha? I'm sure it is a question you've been asking yourselves too. I know you've been interviewed by the police a number of times already, but now that you've had a bit more time to think about it, and looking in hindsight, is there anything unusual that happened that's come to mind, or any thoughts at all about why?'

They were probably sick to death of being asked why. By the police, by family, by friends and neighbours. It would come up with every cup of tea served to caring and well-meaning visitors, and every time it would re-open their very fresh wounds.

Justin blew on his already cooling tea, head inclined like he was contemplating the question. He put an arm around the small blonde missile who had detached herself from Nana's leg and attached herself to his, complete with chocolatey fingers. On the way she'd picked up a unicorn toy with a very impressive pink mane.

'Can I ask you what you think? What sort of things you're looking at? My mind is just swirling at the moment, coming up with all sorts of crazy ideas.'

'We have to look at every possibility, no matter how unlikely or crazy, because this is such an unprecedented crime in New Zealand. In my mind, it has to centre around the baby, around Hope. I've looked into baby-trafficking, which isn't a thing here, or baby-snatching by people who are desperate for a child of their own, for whatever reason. But to me, it has to be more than that for someone to do something so ... brutal. In the past, newborn babies have been taken from hospitals or homes, not...' I let the sentence hang. Even though she would be too young to understand I still felt uncomfortable having this conversation in front of little Charlotte.

'Yeah, I had been thinking about that too. They'd wait until after a baby was born.'

'Which to my thinking makes it about the baby itself.' I had to phase this bit very carefully, but Justin and Helen seemed to appreciate bluntness, so I went with it. 'Likewise, in cases where a baby was taken in a dispute about paternity or custody in a broken relationship, there has been nothing this drastic happen before.'

'Oh,' Justin said. 'I hadn't thought about that.' He laughed then. 'I can assure you that there's no question as to Hope's paternity. This baby was very planned.'

I couldn't help but think even the best-laid plans could be derailed by the impulsive and unpredictable nature of lust, but this wasn't the time or place.

'And anyway,' he said. 'I've got the paperwork to prove it.'

'The paperwork?' Most couples I know didn't rubber-stamp the dates of their shags to prove it had happened. Mind you, if they were actively working on fertility control and family planning, they might have written them down. A brag sheet of sorts. In fact, there was probably an app for that.

'Yes. We had amniocentesis done when Ali was pregnant with Hope, so we know her genetic make-up. I'm definitely the dad. I'm in the clear.'

I knew from my own consultations with my midwife that amniocentesis was offered to older mothers to detect chromosomal disorders that became more prevalent with age, but I didn't think that this couple were old enough for it to be a potential issue.

'Was there any particular reason for the amniocentesis?' They must have had their reasons, because it was an invasive procedure, so not one to be taken lightly. It was certainly not something Paul and I had considered doing.

It was Helen who responded to the question.

'We have an family history of a serious genetic disease. Those who are born with it seldom live to see their third birthday, and if they do, they become seriously disabled. I lost a sister to Tay-Sachs before I was born. My mum said there seemed to always be one in each generation. Some members of our family carry the gene, and because it is so serious we all get screened for it. We found out Ali was a carrier, like me, and I would have passed it on to her. It's one of those diseases where, if both parents carry the gene, there's a one in four chance of any children inheriting it from both sides and ending up with the disease. So when we found out that Justin's family also carried the gene, Justin went and got tested too.'

'Turns out I was a carrier as well,' he said, with a shrug of the shoulders.

'Because of that, Ali and Justin decided to go get the amniocentesis. That way, if the baby did have the double whammy and the disease, they could make some decisions. We all supported them with that, and understood the implications.'

Lordy – I was glad that wasn't something Paul and I had needed to consider.

'We did the screening with Charlotte too,' Justin said. 'As you can imagine it was a bit nerve-wracking, but as it turned out we were lucky with both of them, it felt like we'd won the lottery.'

Oof, I could imagine. And I could certainly understand why they would have the amnio, but, man, armed with that knowledge it would be a very difficult and emotional decision to make, either way. Not a position I'd want to be in. The only unfortunate thing that ran in my family was the lack-of-height gene – for the women anyway.

It did get me thinking about the information you'd get from amniocentesis. I knew that you could find out the gender, and of course some chromosomal and genetic disorders. I'd have to go and do a bit of research, see if there was anything there that would help make some sense of this case.

Baby Hope started making some nuzzly, grunty, 'I'm awake' noises in that 'cute for now but it's going to build into a grizzle very soon' kind of a way.

'Someone's waking up from her nap,' Helen said. 'She's due for a bottle around now. Sam, do you want to hold her while I get it ready?'

'I can sort that, Helen,' Justin said, and got to his feet. The speed with which he volunteered made me suspect he needed a break from the conversation. I'd noted a number of moments where his eyes welled up when we were talking and had to remind myself it was still all very raw for him – for all of them.

'How about you come and grab Hope on the way, Justin. I get the feeling the detective here would like a cuddle.'

I didn't need asking twice.

'Sure do. Hand her over.'

CHAPTER 32

Despite the fact I lived with the guy, and worked with the guy, I felt like Paul and I hadn't had any couple time in ages. The rigours and task allocations of the case meant that we weren't often in the same space at the same time, and if we were it was in the presence of the multitudes. Tonight Maggie was out at the movies with Rudy, so it was just the two of us, well, almost three of us. Four if you counted the cat who was curled up on what was left of my lap. It felt an absolute luxury to be parked on the sofa at home, ensconced in my PJs and fluffy slippers, snuggled up to the man, hot Milo in hand, watching crap TV.

'Is it odd to feel guilty because this pregnancy is going so well, and everything is straight forward and there's no drama when not everyone is so lucky, especially, well, you know...?'

He gave me a little squeeze.

'I wouldn't say odd. I think I'd say it's stupid, ya dumb nut.' Paul was always great with terms of endearment. He was right though, it was silly to feel bad about being happy, and although my head knew this, I still couldn't help it.

'How did your visit with the family go today?' he asked.

It was getting to that time in the evening when Bubs started to get a bit active, usually when I started relaxing. I could feel the first fluttering of her movements. Would she be this predictable when she was on the outside?

'It was great, actually. It felt such a relief to finally meet them in person. Being deliberately excluded from contact was really hard, and I don't know if this sounds weird, but seeing them and feeling what they are going through makes it easier, if that's the right word – to fight for them, to fight for justice for Aleisha. It shouldn't make any difference. I know that I would put in the same work and strive for them whether I had met them or not, but it feels far more personal now.'

'I've gotten used to your level of weird. Nothing you say surprises me anymore.' He gave my hair a scriffle with the arm draped around my shoulder.

'You do realise I'll take that as a challenge?'

'That doesn't surprise me, either.'

'Touché.'

Torie the cat, or Queen Victoria, as we called her when she was naughty, had been leaning against one side of my belly, and I could feel Bubs giving her a few prods from the inside. Her Royal Highness looked mildly perturbed. She then looked almightily perturbed when Bubs gave a massive kick that I swear jolted the cat off her spot. With an extremely unimpressed look on her face, she moved position around to the other side of my lap and resettled herself, out of the firing line.

'I did learn something interesting when I visited them – something that hasn't been noted or recorded earlier as far as I'm aware.'

'Oh? What was that?'

'We got onto the topic of affairs and illegitimate children.' Paul sputtered on his Milo and almost spat it across the room.

'Say what? How?'

'Ha – I said something that surprised you! I win.' He gave me the side-eye. 'It came up in conversation. I'd made a comment about paternity...'

'I don't know that I even want to know how that topic of conversation came up. It's not the sort of thing most people would talk about when meeting the family of a victim of crime involving a baby. Tactful – not.' If his left eyebrow could have risen any further it would have been embedded in his hairline.

'It just sort of accidentally popped up – not something I purposefully asked about. And Justin Newman was laughing when he told me the baby's parentage wasn't in question. It wasn't a whoopsie, or awkward moment, if that's what you were wondering.'

'So maybe not quite so bad as I had imagined. What was it that you managed to find out that they hadn't mentioned before?'

'That Aleisha Newman had an amniocentesis done – to the baby to screen for some really awful genetic disorder that runs on both sides of the family. They had the procedure when they were expecting Charlotte, too – their first child. The thought of having a monstrous great needle going through me and being so close to something so precious gives me the willies, so it must have been a huge concern for them to risk it.'

'I can tell you now, if you'd needed amnio, I wouldn't have been there to watch.'

'Great support you'd turn out to be. I didn't know you were squeamish about needles.'

'I'm not. I have no problem them sticking them into me, but it's a bit different watching someone do something risky with a pointy sharp object to people that you love.'

And there he confirmed what I'd known all along: that he was a big softie with a hard-shell exterior. And that he had the knack of a good save.

'Fair enough. I'll let you off the hook. You do have to be there for the birth though, squeamish or not.'

'Wouldn't miss it for the world,' he said with a wink. 'It is inter-esting that they had amniocentesis. I know when Smithy interviewed the husband, he was very thorough and asked a lot of questions about the pregnancy and who was involved in their care, but Justin didn't mention it then. You do have quite the gift for finding things out.' If I wasn't mistaken he sounded almost proud. It was very endearing. And he wasn't wrong. Maybe I just had one of those 'tell me all about it' faces. Or gave off the kind of vibe that made people feel comfort-able offloading all sorts of stuff. I was often amazed what people would confide in me about, and not just in the job, but in everyday life. Friends and strangers alike.

'I know. To be fair, it probably helped that the initial shock is wearing off and they've had some time to reflect on things. But it's got me to thinking more about why someone would do something as desperate as murdering a woman for her baby. The fact that Hope has been returned tells us it wasn't about possessing or having a baby – or selling a baby, baby trafficking, that kind of thing.'

'Unless the publicity around Marty The Fly's failed financial enterprise spooked them, and they decided to quit and run.'

'Long shot, and please don't mention Marty. I still want to wring his scrawny little neck.'

'You'd have to join the queue.'

An accurate observation.

'As I was trying to say, before I was so rudely interrupted by talk of that waste of space, I was already starting to think that it was something about Hope herself that was pivotal to all of this, some specific characteristic that made her the target, with Aleisha the unfortunate person standing in the way. With the amnio, Justin and Aleisha had a full screening for everything, including the disorder that plagued their families, so that information was out there, on their records. As well as that, yesterday I went down to the crime scene because I'd wanted to see for myself where it had happened, get a feel for it. I saw something there, something that sparked an idea. It was the boys' tag. They hadn't got very far along with it before they discovered Aleisha, but it was going to be their name: "BloodBroz", short for blood brothers.'

'Not a bad name.'

'Pretty catchy. But the name prompted me to get thinking about blood and whether there was something medical behind this case, some health motivation. Justin talking about the amniocentesis has just reinforced that idea.'

'So what are you going to do with this information and with the spark?'

'I'll run it by Smithy in the morning, but I want to check back on basically any recent reports that have involved a baby and odd medical concerns. Take it out broader than abductions, and see if there have been any common threads. And I'll find someone to talk with about exactly what sort of things an amniocentesis can show, along with the chromosomal stuff.'

'Another phone call to your pet pathologist?'

'If you're referring to Alistair, then maybe.' I don't know that Paul had ever gotten over me describing Alistair as being like the class goldfish that someone took home to look after for the school holidays. 'Or I was thinking of our midwife, Naomi, because a midwife would have a pretty good idea. Otherwise one of the obstetricians I met at the hospital or someone at the med school. There are a few good options.'

'The more I think about it the more it makes sense that there could be something medical behind this.' Paul put his empty mug on the side table and reached across to give Torie a rub around the ears. She started to purr her appreciation. 'Perhaps we should go back to Justin and ask if he can think of anything unusual that had happened around Aleisha's treatment and investigations while she was pregnant. It might trigger something he hasn't really thought about before. It's as good a lead as we've got so far.'

'It's worth a try.'

During our conversation I had felt that odd, squirmy and slightly gross sensation of the baby turning herself around. The purpose of her movements soon became apparent as I felt a hefty kick against the very spot where Torie was now leaning. The cat was nonplussed, but had apparently had quite enough of this invisible onslaught. She vacated my lap in a big hurry.

I couldn't help but burst out laughing, and Paul sat up, his legs having been used as a runway for the feline scramble off to the side. Judging by the pained expression on his face he'd have the claw marks to prove it.

'What the hell was that about?' he said in the direction of the escapee. 'Whatcha doing ya crazy, fluffy mutt?'

'Oh my God, Paul,' I said trying to control my mirth. 'We're in for some trouble.'

'What do you mean?'

I placed my hands on either side of my belly and gave it a little jiggle.

'This girl isn't even born yet, and she's already terrorising the cat.'

CHAPTER 33

'Can I speak with you a moment?' I asked Smithy.

We'd just had the morning briefing, which didn't add anything new and significant to the case. We were still waiting on the forensic evidence results from ESR, so that avenue of pursuit was on pause. The euphoria of finding baby Hope had by now evaporated, and had been replaced by a glum frustration that there were no strong leads combined with a determination to keep putting in the legwork, covering all of the bases and marching relentlessly onwards, however slowly.

I'd talked with Smithy before the meeting about uncovering the Newmans' amniocentesis and wanting to pursue potential medical motives in the attack and kidnapping. Thankfully he was very receptive to the notion and had made a small mention of it at the briefing by way of a heads-up to the team and to stimulate more thinking. Until there was a concrete link found, the investigation would still take a broad-brush approach.

Smithy gave me a look of 'what do you want now?' His resting face was one of abject suspicion, though, so I didn't read anything into it.

I'd cornered him in the kitchenette while he was preparing another of his mouth-puckering coffees. Last week's dishes were still in the sink.

'What can I do you for?'

'I have another proposal for you.'

'Not marriage? I thought you were spoken for, and I'm not that kind of a guy.'

I gave him my very best 'funny, haha' look.

'Duly noted,' I said. 'This has to do with the investigation.'

'I figured as much.'

Rather than bite back and continue the pointless banter battle I pitched straight in.

'You know how the Newman family asked to see me, and now I've met them?'

'Yes?'

'And they shared some things with me that they hadn't with you or the others.'

'Yes?' That one came with an extra dollop of suspicion.

'I was wondering how you would feel about me going back to see them and continuing with that line of enquiry? I know I'm not part of that team and you were planning on going yourself, seeing as you were one of the first detectives to talk with them. But can I go, or at least go with you?'

Smithy's eyes narrowed. From past experience I knew this didn't bode well.

'You don't think I'm capable of following up with the Newmans myself?'

Not the response I was expecting. Our conversation earlier this morning had gone well and didn't have the grumpy undertone. I didn't know what had changed to put him in a mood. Maybe he'd been DI Johnsed?

'No, of course not. It's just that I feel like I've built a good rapport with them, and they are comfortable around me. When people are relaxed they are more likely to remember things or connect things that could be useful. I thought we could make the most of it.'

'I am aware of that, so you don't need to quote your psychology manual at me. What's the female equivalent of mansplaining?'

Well this certainly wasn't going as planned. I hoped my face didn't look as surprised as I felt.

'I wasn't—'

'Womansplaining?'

This was getting beyond amusing and now it was my turn to start getting shitty. I took a deep breath and suppressed the urge to get snarky.

'All I wanted to do was ask you if I could continue the conversation with the family about the amnio and the medical things.'

'Because you didn't think I was able to do that, that you're better at this than me.'

Oh, bloody hell. Now the conversation was on the loop of death, and it was apparent there was nothing I could say that was going to salvage it.

'Don't be stupid. It wasn't that at all, and you know it.' There was no point in tiptoeing. 'What has brought this on? All I did was make a simple request, and now you've gone all defensive and are making out that I don't think you can do your job. You know damn well that's not true.'

He banged the coffee mug in his hand down onto the bench with unnecessary force, and a fair amount of it slopped over the side. The anger behind it made me flinch, and my nervous system reminded me he was a well over a foot taller than me and twice my weight.

'Oh really? Ever since the Powell case you've treated me differently, like you think I've lost it, that I'm not up to it anymore. Why do I feel like you're always judging me?'

Wow, I didn't see that coming, but there it was, right out in the open. The simmering past come to the boil. We'd skirted carefully around any conversation about what had happened to Gideon Powell in the interests of continuing a professional relationship, but I was never satisfied that Smithy didn't have some hand in it, and it was an uncomfortable grey area in my usually black-and-white views on justice. Well if he was going to stand there and out the issue front and centre, then so be it. Looked like now was going to be the time and the place.

'So why does your conscience think I'm judging you?' I asked.

'It's got nothing to do with my conscience. My conscience is clear. It's fairly obvious you don't trust me anymore, and I don't know what I can do to change that.'

Trust. It was a complex issue.

'Well, you could be honest with me, for a start.'

'I have been honest.'

'Have you? Have you really? Because you've never given me a definitive yes or no answer when I've asked you about what happened to Powell. You've always hedged.'

'Well how the hell should I know? We've never managed to close that case despite all the man hours thrown at it. I know you've got it in your head that I had something to do with his death. But my injury was a coincidence and caused by me being a clumsy oaf.' Granted, he had never been known for his gracefulness. 'You can check my medical notes if you want. And if you really want to be particular about it, the DNA evidence was not mine.'

'And was that luck or design?'

'Jesus Christ, Sam, what sort of a man do you think I am? Do you think I'm a murderer?'

That implied premeditation.

'No, I don't think you're a murderer.' I had to phrase this carefully. 'But I do think that you are the kind of man whose loyalties would seek some sort of vengeance for a friend, and that in the heat of the moment, could make an error of judgement.'

His face was stony as he weighed up what he was going to say next.

'You have to take my word: I didn't have anything to do with his death. There's your definitive answer. Take it or leave it.'

'Well, at the moment I'm struggling to trust you, and it's going to take more than words for you to earn that back.' We stood there in stalemate, neither of us willing to back down.

Smithy looked off to the side and sighed before looking me back in the eye.

'It was a tough time for you back then, Sam, and I think you were looking for things that didn't exist.'

So now he was gaslighting me too.

CHAPTER 34

For the second time this morning I left a short message on voicemail. The first was to my pathologist pal, Alistair, who was usually on the sharp end of the job on a Monday morning, catching up on what had been stored in the chillers over the weekend. The second was a more carefully worded message to Naomi, my midwife, to make sure she realised the reason for the call was not urgent and about work, rather than my needing her services for an untimely arrival. We didn't need any panic stations. Hopefully between the two of them I would get the information I needed about amniocentesis. I always found it way easier to talk, in person, with people I knew when I needed information rather than cold calling. I didn't really do telephones, so cold calling rated up there with dental appointments and being on traffic patrol. I did have a recommendation of a tame obstetrician, so there was a plan C, but I hoped it wouldn't come to that.

My rather heated and awkward conversation with Smithy had prompted a need for a walk around the block to regather my composure. That regathering had also involved a coffee and a sausage roll that I was already regretting.

I turned my attention back to previous cases with anything that had involved babies, but this time through the lens of potential medical connections. Logic was telling me that I should narrow it down to cases that had occurred within the last five years. To my mind that time frame was still a bit broad, but the numbers weren't huge, so it wasn't like I would be overwhelmed. I also discounted any cases where a successful prosecution had occurred, which included the two most recent Dunedin instances of kidnap. A number of those convicted across the South Island had completed their custodial sentences and to my mind were unlikely to re-offend. Those cases had been more about people desperately wanting a child to the point of doing something irrational, and were the kinds of incidents where, although justice was served, it was still terribly sad and you felt deeply for both the victims and the guilty.

One stumbling block to this train of thought was the completeness of our records. The police files contained profiles and interview transcripts, observations and some medical information that was relevant to those investigations, but not full and comprehensive information about those involved. So there would be an element of following up and reopening the dialogue around that if needed. I wasn't going to be lacking in things to do.

There was one element of my background investigation into cases involving babies and hospital admissions or medical reporting that I had been putting off. Every time I had been involved in investigating a certain type of case I had been left feeling sickened and traumatised, and I knew that looking back into them was going to be like picking the scab off old wounds. These were the instances where parents had harmed or killed their own children. Where the very people who were supposed to love and care for the most vulnerable had instead turned their hands against them in sometimes utterly cruel and unfathomable ways. Unfortunately, New Zealand had some of the worst statistics in the world when it came to the domestic abuse of children. The thought that on average a child died every five weeks was horrendous. Yet every time another child was murdered at the hands of a parent or caregiver, there was a massive public outcry – 'this must stop', 'something must be done', 'the system is broken' – and there were promises to enact change, train people working with children to identify abuse, address inequity and poverty and social deprivation, and those huge underlying societal drivers, to support communities and families to be good parents, to stop that kind of atrocity from happening again. But nothing ever changed. Children were still being beaten, broken or killed at the hands of their supposed loved ones. The sad truth was, even though New Zealand was a small country, we didn't seem to be able to protect our most vulnerable *tamariki*. The statistics were appalling, but of course, they only counted the reported cases, the ones where children were injured enough to need medical attention, or where abuse had been picked up by child-care centres or schools. It didn't count the invisible ones, the God knows how many children who suffered abuse every day. Fuck, even thinking about it was getting me down.

CHAPTER 35

The vibration of my phone bumped me out of the little daze I had slid into. I wondered how long I had been staring at that particular page. I scanned around the room to see who was still here, and was pleased to see only Sonia. Hopefully I hadn't nodded off and been snoring, but she wasn't giving me funny stares, so I think I was in the clear.

The caller ID revealed it was Naomi returning my call. It was good timing.

'Hey Naomi, thanks for calling me back.'

'No worries, Sam, is everything okay? I got from your message that this was more work-related, and you didn't sound like you were wildly panicking, but I just want to check up on you first anyway, just in case.'

General panic levels were rising, but the needle hadn't swung across to wild as yet.

'Everything is absolutely fine on that front, thank you. Couldn't be better.'

'That's what I like to hear,' she said, warmth in her voice. 'And well done on finding the baby, by the way. I heard about it on the radio. That must have been a relief to everyone concerned.'

'Thanks, it sure was. It was blind luck, really. I got to meet her family, which was great. Sad, but great. That's the reason I wanted to talk with you. I wanted to pick your brain about something that came up in conversation with them.'

'Sure, how can I help?'

'One of the things they revealed was that the woman had an amniocentesis performed earlier in her pregnancy to screen for a genetic disorder that ran in both sides of the family. They talked a little about it in our antenatal classes, and I recall you talking about it to me back when we were first talking about ultrasound scans and blood tests, and all of the things they screen for in pregnancy.'

'Yes, it's one of the things we're required to raise with couples so they can make informed decisions about their antenatal care.'

Knowledge was power, and from my very recent experience of the scary realm of bringing a new life into the world, every bit of information helped. Although, I could also see how too much information could be overwhelming. Some of it had triggered my tendency to over-think.

'What I'm wanting to know is the range of disorders and problems it can pick up. And also how that is all tested for.'

'I can help with the basics of some of that. An obstetrician or paediatrician would be able to give you a more comprehensive list of conditions that can be detected. But for a starter you can tell the baby's gender, blood type, including Rhesus factor, which if the baby and the mother are opposite can sometimes cause complications. There's Down's syndrome and other chromosomal disorders.'

'Paternity?'

'Yes, although it is an invasive procedure so people wouldn't have it done exclusively for that reason. Genetic conditions such as cystic fibrosis can be detected, or spina bifida and neural-tube defects.'

'So it can detect a lot.'

'Yes, and is ninety-nine percent accurate as well. Of course, it can tell people what's wrong, but can't tell them the severity if their baby does have one of these conditions. That's why it's a tool that goes hand in hand with conversations with their maternity carers, or even genetic counselling. As you can imagine, any news like that would be a shock to a couple.'

All any of us wanted was to have a healthy and happy baby, so yes, I could imagine – and had done so regularly and in great detail at stupid o'clock in the morning when I was uncomfortable and couldn't sleep.

'And what about the actual logistics of it – the procedure, testing, that kind of thing?'

'It's usually done at the fifteen-to-seventeen-week stage by an ob-stetrician, and done with the guidance of an ultrasound, so in a hospital or private practice. It doesn't actually take too long, I'm told. Then the sample is sent off to the lab for testing, and we wait for the results. That's about as far as my specific knowledge goes, but if you want, I can email you some articles with more detailed information.'

'That would be really useful, thanks.' I thought about where to take this line of enquiry now I was armed with a bit more knowledge. 'I guess my next thing would be to chat with someone at a lab to find out a bit more about their procedures.'

'If it helps, my husband Michael works at one of the labs here. If he can't answer your questions, he'd be able to put you in touch with someone who could.'

'That would be brilliant, thanks.'

'I'll text you his details.'

'Look, thanks so much for all of your help.'

'No problem. Hopefully it helps you get some answers and find who did this. I can tell you, it's the hot topic of conversation with all of my mums, everyone's really freaked out by it.'

'I can imagine. I'm freaked out by it.' And I wasn't joking.

'Oh, and one last thing, Sam.'

'Yes?'

'Don't forget your appointment tomorrow.'

Crikey, I was glad she'd reminded me. In all the excitement of the case my midwife appointment had completely slipped my mind. That would have been a bit embarrassing.

'How could I possibly forget. I'll see you tomorrow.'

CHAPTER 36

It was such a beautiful day, I decided to go out and make the next phone call from the closest patch of grass, which happened to be situated in The Octagon. I plonked myself on the steps in front of the statue of Robbie Burns, which today was artfully adorned with some unfortunately placed bird poo. I wondered if the Scottish Bard ever imagined his likeness would be prominently positioned in a city on the other side of the world to be admired by tourists and pigeons alike. He'd written 'To a mouse', and 'To a louse', so perhaps his sense of humour would extend to a poetic ode to the indiscriminate bowel habits of birds.

Before I worked up the gumption to make the call I enjoyed watching humanity walk by. People-watching was one of my favourite sports. Dunedin seemed to bring out some superb fringe specimens. The advantages of living in a city that wasn't too up itself.

I was getting heartily sick of being a desk and phone jockey and was really missing being out in the field. I felt highly envious of Paul, Smithy and the crew out interviewing people in person, visiting sites and following up on leads. I had a cunning plan that would hopefully get me doing something a bit more interesting than exercising my fingers on a keyboard and my eardrums on a phone, but still at the low-risk end of the spectrum to keep the cotton-wool brigade happy.

'Michael speaking.'

'Hi, Michael, it's Detective Sam Shephard here.'

'Oh, hi, Detective. Naomi said I might get a call from you.' Great. At least I didn't have to explain from scratch, which made life easier. It wasn't so much of a cold call, but a luke-warm one. 'She said you were researching lab testing and amniocentesis.'

'Yes, if that's something you can help me with.'

'Hopefully I can help a bit. My work at the lab is fairly generalist, but fire away, what were you wanting to know?'

'I think for starters just a basic run-down of the procedures you use to process the samples. Is it okay just to talk about this over the phone? Or I can come down to the lab and talk with you there if that works better, see how it's done?'

My fingers were crossed in the hope he'd give the desired answer and invite me down to the lab. I loved looking in labs.

'The phone is fine, I can describe everything. For security reasons and sterility reasons, we're not allowed to have any unauthorised people visit the lab, other than med students and people in training, so unless it was extraordinarily important I can't accommodate you there.'

Damn, that's where my cunning plan fell down. I felt ridiculously crushed at not getting the chance to go in person. But I supposed it was worth a crack.

'That's okay, and understandable. It's just a general enquiry really,' I said. 'Phone it is, then.' Hopefully my disappointment didn't show in my voice. 'So what happens with the samples once they get to you?'

'Let's take a little step further back from that. The samples are collected at the hospital – they're clearly labelled at the time of the procedure with barcodes and identify the donor with their name, date of birth and NHI number. As you can imagine, getting the samples mixed up with anyone else's would be an utter disaster, so the chain of identification is very careful.' I imagined there would be serious consequences, far beyond the embarrassment of stuffing that up, if samples were accidentally swapped. People were making some serious and life-changing decisions based on that information. I shuddered even thinking about it. 'We have our own courier who picks them up, so that is all very secure.'

'So you don't reply on a commercial company?' My own experiences with so-called same-day or even overnight delivery hadn't been too flash. And the fact you paid more for the super-service that failed to deliver always grated.

'God, no. When samples can be temperature sensitive, they can't guarantee delivery within the time frames we need.' I guessed precooked specimens weren't a good thing.

'So what happens when you receive the samples?'

'When they come to us we process them by first separating out the baby's cells from the amniotic fluid and then undertake the testing from there. There are specific proteins that can be found that indicate some of the chromosomal disorders. We undertake DNA analysis, and do a broad sweep of tests in addition to any specific tests the physician may have requested if there is a family history.'

Like in the Newman case. It sparked a vague thought in my mind, but one I couldn't quite put into words, so I went for the simple.

'And how long does it take for results to get back to people?'

'Some things are quite quick, a matter of days, but some of the more complex analysis, where we are growing cultures of cells, can take up to a couple of weeks.'

'So you'd report those as they come, or wait until they were all ready and notify in one hit?'

'Oh, definitely as they come. As you can imagine, people can be really anxious about the tests and what they might mean for them, so as soon as they are verified, we pass them on.'

'So who do they go to?' I was guessing it wasn't straight to the patients.

'They are sent directly to the obstetrician, who then contacts the family and any other medical providers involved in their care. They get the job of explaining the results, and then, if they are not great news, talk about the options available, that kind of thing."

'I wouldn't envy them that task.'

'Me neither. I'm happy doing the invisible bit behind the scenes.'

And with that I finally pinned down the thought that had been skittering around the edges of my consciousness.

'So in terms of the information you get from the testing, who has access to it? Obviously the obstetrician and whoever they pass it on to.'

'Well, yes and whoever can access their computer records there, I suppose.'

'What about with your systems at the lab?'

'Here?' He paused for a bit. 'The person who actually does the testing and enters the results, and the person who verifies the results for anything that was complex, or who does quality-control testing, which is a continuing process. I guess most people here have access to results. But we have to sign confidentiality agreements as part of our employment contract.'

'What happens in the lab stays in the lab?'

'Haha, yes indeed.'

CHAPTER 37

Dunedin in the spring was nothing short of spectacular. We'd hit that sweet spot of the day when the wind had died down to a mere flutter, the soft light of the longer evenings was kinder on the eyes than winter's low, angled glare had been, and the temperature hadn't yet dropped to Antarctic with the setting sun. The last rays backlit the swathe of daffodils, giving them an ethereal golden glow under the semi-skeletal canopy of the large trees sporting that vivid, first flush of new-growth green.

In the name of exercise and blowing away the day's cobwebs, Maggie and I had come down to the Botanic Garden for an after-dinner constitutional. Despite the ghosts of cases past, it was one of those havens in the city where I could breathe in nature and feel the day's tension melt away.

We'd been walking along in companionable silence, listening to the rising clamour of the birds as they settled in for the evening, and the lessening chatter of students as they shortcut through the park on their way home to flats in the Valley.

'Can I ask a question?'

'Of course,' I said. 'But I reserve the right not to answer it.'

'Suspicious wee critter aren't you?'

'Always.' I'd been around Maggie enough to know that when she started a conversation with 'Can I ask you a question?' it was usually a question I wouldn't like. The kind of question that fell into the 'you're about to get a serious talking to' category. I noted the neutral territory, the absence of Paul and the fact Maggie had suggested the outing in the first place.

The cow had set me up.

'And pray tell, what would that question be?'

She laughed. She knew she'd been sprung.

'Well, I was just wondering when you were going to set up the baby room?'

That wasn't too bad. I was expecting something more challenging. Maybe I'd misread the situation.

'And why are you putting it off?'

And there it was.

'We're not putting it off, we've just been busy.'

'Too busy to create a welcoming space ready for your impending bundle of joy, the biggest moment of your life?' The way one eyebrow raised provided just the right level of derision.

'We'll get on to it.'

'When?'

'Soon. I'll have lots of time on my hands in a week or so. It will give me something to do.'

'Hmmmm,' she said, and walked on.

'What do you mean by "hmmmm"?' I asked.

'I mean hmmmm.' If she was trying to make another point, it was a bit lost on me. We'd wandered further across the lawn to the sunken herb garden and had started walking down around crazy-paved, circular stone tiers.

'How about you save me the guessing and come straight out with what you're thinking.'

'But that would be no fun.'

'They're going to shut the gates soon, it might save us being locked in for the night.'

'Fair call. The point I'm trying to make is it feels like you are putting it off. I don't know if it's because you're in denial that actually, you're about to have a baby, despite the rather large evidence. I don't know if it's also a way of saying you're still not quite sure how things are going to work out with you and Paul. It could be that you're afraid of the changes ahead. And it could be all of those things.'

She'd summed the situation up nicely – she was good like that.

I sat myself down on the steps between tiers, ran my hand through the lavender, then raised it to my nose to inhale the scent. Maggs parked herself beside me.

'Is that such a bad thing?' I asked.

'I'd say it's a pretty normal thing. But you've always been the kind of person to face new things head on, roaring like a beast. This doesn't feel like you. What's changed?'

That was a horribly complex question, and I wasn't sure how I could articulate it and make any sense at all. My brain was swirling with thoughts that ranged from fears to anticipations to questions, and I wanted to express them to her, but it was like trying to make sense and order out of three jigsaw puzzles shaken together in one box, with no cover pictures to go by. Maggie, bless her, recognised the spinning-ball-of-death expression on my face and gave me a little affectionate punch on the arm.

'Bullet point it.'

'What do you mean, bullet point it?'

'Give me a list of your concerns, not more than five words per item, quick fire, so your brain doesn't engage too much. Then I'll systematically work my way through them, pick them to pieces and destroy them.'

Her methods probably wouldn't appear in a text book anytime soon, but Maggie was just the kind of therapist I needed. I took a deep breath and dove in.

'Dad died.

'Mum mummed.

'I'm fucking pregnant.

'What if I'm a shit mum?

'Do I love Paul?

'Does he love me?

'Will we last?

'I'm fucking pregnant.

'Career and baby?

'Pregnant woman died.

'I'm fucking pregnant.

'It's gonna hurt.

'You're leaving.'

With the last statement I could feel my vision blurring, and I had to turn aside for a moment and examine the leaf structure of the lavender more closely.

'Okay,' she said. 'That's quite some list. I shall dive on in.' She did that classic interlock fingers, turn them inside out and stretch your arms out thing, readying for action.

'Yes, he did. Jock was an awesome man and he'd be so proud of you and pissed off he didn't get to meet his grandchild.

'Your mum loved your dad and did what she did and does what she does because she cares.

'Why, yes you are pregnant, isn't it great?

'You won't be a shit mum. And hey, even if you are, you're still going to be a better mum than your mum. The bar is set low.'

That one elicited a snort-laugh.

'The next one: do I love Paul? I can't believe we're still having to have this conversation. You are a classic commitment-phobe. Get over it. Let yourself love him.

'He worships the ground you walk on and has done from the moment he met you. I was there when you guys met in Mataura, remember. He still looks at you the same way. Most people would kill for that. And he loves you despite you, so there's a good sign.'

That comment deserved a thump.

'Will we last? I refer back to my earlier comment. Why, yes you will, if you let yourself love him, and let yourself be happy. About bloody time you did.

'What was next?'

'I believe it was "Fuck I'm pregnant",' I said.

'Why yes you are, Isn't it awesome?

'A gazillion women before you have managed to juggle career and a family. No one said it would be easy, but, hey, you're always up for a challenge. You'll find a way to make it work. Just don't try to be a superwoman. That whole "women can do everything" line – load of rubbish. You do you.

'The woman was murdered. She didn't die of pregnancy. And you'll figure this case out. You always do. That is your superpower. Trust yourself. Trust your instincts. Trust your processes, even if others aren't so confident in them. Fuck them.

'Next?'

'I'm fucking pregnant.'

'Why yes you are, it's frigging amazing.

'And I'm sure it's going to hurt – it's going to hurt like hell. That bubba is going to have to get out of you one way or another, that's the way it works, but, at the end of it all you'll finally get to meet that special little girl, and your life will never be the same, but in a good way. I can't wait to meet her. Hurry up and have her.'

She took a pause before addressing the last item on my list.

'I'm leaving your house, but I'm not leaving your life. You don't get rid of me that easily. It's going to be a big change for both of us, and I'm struggling with the thought of it too. But the reasons for that change are really positive for both of us. *We* will be fine. We'll be better than fine.'

'I guess we will.'

'Of course we will. Love you, bestie.'

'Love you too, Maggs.'

We wrapped each other in a big embrace.

'Anything need clarification?'

'No.'

'Feel better?'

'Yes.'

'See, that was easy.'

CHAPTER 38

I clambered up onto Naomi's examination table. This involved a very inelegant manoeuvre – reversing in, hoisting my butt up first and then swinging my legs up and around. There was nothing graceful about being pregnant.

'You're looking very spherical there,' Naomi said with a grin. 'On the home stretch now.'

'Thank God,' I said.

I was at that awkward stage in pregnancy where I desperately wanted this critter out, because, damn, if she got any bigger I might explode, and everything was getting uncomfortable, but the thought of giving birth, like actually getting something that big out of what was a very small orifice was kind of terrifying. I liked to think I had a pretty reasonable pain threshold, but the anticipation of the pain that might be involved in pushing this gal out had me cowering at the sook end of the bravery spectrum. My hyperactive imagination was not helping.

'When do you finish work?' she asked.

'End of this week. Then life's going to change a bit.'

'Just a little.'

Naomi was a young professional woman who juggled what was an unpredictable job and family. One of the things that was concerning me was how I'd handle that work-life juggle when it came time to return to the job.

'How do women do it?' I asked. 'How do they manage going back to work with a baby. I mean, how do you manage it with a child?'

'Well, women find a way. It depends on your partner and their work situation, how much your family can help out, daycare. Some women go straight back to work, and their partners stay at home and look after baby. It's a juggle and everyone is different. For me, with my hours, we rely on childcare and family. But best-laid plans can get thrown into disarray, especially if you have a sick kid, so you have to be flexible. Don't worry, you'll find a way that works for you both, and you've got a while before you have to nut that all out.'

'You're right, I guess. Sorry, I probably sound a bit pathetic.'

She shook her head. 'Sam, you sound like every woman who comes through that door. Self-doubt comes with the territory. Let's have a listen to her heart and do some measurements.'

Hearing the *woosh, woosh, woosh* sound that came over the small handheld device made me realise I'd been holding my breath, that a little part of me was worried that something could be wrong. I couldn't help the smile that spread across my face, a smile mirrored in Naomi's.

'Well that's a hearty sounding heartbeat,' she said with a little lift of the eyebrows.

'Sure is. She gets that from my side of the family. All the good stuff comes from my side.'

'Naturally. I'm sure Paul's genes are only responsible for the dodgy stuff and any poor behaviour on her part.'

'Spoken like a fully signed up, card carrying member of the sister-hood.' Although if I was being honest, any impulsive or bad behaviour was more likely to come from my side of the family – my personal track record wasn't exactly angelic.

'Hey, thanks for recommending your Michael to me about the lab-testing side of things. He was really helpful.'

'That's okay. He said he was really happy to help. Let's just slip the blood-pressure cuff onto your arm, see how it's doing.'

'This case is probably not doing my blood pressure any favours.' She pumped the sleeve up to that point of pain where you felt you were going to have permanent crush injuries, before releasing the valve. That little release sound was a welcome relief and I watched the little bubble on the sphygmomanometer drop, do it's little uppity dance as I experienced that weird tapping sensation, and then drop some more.

'That's looking absolutely perfect.' She slid the cuff off and then indicated for me to sit up a bit. 'Just going to have a listen to your heart.'

'Can I ask you a couple of quick—' Naomi gave me a little finger wiggle and pointed to the stethoscope ends in her ears.

'Deep breath in ... and out.' She shifted the blessedly warm stethoscope head elsewhere and repeated the process. 'In ... and out.' She removed the contraption from her ears and grinned. 'Bit hard to hear if you're talking. But that's all sounding right as rain. What were you going to say?'

'I was just wanting to ask you a few questions about maternity stuff in general – well, about health information actually.'

'Is this still for that hideous case?'

'Yeah. You don't mind, do you?'

'No, that's fine if I can help you out. How's it going, anyway?'

'Slowly. Nothing helpful to go on so far. But like all things, we'll be systematic and thorough and something will come to light. It always does.'

'Slow and steady wins the race, as they say.'

'It's just a bit too slow for my liking. It would be good to feel like we were really on to something before this little one decides to make an appearance.'

'Clock's certainly ticking.' She started putting things away. 'So what did you want to know?'

'It's around health information. I know it's all very secure, passcode-protected, etcetera, but who can actually access, say, for example, my records?'

'Well, there's a difference between who can and who should.'

'What do you mean?'

'Obviously your GP and practice nurses can access your information – they've probably put most of it on the record. Anyone who needed to treat you if you were admitted to hospital, a specialist. I can because I'm your lead maternity care.'

'Yeah, makes sense.'

'But a lot of people have access to the data. Anyone who works in the hospital health system can go in and look up records within that system, but ethically, they can only do so for patients under their care. I can access the system and look up your records, but I shouldn't look up the records of anyone not under my care – like Paul's, for instance. That kind of thing could get me struck off the register.'

'So they actually audit that kind of thing?'

'Yes. Good example: you remember a number of years back when one of the All Blacks was admitted to hospital? There was a bit of speculation as to why, and a whole group of people got sprung because they'd accessed his health records just to be nosey, when they had nothing to do with his care.'

'Actually, that does ring a bell. It was in the newspapers, and if I recall correctly a few people lost their jobs over it.'

'Yes. One of the first things we're told is to mind our own business and not get tempted to check out what some celebrity starlet of the week got admitted for. And absolutely don't share anyone's private information, especially not with the media.'

'Well, I have to say it's good to know those safeguards are in place. I sure as hell wouldn't want people to know what brand of haemorrhoid cream I'd been prescribed.'

'I'm sure the world is dying to know,' she said, with a grin.

'And how hard would it be to change someone's information?'

'In what way?'

'Say, for example, their blood type? Would there be a record of the change?'

'I honestly don't know. I've never needed to change anything. If there was some kind of amendment needed I've always just made it in the patient notes, which also logs the date and time. So can't help you there, I'm afraid. It would be odd to have to change a blood type – they don't usually get that wrong. Why would you want to do that?'

'No reason really, just thinking out loud, trying to get my head around how people would find things out.'

'Well, like I said, lots of people can get into the patient information management system. But only a specific few can legitimately access someone's files.'

'And there isn't one big national system, is there? Where everyone's, say, doctor's records and hospital visits and prescriptions and everything is stored?'

'No, no such luck. Everyone runs different software, and not all of them are compatable or talk to each other. So it's not very helpful really.'

'What about the NHI number? That's a national thing.'

'Yes, but NHI numbers are more for identification, and recording demographic rather than health information. They're so people can access services.'

'That makes sense. I hope you don't mind me asking you all these weird questions,' I said. Sometimes it wasn't a good thing to be a colleague or friend of a detective. We shamelessly milked everyone for information.

'No, not at all. It makes a nice change from being quizzed about stretch marks, cervix dilation or pelvic-floor muscles, or that oldie but goodie: how long will labour last?'

At the mention of pelvic floor muscles I realised I'd forgotten to do my exercises today so went into clench and lift mode.

'Speaking of which, how long can I expect to be in labour?'

'Haha. How long is a piece of string? We're midwives, not clairvoyants.' She clapped her hands together and gave me a big smile. 'Well, that's us all done. Everything is looking absolutely perfect. I'll see you here next week, same time, unless of course someone decides she can't wait any longer and wants to make a grand appearance.'

'She bloody well better not. I'm not ready for her quite yet.'

'Well, experience tells me they run by their own schedule, both before and after the big moment.'

'And that's precisely one of the things that terrifies me.'

CHAPTER 39

It was a testament to my levels of frustration and phone-ophobia that going to the morgue was more favourable than picking one up. If I didn't have to make another phone call in my life, I'd be a happy girl. I was all phoned out, feeling phone deaf, ringing my hands in consternation and ready to call it quits and put my day on hold. Yes, it was so bad that I was even playing pun wars with myself. Sometimes I really did wish my head would shut the fuck up.

I'd texted Alistair ahead and arranged to meet him at 11.00am. Unfortunately I was very familiar with the morgue at the Dunedin hospital. It was one of the hazards of the job. I had attended a few postmortems in my time, and some had been more confronting than others. Overall though, odd as it may seem to some, I viewed the morgue as a comforting place to be. For families it meant that they had experienced a devastating loss, but the postmortem started the process of finding answers for them. If the death was unexpected, they'd find out the cause. If it was as a result of an accident, they'd get some closure. If it was the result of foul play, there'd be evidence that could lead to justice.

I also knew the level of care, respect and professionalism undertaken by Alistair and his associates. People were in good hands.

I descended the stairs to the basement, and sat in the reception area, waiting for him to come and collect me. True to form and exactly to the second, Alistair appeared through the door and waved for me to come on through.

'You're looking a lot more rotund than when I saw you last.'

'Thank you. I'll take that as a compliment. You're looking greyer than when I saw you last.'

'*Touché*, but I won't take that as a compliment.' Alistair was a few years older than me and reminded me of that actor who played

Capote. Throwing shade at each other had been a hobby since our school days.

He led me through to the back. I couldn't believe how thrilled I was to leave my office, even if it was just to go to someone else's office. Geography was everything. His was also a shared space, but we were lucky enough to have the place to ourselves.

'Are you sure you've still got three or four weeks to go, because that thing looks huge on you.'

'So we're a gynaecologist now, are we?'

'Haha, no, couldn't think of anything worse.' That kind of made sense, because on the farm, back in the day, he'd been squeamish about the animals giving birth, but was perfectly happy prodding the dead things. 'So what did you actually want to see me about? Because as you well know, maternity things aren't my forte.'

'I just wanted to see if you knew much about amniocentesis and the conditions it picks up?'

'Well only the basics of what I learned on the gyno rotation at med school for the amnio. For the conditions, we occasionally see very young babies here if they have died from a condition that's the result of a chromosomal or genetic disorder, or from anencephaly.'

'That's the one where part of the skull and brain are missing?'

'Yes. But often for those kinds of cases, because they have a diagnosis for a fatal disorder and they have had regular and ongoing medical care for it, we don't need to perform an autopsy. The physicians are confident about the cause of death and can sign off the certificate. For something as extreme as anencephaly, it is clear from an external examination and the poor things only survive days, if not hours, if not stillborn.'

I was starting to feel thoroughly depressed by this conversation. Maybe visiting Alistair wasn't such a good idea after all.

'Do we get many cases like that in Dunedin?'

'No, maybe three or four a year, if it's a bad year.'

'That must be awful for their families.' The magnitude of that understatement was not lost on me.

'Yes.' Or him. Both of us stared into space for a bit, my mind trying hard not to imagine myself in that position. There was enough to worry about already with bringing a new human into the world without adding that to the clamour in my head.

'That's all I can help you with really. An obs-gyno or paediatrician is your best bet if you want detail.'

'I've got that sort of covered. It's just that sometimes you offer a different take on things. Please take it as a compliment that you're weird. It can be useful.'

'Compliment accepted.'

'Actually, there was something else I wanted to sound you out about, seeing as you've probably been thinking about it anyway.'

'Oh, and what was that?'

'When I spoke with you about the postmortem results for Aleshia Newman, you dropped the wee bombshell that the perpetrator took the baby, placenta and all. We'd flippantly commented that maybe they were in a rush, so just grabbed the kit and caboodle and ran.'

'Hmmmm,' he said with an almost suspicious tone.

'What if that wasn't accidental or unplanned? I guess what I'm asking, in its most basic form, is, what could you do with a placenta?'

'That's a good question, and it's wise not to make any assumptions as to why that happened. And by the way, even though you think I'm weird, no, I hadn't been dwelling on that odd detail.'

'I didn't think you would have.' That was a lie – it wouldn't have surprised me in the least if he had.

'Placentas are interesting. They are the life-support for a growing baby, that mystical link to the mother. So in some cultures they are seen as precious, and they are given ceremony of their own.'

That was something I hadn't thought about, but now that he mentioned it I realised it was very important for some. In fact Mike and Sheryl had saved the placentas from my niece and my nephew; they were each planted on the farm with a tree. I remember being sceptical when the family was invited along for the ceremony, as it were, but it turned out to be rather special and a very symbolic earthing of the child to the land.

'From a medical perspective they are interesting too. Not so much the placenta, but the umbilical cord. Cord blood is sometimes taken as a source of stem cells, which are cells that basically have the potential to become any kind of cell in the body. So they can be used to treat a number of conditions that conventional medicine wouldn't be able to.'

'Such as?'

'Repairing damaged tissue, like cartilage in joints. Stem-cell therapies are being developed all the time. It's a growing field. They are looking at their use in heart disease, or brain disorders, such as Alzheimer's. There's also things like treating blood diseases such as leukaemia, or genetic blood disorders.'

'So there is a demand for them?'

'Yes, there is more and more research into treatments using them. But there are other sources they can be harvested from, other than cord blood, although cord blood is a useful and higher-concentrated source.'

'Black market trade?' I said, half joking.

'If you're thinking this case, it's a pretty brutal way of acquiring them. There are much easier ways.'

'Such as?'

'Well, you could just ask someone for starters.'

True.

'And they can be sourced from bone marrow,' he continued.

'That would be less brutal.'

'But still a bit of a procedure.'

'Hmmm.' I was imagining monster needles being inserted into uncomfortable places.

'But getting the cord blood is all well and good, it's storing it and then getting them processed, and even getting on a list with specialists to do the treatments, that is the problem.'

'Are these treatments available in New Zealand, or do people have to go overseas?'

'I think there are a couple of private practices here that do them, but I couldn't say for sure.'

'Ah well, it feels like a very long shot, but it gives me something to think about when I've run out of ideas to follow up on the baby front. Thanks for your help.'

'Don't think I was that much of a help.'

'Always nice to have an excuse for a catch-up, and anyway, I was going stir crazy being stuck in the office, so it was good to escape.'

'In that case, glad to have been of not very much assistance.'

CHAPTER 40

I wandered my way back along to the police station, having a slight moment of panic when greeted by a wall of medical students pouring out of the Red Lecture Theatre, but they spread around me, making me feel like Moses parting the Red Sea. The walk back also took me past a baby shop, and I couldn't resist the siren call of cutesy things luring me from the window. We had everything we needed for the lump in the bump, and then some, courtesy of hand-me-downs from siblings and friends, and Mum's knitting and shopping prowess, but it didn't stop me oohing and ahhhing over new and shiny things. I stood inside the store, holding up an intolerably sweet little ivory-coloured jacket with cartoon-style kiwis on it, and matching it with some cinnamon jodhpurs.

My left-field conversation with Alistair replayed in my head. It didn't make sense that someone would do something as extreme as cutting a baby out of a woman just for the placenta. It still felt to me that it was all about the baby, but at this point, with no great leads, nothing was off the table. What if someone needed stem cells for whatever reason. Would it be enough to kill for? Kill Aleisha Newman for?

The image of her last moments crept into my brain, playing like an old-school noir movie, and I could almost feel the trace of cold steel across my belly. In fact I could feel it, or something like it as the wave of a Braxton Hicks tightened across my abdomen, making me buckle at the knees. A rush of heat washed up my face and suddenly standing in a baby shop surrounded by women in varying degrees of pregnancy immersed in newborn-sized clothing didn't feel like such a good idea – not a good idea at all. The small items in my hands gained a weight that felt unbearable and I bunged them onto the end of the rack in front of me before beating a hasty retreat out the door.

CHAPTER 41

Escape was in order. My hormones were telling me that I needed ice cream, and my heart was saying I needed to be by the sea. Consequently I jumped into the car and took myself out to the only place in Dunedin that achieved both. It was near enough to my lunch break, and to be honest, no one was paying any attention to what I was up to. I didn't need to worry about the clock police.

The Pacific Ocean was in truculent mood, matching the threatening skies. A flotilla of surfers were making the most of the conditions, bobbing up and down on the swell, breaking off in ones and twos to find their feet and surf the wave in. I leaned against the rail at the St Clair Beach esplanade and savoured the zest of the pear and blue cheese ice-cream from the Patti's & Cream truck. The savoury sweet combination along with the satisfying crunch of the waffle cone hit my fickle food mood perfectly. The meditative soundscape of waves crashing on the exposed boulders below me helped to quieten the continuous chatter in my head, and watching the surfers and their varying degrees of success tuned me into the moment. It felt good to breathe in the fresh air and its delicious tang of saltiness with just a hint of seaweed. An outburst of squawking pulled me away from my thoughts, and I turned around to see a scrum of seagulls fighting over hot chips. Some little girl was getting immense pleasure out of tossing a chip into the melee and watching the squabbling that followed, her squeals of delight competing with the birds' shrieks. She crouched down in preparation for each throw then sprang up into a little jump with the toss. I couldn't help but grin at both her enthusiasm – and the birds'. I could see her grandmother's face moving between hilarity and concern she was going to get mugged by the over-enthusiastic gulls. We made eye contact and a spark of recognition leapt between us. We gave each other a wave, and I wandered over in their direction, making sure to give the seething mass of seagulls a wide berth.

'She's pretty game feeding that wild bunch. I'm surprised they're still going for the chips on the ground and not trying to nick off with the whole packet.'

'I know, it's a bit more fraught than feeding the ducks.'

'She's loving every minute of it, though.'

'Until one of them decides to get a bit too close.' As if on cue, one of the bolshier birds started ignoring the scramble on the ground and began hassling the bearer of the gifts. 'Come on, Charlotte, I think that's enough now. Let's go.' Helen Freeman grabbed her grand-daughter by the hand and lead her away from the group. Charlotte tottered along, all the while craning her head around to watch the last of the squabblers and the ever-hopeful entourage that followed behind, just in case.

'Hungry birds,' she uttered. 'Chips.' Touch wood the bundle I was carrying would turn out to be that adorable.

'How are you all going, Mrs Freeman?' I asked.

'Please, call me Diane, Detective.'

'As long as you call me Sam,' I said in reply. We walked along a little further, until the last of the seagulls had given up on the little person as a food source and gone in search of some other sucker.

'The ice cream looks good,' she commented. 'What flavour?'

'Pear and blue cheese.'

The look on her face said it all.

'It's really good,' I said in its defence.

'I'll take your word for it.'

'Just the two of you out and about today?' I asked.

'Yes, Charlotte needed a bit of attention and was getting a little bit cabin feverish, which isn't surprising given we've been pretty much stuck at home trying to get used to the new baby in the house. It's been a while, and I'd forgotten just how much time they consume, and how tired they leave you. Sleep is a bit of a novelty.' She glanced down at my rather obvious belly and gave a little laugh as she pointed towards it. 'I guess you're going to find out that soon enough. Your first?'

'Yes,' I said. 'My mum keeps reminding me just how much sleep she didn't get once I arrived on the scene. Apparently I was a bit of a shocker in that department.' She also constantly reminded me that my brothers were such good babies, bless her.

'Oh well, good luck. Hopefully there won't be any karma for you there.'

'Fingers crossed. Although, I get the feeling my mum kind of wishes that I get a taste of my own medicine. A bit of delayed revenge.'

'Oh, I doubt that,' she said.

'You haven't met my mum.'

She gave a broad smile and a knowing nod.

We'd pretty much walked the entire length of the esplanade down to the saltwater pools complex. The outdoor café tables were bustling with humans and an assortment of canine companions. Charlotte was pulling at her gran's arm in an attempt to get closer to the pooches, but Helen held her back, and we stopped at a distance that ensured she could look and wave and chatter at them, but not get close enough to touch. She seemed pretty happy with the arrangement, crouching down and clapping her hands, trying to invite the fluffy mutts to come to her.

'It's very handy that we bumped into you today, because I was going to give you a ring anyway.'

'Oh?' I said. 'Anything wrong?'

'No, nothing wrong, besides the obvious. It's just I had been thinking about everything after you came to visit. And there was something that Ali had mentioned that I didn't really want to say in front of Justin.'

'Oh, why was that?'

'Well, you know, sometimes daughters tell their mothers things that they wouldn't tell their husbands.' I had heard this from a number of friends, but it wasn't something I had experienced. In many ways I felt envious of women who had that kind of a relationship with their mum. Mine wasn't quite that comfortable. Things I told my mum in confidence tended to get turned around as ammunition to ping me with. She was the queen of the ping.

'I figured that because Justin didn't say anything about it to you that Ali hadn't said anything to him – probably didn't want to worry him. So I didn't want to mention it in front of him in case it made him feel bad about Ali not saying anything to him.' My mind was struggling to follow the awkward way she was describing the situation, but I got the general gist. 'So I hope you don't mind me not saying anything at the time.'

'No, no. It's not a problem, you're telling me now. So, what did she tell you?'

'We'd been having a conversation about the weird things people say to pregnant women, or ask pregnant women. I bet you can relate...'

'Oh, yeah.'

She adjusted her position against the railing as Charlotte stood back up and leaned into her gran's legs. Despite some trying, none of the dogs had managed to get close enough for pats so she'd given up on that.

'One thing that did strike me as odd though, especially in light of what happened to her, is she said someone had asked her if, when she had given birth, they could have some blood from the baby's umbilical cord.'

'Really?' I felt my eyebrows rise and a few cogs in my brain start whirring.

'Yes. Strange, huh? Of course she said no, that was just too weird.'

'Did Aleisha say who asked her?'

'Not a name, but she did say that the lady said she needed it for a sick child that had some rare disease the blood could help with. That it would save their life. I think Ali was almost feeling a bit guilty for saying no, was wanting reassurance that she'd done the right thing.'

'So it wasn't someone she knew well – a friend?'

'No. I think if it was a friend who asked she would have considered it. This just seemed to be from some random person.'

'Yeah, I can see why that would be really odd.' It was a step or two beyond odd.

'I told her she needn't feel bad about it. Who knows if the person was telling the truth or was just a crack-pot. Ali could be a bit of a softy sometimes. She always did have a good heart.' I could see Helen's eyes welling up before she looked away out to sea.

'I think you were right, and thank you for telling me. If you remember any more details, please get in touch. It's certainly given me something to think about.' It was more than giving me something to think about, it was triggering red flags everywhere.

'Yeah, well anything to find out who did this to my girl. It's absolutely killing us all. And poor Justin. He's got all this and a baby to cope with. He's being strong and is utterly incredible, but he's heartbroken, we all are.'

'It is the worst thing that could ever happen to a family.'

She looked back around at me then, the tears running freely down her face. 'I can't believe that I'm burying my daughter tomorrow.'

There was nothing I could think to say in response. Words were inadequate, so I did the only thing that could offer any comfort and wrapped her in a hug. Having a grown woman clinging to you and sobbing in such pain was something you never want to experience in life. I recognised a woman who had been holding it together for everyone else and pushing aside her own grief, her own needs. She had lost a daughter. It made me think what it would be like for my mum, should anything happen to me. Despite our often tense and complicated relationship, it was not lacking in love. She would be desolate. I closed my eyes and hugged Helen even tighter. The pressure of my belly against hers must have irked my passenger, as I felt an almighty kick slightly left of centre. Judging by the gasp from Helen, she felt it too as she pulled away and gave a raspy laugh.

'Oh my.' She reached out and laid a hand on the offending spot. 'God bless the little darling.'

'Oh, sorry about that. I hope you don't mind.'

She shook her head. 'No, no, don't be sorry. I don't think you'll ever know how special that was. That was something I never got to feel with Ali, something I was robbed of. I was supposed to be here for the weeks leading up to her having my grandchild – to share in the birth not her funeral.'

I placed my hand over hers, felt the protests of my girl still beating through.

'Promise me something, Detective. Promise me you'll find who did this, who did this to my girl, and you make them pay for it.' She reached over and pulled Charlotte into the huddle. 'Please, do this for us.'

I looked at her, then down at the wee poppet who would grow up never really knowing her mum, swallowed back the lump in my throat, but couldn't hide the tears that blurred my vision.

'I'll find them,' I said, and meant every word.

CHAPTER 42

The trip to St Clair Beach had dragged me out of my slump and had been helpful on many levels. Firstly, the ice cream had hit the right spot, and I no longer felt the need to hoover up every sweet thing that wasn't nailed down. And, of course, meeting up with Helen Freeman and Charlotte had been the icing on the cake, or perhaps the chocolate flake in the ice cream. My mind still echoed with the gravitas of my promise. It wasn't made lightly.

Her revelation that Aleisha had been approached by someone about getting some blood from her soon-to-be-born child's umbilical cord had all sorts of alarm bells ringing in my head, particularly after my conversation with Alistair. He'd said the reason someone would want umbilical cord, or the blood from one, was to get stem cells. I'd taken a brief look into them earlier when doing a general information sweep, but it was time to take a deeper dive. An afternoon of serious web searching was in order.

Although I was always loath to rely on Dr Google, it was a useful first filter. There were some organisations that I trusted to provide accurate and useful information, and plenty I didn't. I went to my go-to sites first. I was looking into the hows and the whys.

The hows came up with more detailed explanations of the things Alistair had mentioned. As he'd said, there were easier ways of acquiring stem cells than from cord blood – such as from bone marrow. We'd all heard of bone-marrow transplants for diseases of the blood, like leukaemia. The technology had advanced, and now scientists were able to create stem cells that could transform into other tissue cells around the body. How that happened was beyond my high-school grasp of science, but the concepts were fascinating.

It begged the question, why cord blood rather than the good ole-fashioned way? I added it to my list to brainstorm with the team.

As to the whys, the list of diseases that could be treated with stem-cell therapies was growing all the time as the research and technology developed. The tried-and-true involved diseases of the blood. The hopeful included research into spinal-cord injury and other tissue repair, recovery from stroke, diseases such as Parkinson's, and Hunt-ington's and repairing hearing loss. That was a lot of hopes pinned onto a tiny cell.

I found myself most drawn to the diseases that affected children. Helen's words echoed in my head: *The lady said she needed it for a sick child that had some rare disease. That it would save their life.*

The more I thought about the extreme act of cutting open a woman to steal a child and placenta, the more certain I was it had to be motivated by something personal and dire. Maybe it was because my current situation clouded my judgement, but the only thing I could think of that would elicit that kind of desperate response would be the health of a child.

I had found myself asking that question: what would I do for my baby? And even though this poppet wasn't even born yet, the defini-tive answer was anything.

Someone had asked our victim for a very personal donation.

We really needed to find that woman.

CHAPTER 43

Last night I'd finally stood at the door of the baby room and contemplated diving in. But one look at the enormity of the task had
produced an attack of paralysis by indecision, which had required
immediate therapy with Milo and Toffee Pops. This morning I was
feeling a tad guilty about the cop-out, Maggie's words ringing in my
brain. And these thoughts had insisted on intruding while I continued my research into childhood diseases – probably as a diversion
from the depressing topic, if I was being honest. It meant that by
10.00am I was well and truly ready for a change of task and scenery.

My hormones had demanded a visit to Side On Café this time,
and a date with a Danish pastry and a hot chocolate. I wasn't quite
sure what excuses I would use for my food obsession when I wasn't
conveniently carrying a voracious, sweet-craving parasite. I was sure
I'd come up with something convincing, though. I liked the semi-in-
dustrial feel of the place and the fact I could sit there and see the
ovens my treats came out of. We were constantly being told we should
get closer to the origins of our food. I was brought up on a farm and
had shot dinner before, so that was a big tick in that department. As
far as I was concerned, this counted too.

I was scrolling through my Facebook feed, enjoying the array of
felines that seemed to take up most of it, getting annoyed by the
number of baby-product advertising posts, and wondering how
Mum's fishing in the knitting group was going when a message from
Paul flashed up:

Where u?

He didn't believe in wasting keystrokes.

I sent a photo of my half-eaten morning tea.

I watched as the three little dots did their Mexican wave.

Surprise surprise.

Heart smiley wink
Guess wot?
What?
U never guess.
Then why ask?
Coz.
Eyeroll emoji
Another baby.
?
Found another baby
WTF?
Yup.
He? She?
She
Where?
St Patrick's.
Safe?
Yup
Poo emoji.
Yup.

CHAPTER 44

My stomach wasn't feeling the happiest after guzzling down the remainder of the hot chocolate and stuffing too much pastry in my mouth at once in my efforts to get back to the station to find out what the hell was going on. Fortunately it was only a short waddle down the road, but I could feel all manner of things sloshing and protesting inside me, including the child.

My mind ran a rapid-fire series of questions as I wove my way through the scattering of folk waiting at the stops along the bus hub. Fortunately for me, people took one look at my condition and cleared a path.

Whose baby was this?

Why did they leave it?

Whose baby was the other one?

Was the baby I found the Newmans' baby, after all?

We'd assumed it was, but what if it wasn't, and this new baby was really the Newmans' and they'd been busy loving and bonding with the wrong one?

How would we find out whose was whose?

Actually, I answered that one before the thought had entirely formed in my head, DNA testing would show that, but how quickly would they get the results back? Would a quick blood typing settle it?

And in the meantime, what would happen with the babies?

Would they leave Hope with the Newmans?

How would the family feel about all of this?

Hadn't they been through enough already without having to doubt if they even had the right child?

Jesus, it was the stuff of nightmares.

CHAPTER 45

This investigation was starting to feel like a juggling act in which, every few seconds, someone tossed in a new ball. First there was a murder that turned into a murder-kidnapping. Then a baby turned up. And now there were two babies. Chuck in a ransom for a baby that wasn't even there to ransom, and it felt like we were diving to catch the balls as they fell. Everything we were doing was reactive, rather than implementing a considered plan of attack. It sucked, and my frustration was shared by everyone else on the team. Chuck in the unrelenting attention of the media and those higher up in the police food chain demanding results and it was a recipe for stress and a mess.

For now my efforts were pointed in the direction of finding the mother of the latest arrival. From the moment she was discovered and rushed to the hospital for a check-over it was clear this baby was a fresh-out-of-the-oven newborn. She had been left in the sanctuary of a church. She was still covered in vernix, that creamy coating that protected babies' skin, and instead of being carefully clothed and wrapped in blankets as baby Hope had been, she had been naked and loosely bundled in a puffer jacket, complete with her umbilical cord and placenta still attached.

She was a small baby, weighing in at six pounds two and looked to be of European heritage. Other than being dehydrated, she was healthy, had good levels of alertness and was perfectly formed. The attending paediatrician's comments were that we really needed to be searching for the mum, because in her experience working overseas, babies abandoned like this were often from teenage mothers who had been hiding their pregnancies, or mothers who were homeless and vulnerable. She was hugely worried that there was a woman out there who had just given birth, probably alone, and was in dire need of medical attention, as well as emotional support. The thought of anyone giving birth alone was terrifying, and now I was worried about her too. My hyperactive and hormone-doused imagination was working overtime on worst-case scenarios, and I had to reign it in to focus on the task at hand.

The puffer jacket she was found in was a black Kathmandu brand, pretty much standard issue in Dunedin, as they were often on sale, and everyone loved a bargain. It was frequently the first purchase of the hordes of teenagers escaping home and invading the University of Otago, particularly the Aucklanders who discovered pretty quickly the vagaries of our weather, and that short shorts and flimsy tops were going to get you hypothermia rather than a tan. In Dunedin it was perfectly acceptable to wear a puffer jacket to the beach in the height of summer. The coat was a women's size fourteen, which was the average Kiwi woman size, so that didn't narrow the field down any. Alas, the previous owner hadn't conveniently sewn their name onto the collar, or their mum hadn't.

The news of this second baby had got out pretty quickly as the main media outlets covered the story from our statement. The police had wanted to make it clear this was a freshly newborn child, and that it was unlikely related to the current murder investigation. The release was carefully worded to stress that the police's primary concern was for the mother, and that she was safe and not in need of medical attention. Whereas the local rag had played that angle, other media hadn't been so kind and were vilifying the mother for abandoning a vulnerable newborn, no thought given to her circumstances. It was with disgust that I noted some of them had even headlined it on their websites under their 'crime' banner. It wasn't a crime, for fuck's sake. Something like that was only ever done out of desperation. I'd made the mistake of reading some of the comments beneath the articles, and that had made me angry. Then I made the worse mistake of following the story as it spread across Twitter and other social media, and that had left me feeling sick. People could be so bloody vicious. The vitriol was appalling. I could imagine the poor mother out there somewhere, clicking on the news to make sure her baby was at least found safe, and being bombarded by a wave of hatred and self-righteous indignation. It was not going to encourage her to come forward – if anything it would guarantee that she never did.

I'd already been on the phone to the welfare agencies and charitable organisations that worked with our homeless to see if they had been supporting any women who had been expecting, but that had been a dead end. Next step was to phone the high schools – the girls' and co-ed ones – and then the university halls of residence. Others in the team were out door-knocking at the various shelters and boarding houses around the city and following up with medical practices and urgent medical centres. We could strike it lucky, or we would have to rely on someone ringing in concerned about a friend or a relative.

It was too many balls up in the air.

CHAPTER 46

After what had felt like a futile day at work we got brave and assembled the cot. We felt so proud of the fact we'd managed it without a) having a concerning number of bolts left over, or b) having a flaming row, that we thought we'd reward ourselves with a session on the computer, looking up how you could store cord blood. Yes, we were that sad couple.

It was all well and good getting cord blood, by means fair or foul. But once you had it, what did you do with it other than bung it a container and put it in the fridge? A quick hunt had revealed that cord-blood banking was available overseas, and then a little further digging revealed, lo and behold, it was an actual thing in New Zealand. Who knew? There were companies that offered that service here, for a fee, of course.

'Click on that one,' I said, directing Paul from my wingman position standing by his shoulder. My back wasn't up to hunching over a keyboard at this exact moment in time.

He duly clicked as commanded and the 'How much does it cost?' question on the FAQs menu opened up.

'Doesn't actually answer the question, does it?'

Saying 'pay a deposit' then giving the deposit prices for cord blood, or cord blood and tissue, was cheating as far as I was concerned.

'They probably only let you know when you're most of the way through the enrolment process and unlikely to back out.'

'Lure 'em in, get them hooked. But the deposit price isn't too bad,' Paul said.

'I suppose not. For everything else on the planet most deposits are around 10%, so doing the maths, we could stab a guess at fifteen hundred dollars – two thousand, five hundred, all up.'

'Ouch. That's not so appealing.'

'And looking at how it's cryo stored, there's probably an annual fee as well.' I wondered how long you could store samples like this before they became unusable? I know there were things lurking in our freezer that were probably way past their best-by date, and some mystery meats that had been there for years. They were a casserole waiting to happen. There wasn't any information on the website about the ongoing costs.

'Mind you, if you were needing to go down this path as a medical solution, then I guess you'd just do it and the cost wouldn't come into it.' I had to agree with him there.

'I know if it was us we'd find a way, even if it meant mortgaging the house.'

'Um, small problem there – we don't have a house to mortgage.'

Fair point. I didn't think our landlord would be too impressed if we tried to sell her property out from under her. And we weren't going to be able to afford to get on the property ladder anytime soon.'

'We'd have to sell a fair few cheese rolls to fundraise it.'

'Doable, though.'

True. Everyone down here loved a cheese-roll fundraiser. So families were peddling them, and there seemed to be continuous supply of the rolls at work. The local schools' sports and arts economy relied on this kind of fundraising.

'I see that they send you out a kit that you take along to the birth, and you get your lead maternity career, obstetrician or midwife to do the collection. Then you call the courier to pick it up. But does it say anything about the actual timing of when you take the sample? How soon after the birth?'

There were so many scenarios I'd played in my head about the killer's motive, and how Aleisha had been killed down that isolated alley. If the whole thing was in fact motivated by getting samples, given the environment, did they get them at all and did they get them in time? And I didn't want to even think about the potential for contamination down there. It wasn't exactly a sterile environment.

'Good question. Wouldn't have been easy doing anything down

that alley when you were worried someone might come along. And bloody dark for starters. They might not have actually managed it.'

Sometimes I wondered if Paul read my mind. I was pretty sure Maggie could. Maybe it was an easy read.

Paul clicked through a few more screens before finding one with the relevant information.

'Says here it has to be immediately after the birth for the blood, once the cord has been clamped and cut. Cord-tissue sample is taken once the placenta is delivered.'

'I'm pretty confident there wouldn't have been any handy health professionals down the alleyway in the middle of the night, so they would have just had to do it themselves.'

'It would have been past most health professionals' bedtime.' He scrolled down a little further. 'It states it's painless for the mother and baby. If the kit had everything they needed, if indeed they just happened to have a kit in an alleyway in the middle of the night, then yeah, it's a possibility.'

A shudder shook through me. I was also pretty confident that the mother in this instance experienced a shit ton of pain.

'Can you remember from the reports how the baby's cord was tied off?' Paul asked.

'There wasn't anything tied around it when I saw her being examined in the hospital, and I don't know if they can tell what was used after the fact – seems unlikely. It would be interesting to know how they did it though. We can check in the morning.'

Paul reached over, absentmindedly grabbed a couple of scorched almonds from the bowl on the table and shoved them in his mouth.

'So you've managed to get a sample, courier has picked it up, and it's safely with the storage company. Then what?'

I managed to interpret the sentence through the chewing. I was glad he was facing away from me. My brain was still processing information from a few steps back.

'Wonder if we could get a warrant for information from the blood banks on any recent deposits?'

Paul was accustomed to the backward-and-forward way I operated and was able to keep track.

'Not based on our supposition and reckons.'

'Didn't think so. We'd have to be pretty certain this was the path taken.'

'Yup.'

'So back to your original question: then what?'

'Yeah, it's all very well and good if they've got the blood for the stem cells, but then what do they do with it? They're hardly going to be able to do a transplant themselves, are they?'

'Not unless they're cancer specialists or haematologists.'

'Even if they were, I'm sure there's processing and dealing with the cells involved. That's hardly something you could do in the kitchen at home.'

'Certainly not in ours.' Dishes and clear benches weren't our strong point, or priority. As far as I was aware, no one had died from not doing the dishes, or any kind of housework, really.

'And how would they treat the child without arousing suspicion?'

A few things that had been swirling in my brain did a little clunk into place. The sensation felt a bit like an ear pop.

'Oh, that's quite clever really.'

Paul looked up at me with a quizzical expression on his face.

'Not me, I take it?'

'Well, not this time. Them.'

'Enlighten me.'

'I've been wondering – why the cord blood, if there are far more easy and available ways of getting stem cells, from bone marrow, et-cetera?'

'Yes?'

'Because with cord blood, if you had a willing donor, or in this case, if you stole it, for want of a better word, you can get the cells without needing a hospital procedure.'

'So you can fly under the radar, as it were.'

'Yes. To go to those extremes they must have tried treatment through the existing systems, but there hadn't been any matches or success, so they found an alternate route.'

'Makes sense?'

'But wait, there's more.'

'There always is,' he said.

'By getting the samples stored by a third-party company, a professional company with a good name, they immediately legitimise them.'

'Laundered.'

'Precisely. That gives them the option of seeking treatment privately without arousing suspicion. They can just say, "Hey, we've got these samples that were donated to us. Can you use them for treatment? We'll pay."'

'Money always talks. Wonder if there's a way of hooking back into the public health system if you come to light with the donor goods? We'll have to check that.'

'Add it to the list.'

He went back for another round of almonds. 'You know, it all sounds feasible. Fantastical, but feasible.'

'In the absence of other theories, I think it's a line of enquiry worth pursuing.'

I'd been trying to resist the scorched almonds, but gave up and grabbed a fistful before Paul ate them all.

'But where would you even start. I mean properly start?' I asked.

'Well, there must be a limited number of children in Dunedin with disorders that would need a stem-cell transplant, so we could start by looking there.'

'I don't fancy our chances of being given any specific information on families that are dealing with that, Privacy Act and all. And even if we could, that's going to be tiptoeing on broken glass with a hugely stressed and fragile group of people.'

'Is there anyone you could talk to – sound them out, see if it's even a possibility?'

I thought back to the list of people I'd had in mind when enquiring about the amniocentesis. There was the paediatrician from the hospital. 'I've got someone I could try.'

'We can talk with Smithy about it in the morning, give him the whole scenario, see what he thinks.'

'How about you talk with him, might be better coming from you.' Last time I made a suggestion it didn't go down so well.

'Why? Is there something going on there?'

'We're not quite seeing eye to eye at the moment.'

'What did you do to piss him off?'

'Why do assume it was that way around?'

'Was it?'

'Yes.'

'I rest my case.'

CHAPTER 47

Being in one position for any length of time was becoming a bit of a challenge. I was immensely grateful that work, to keep the health & safety gods happy, had splashed out and we all had adjustable-height desks now, so sometimes I stood, sometimes I sat, depending on how the mood, the aches and the kid took me. Over the course of a day the aches did a random shuffle through my playlist of sore feet, sore back, and that disconcerting feeling like someone was trying to prise your pelvis apart from the inside by ramming a large object through the middle. At this stage my sit bones were complaining louder than my back, so it was time to go up in the world. The sooner this poppet was out the better. I fiddled with the control and listened to the gentle whirr as the desk level rose to standing height. It was always slightly disappointing that the mechanism was so smooth and slow, as a part of me would have loved to see it go rogue, jerk and take off skyward, sending pot plants and computer screens flying everywhere.

'That's right, stand up, Shep,' a voice piped up from across the room. 'Oh, you are standing.'

Unfortunately, some in the office enjoyed giving me grief about the fact that the sum height differential between standing and sitting was less than a foot. For this particular someone, the joke never got old.

I looked over at the offender and started scratching an itchy spot on my face with my middle finger. 'You'll keep. You just wait till we get home.'

'Promises, promises,' Paul said, and gave me a wink.

A wee snort came from the direction of Sonia's desk.

The opportunity for retaliatory remarks was disrupted by a clamour of voices and footsteps in the hallway. I caught a glimpse of some unfamiliar faces before a more familiar one popped his mug around the corner and indicated for me to come on over.

Grateful for any opportunity to move, I headed towards the door.
'Sam, do you mind doing us a favour?'

Paul's approach this morning had been met favourably, so I appeared to be back in the good books. For now.

'Sure, what do you need?'

Smithy drew me out into the corridor. He indicated with his head towards the soft meeting room – the one where we took victims and family to talk with in a more relaxed setting with comfy sofas, rather than the formal and more intimidating interview rooms down the other side, with their tables and chairs and obvious recording equipment.

'Look, we've got the young woman who abandoned the baby. Well, she's pretty much a kid. Her mum's in there too. We're just waiting for the people from Oranga Tamariki, who are due shortly, but would you mind sitting in with them in the meantime, keep them company till the Ministry folk arrive?'

Oh, that would be a fraught and delicate conversation for both parties. Working for Oranga Tamariki – our Ministry for Children – was another job I wouldn't be suited to. I feared I would be far too affected by the difficult and often tragic situations they had to deal with to remain objective and impartial. And the weight of responsibility for making decisions about the placement and care of at-risk children would haunt me.

Today, part of me was curious to see what kind of a woman would give up on a baby, abandon it immediately after birth. But part of me also realised that for someone to be that desperate they would also be incredibly vulnerable. Perhaps the concerns raised previously by some others on the team were right in this instance – given my obvious condition, and the risk of triggering overwhelming memories of a very traumatic moment in the mother, maybe I wasn't the best fit for minding duties.

'You think I'm the right person at this time, considering?' I asked, pointing to my middle.

'Yeah,' Smithy said, unequivocal. 'No offence, but I think she needs a woman, and someone completely non-threatening right now.'

He cocked his head, apologetically. 'Pretty sure they don't want me in the room. And you might want to take in a box of tissues.' I could see why an enormous, untidy and slightly BO-ey lump of maleness wouldn't be the right fit.

'There's Sonia,' I said.

'True. But of all of the women in the immediate vicinity you're the one with the most experience of motherhood – limited as it is – so I think you're it.' He wasn't going to take no for an answer, grabbed the nearest box of tissues and presented it to me.

'Well, if you're sure.' I accepted it with reluctance and wandered around the corner into the room.

I was met by two faces: one looked like she'd been awake for twenty-two of the last twenty-four hours, and the two hours of sleep had been of the *Nightmare on Elm Street* variety. The other resembled a startled possum, a very young startled possum on the verge of tears.

'*Kia ora*, I'm Detective Shephard – Sam. I'm just going to sit with you while we wait for the Oranga Tamariki people to arrive. Can I get you anything to drink? Tea, coffee, a water?'

They looked at each other, the mum quietly asking, 'You right?'

'I'm good,' was the whispered reply. She looked anything but.

'We're okay for now, thanks,' the mum responded. 'I'm Adele. Adele Smythe. And this is Georgia.'

Georgia looked all of sixteen, with her flushed, acne-speckled face, straightened, long blonde hair and braces on her teeth, although she could have been older – or younger, for that matter. I always found it difficult to judge the age of teenage girls with their vast range of maturity and rates of growth. Chuck make-up into the mix and it was nigh on impossible. I'd been this insubstantial height since I was ten and started growing boobs, and back then I looked much older than I was. Hence I got inappropriate and annoying attention from older boys who didn't realise I was very much under age. Fortunately, my mother had been quite forthright in telling them to fuck off, and in training me to tell them to fuck off. It was one of the few favours she'd done me in life.

You couldn't really tell that Georgia had recently been pregnant. She was a fairly solid young woman, dressed in baggy-legged, light-blue denim jeans, a loose white jumper and a too-big black puffer jacket over the top of everything. It was pretty much the standard uniform of most female uni students in the city. The clothing helped disguise her midriff, and perhaps she was also one of those people who didn't show much anyway. I didn't look pregnant from the back, but from side and front on I looked like I'd swallowed a basketball. So who knows, maybe she'd hidden the pregnancy from her family, and the first they knew about it was when the abandoned-baby headline was splashed all over the news and their little girl confessed? It was something I was dying to ask, but it wasn't my place, so my almost tabloid curiosity would just have to remain unsatisfied.

'Hi, it's lovely to meet you,' I said. 'I know you're here under difficult circumstances today, but I'm not here to question you or anything like that. I'll just be waiting with you, and I'm here if there are any questions you have about anything.'

The two women were sitting side by side on the small sofa, legs pressed up against each other, bodies leaning into each other, Adele's hand resting lightly on her daughter's knee. The body language spoke of solidarity and support, and I felt relieved on Georgia's behalf that, to outside appearances at least, her mum was on her side. I didn't think that mine would be quite so forgiving. Of course, all of this first-impressions judginess on my part was working on the assumption that Adele didn't know in advance her girl was going to dump her baby at the local church. For all I knew it could have been at her parent's insistence – a way to solve an unexpected problem. I lowered myself into the armchair angled alongside them and wriggled to find a comfortable position.

'When is your baby due?' Adele asked.

My hands went into automatic pilot, rubbing the top of the mound, my face curling into a smile. 'Just over two weeks' time.'

'And you're still at work?' The tone sounded identical to my mother's on the same topic. Was there a manual for impending grandmothers that I was unaware of? 'When do you finish up?'

I noticed Georgia staring at my rather obvious bump and was beginning to regret accepting Smithy's judgement that I was the most appropriate person for the job. 'This is my last week, so I get a couple of weeks' break before baby arrives on the scene.'

'You'd better hope it doesn't arrive early, then.' Yup Mum and her had the same play book.

'Are you having a boy or a girl?' Georgia asked, before Adele could continue along the party line. Her voice sounded very young, and I changed my estimation of her age down to fifteen, maybe even fourteen. How did I answer her question? Somehow it felt important to be upfront.

'I'm having a little girl, but please don't tell anyone else here. They don't know.'

That elicited a small smile.

'Have you decided on a name yet?' I'd spent many a sleepless night thinking about names. It felt such a responsibility to get it right. A name that would work when they were young and when they were old, one that people could spell and didn't have extra Ys or Ks thrown in for good measure so the poor sod had to spell it out to all and sundry their entire life. A name that was different, but not whacky, one that had some meaning. Also a name that couldn't be abbreviated into something crappy, or where the initials spelt out something rude. There was so much to consider.

'We've got a couple of names we're thinking about, but it really depends on what we feel suits her when she's born. We might take one look at her and decide, ahhhh, she looks like a Gertrude.' That dragged out another smile.

'Are you married?'

'Georgia, that's getting a bit personal.' Adele looked uncomfortable at her daughter's insistent questions, but I waved her away. The girl was talking, that was a good thing.

'That's okay, I don't mind answering. No. My partner, Paul, and I have been together for a little while now, but we're not married. I think our parents would prefer that we were,' I said, 'but this baby was a bit of a surprise, and we didn't want to rush a wedding just because we were expecting.' That turned out a bit more personal than I was intending, but something told me that what this girl needed right now was some frank honesty.

'So you didn't plan on getting pregnant?' I could see the slightly horrified look on Adele's face, but I gave her a tiny shake of my head, and smiled at Georgia as I gave my response.

'Hell, no. We had only been together for a little while really, so the last thing I wanted or expected was to get pregnant. But it happened that way, so we talked about it, and decided that yes, we wanted to have this baby and become a family.'

'I didn't expect to get pregnant either.' Georgia's voice had become very little, and I had to strain to hear her words. She was looking down at her hands. 'And the boy was really upset and didn't want me anymore when he found out.' In that moment I just wanted to reach over there and wrap her in a cuddle. Her mum took her hands, leaned over and gave her a kiss on the cheek. I had to work hard to disguise the lump in my throat when I spoke again.

'I'm so sorry to hear that, Georgia. It must have been so hard for you.'

'I didn't know what to do, I was so scared. I felt I couldn't tell anyone, not even Mum and Dad, and I'm so sorry about that, Mum, I should have told you.' Adele didn't say anything, she just wrapped her arms around her girl and let her cry into her chest.

'I can understand why you would be scared,' I said. 'That's an awful thing to have happen to anyone, let alone someone your age.'

'You're not scared?' she asked, through the hiccoughs.

I pushed myself up onto the edge of the seat and reached out to touch her knee.

'Georgia, I'm absolutely terrified. This is the biggest thing that has happened to me in my entire life. I don't know how to be a mum. I don't know if I'll be a good mum – I might be dreadful at it. I worry about the baby and what if something goes wrong. I don't know how this is going to affect Paul and me, and if that will work out okay. And the thought of giving birth is really scary. To be honest, I'm a nervous wreck.' Somehow it felt good to say those thoughts out loud. They had been creeping around at the edges of my mind, kept at bay by the inner voice that said, *You should be happy Sam, you're so lucky Sam, this will be amazing Sam, be strong.* But the inner fifteen-year-old in me was struggling to deal with the enormity of it all.

'But you're a grown up, and in the police.'

'Yes, but that still doesn't stop me from being afraid,' I said. 'I just have to keep thinking about the good things. That I'll have a little girl to love, like your mother loves you, and it's the beginning of a scary but exciting adventure.'

She paused for a bit, before looking at me with serious and sad eyes. 'Can you understand why I panicked? I didn't know what to do. Why I didn't tell them, why I left her there, at the church?'

My God, this young girl gave birth by herself. My mind struggled to grasp at the enormity and tragedy of a teenager feeling she had no choice but to do it alone, and try and hide that it ever happened. This time I couldn't conceal the tremor in my voice and the overflow in my eyes.

'Yeah, I understand. And you know, other people will understand too.'

'I'm scared they won't let me have her back.'

'I'll help them to understand.'

'You promise?'

'I promise.'

CHAPTER 48

Hospital foyers were never the most welcoming places in the world, but the lobby at the Dunedin Public Hospital bucked the trend. Besides some pretty impressive and colourful artwork and a quirky kinetic sculpture, it had the key to making any place seem friendlier – a coffee shop. Actually, it had two: the appropriately named The Dispensary and The Daily Dose. There was a permanent queue of the caffeine-deprived at The Dispensary, leaning on the tall tables or just mingling and chatting. Scrubs seemed to be the predominant dress code for those going for a smash and grab. The Daily Dose had proper seating and not only lured hospital visitors with caffeine and food, it also helped empty their pockets by providing a selection of toys, trinkets and toiletries for that last-minute cheer-up gift. Between them they gave the entrance a bit of ambience, and the burble of warm chatter countered the often quiet, sterile and impersonal atmosphere I'd encountered in health-care centres in other places.

Hospitals could also be overwhelming, and the majority of people were here for reasons they would much rather not be. I was always grateful for the presence of the volunteers at the St John Hospital Host Information Desk. Kath was a regular who, for years, had been giving her time to help direct out-of-towners, keep some company to those discharged but waiting for family, help people find wheelchairs to transport their loved ones from their cars to their appointments, and generally be a friendly face and willing ear. She was a compulsory stop for a chat.

'You must be ready to pop soon,' she said with a smile as I wandered past.

'Soon enough,' I said. 'I'll be quite glad because this thing isn't getting any smaller.' I gave my belly a rub. 'How's your daughter getting on. She must be due any day now.' Kath was expecting her fifth grandchild, and judging by the pink-and-yellow combo yarn on her knitting needles, it was going to be another little girl. There was always something growing on those needles. Sometimes I thought she did it to have a conversation starter – over the years I'd observed a number of animated discussions with folk that seemed directed at her craft. It certainly made her approachable.

She laughed. 'Stacey's overdue and over it. Just wants this baby born. She's at the "begging the midwife to induce her" stage, but that won't happen for another week unless Bubs decides to get with the programme.'

'Well, wish her all the best from me.'

'Will do, and all the best for you too, if I don't see you before the big day.'

'Thanks, Kath.'

I spotted the person I'd come to meet waiting in the café queue to get served, so ambled towards her, weaving my way between the small clusters of imbibers. Her scrubs were not the standard-issue blue, but a vibrant shade of green and covered in cartoonish dinosaurs. They made me smile, so I imagined they'd also help make her young patients feel a little less intimidated.

'Dr Harris, hi, thanks so much for your time. You must be pretty busy.'

'Hi Detective, and yeah, sorry about only being able to fit you in briefly and timing it for my coffee run. If I don't get one now, it won't happen.' She looked a little embarrassed. 'We're very short-staffed at the present, so it's crazy busy.' Everything around here always looked crazy busy, including the evening we'd met in the emergency department when she'd been the attending paediatrician checking over Hope Newman.

'No apology needed,' I said. 'I appreciate any opportunity to talk.'

She placed her order, handed over her turquoise ceramic keep cup, and we moved off to the side to wait. I resisted the lure of the berry friands sitting in the cabinet. I really did need to put a lid on succumbing to every craving.

'I re-read your email and your query about childhood diseases that could be treated with stem cells. I don't think I can help you much though.'

In my initial reach-out I'd explained I wanted to find out if there were any cases in Dunedin of children who had some of these rare diseases, and I'd mentioned a bit of the why, too.

'We were wondering how much information we can access about any patients and families that might be affected.'

'I understand why you would want to know who has a life-threatening disease as part of your investigation into the recent murder and the motive for it. But there is very little I can tell you. I can say that yes, there are families in Dunedin with children who have some really distressing and life-limiting diseases. But because of patient confidentiality I can't give you any names or details.'

The response didn't surprise me, and given our privacy laws it was to be expected, but it was still disappointing.

'What if we had a specific name or case where we suspected family might be involved, would you be able verify it?'

'Not unless you had a warrant, but I'm not even sure if they would issue a warrant under those circumstances. Look, that poor woman's murder has really shocked everyone around here, and we all want to see whoever did it locked away, and preferably the key thrown away. So I really am sorry I can't be of much help.' She meant it too, judging by the expression on her face.

'Large flat white with sugar for Harris,' came the call from the barista.

'Hang on a tick.' She manoeuvred over to the counter, thanked the staff and wove her way back through the sea of waiting patrons.

'Thank God for coffee,' she announced on her return.

'It makes the world go around,' I replied. 'There is something else I was hoping you could help with. Other than bone-marrow transplants, who in New Zealand does stem-cell therapies? Can it be done under the public health system?'

'No, not at the moment. The only places offering those services that I am aware of are private hospitals or practices, and none in Dunedin. I think the majority only do therapies relating to degenerative diseases in joints, that kind of thing.' She punctuated her sentences by sipping from the coffee in a semi-worshipful kind of a way.

'There may also be some specialists involved in research or clinical trials through universities, but I couldn't tell you those off hand. It's certainly an area that is evolving rapidly. Actually, now I think of it, there is a new clinic in Auckland that has only opened in the last three or four months – it's offering more complex treatments and all of the support services around that, but of course any treatment would be unfunded, so it would be very expensive. I'm not aware of any families from Dunedin who have opted to do that, but then, our most complex paediatric cases are referred to Starship Hospital in Auckland. I could find a contact person for you there who may have the most up-to-date knowledge of what's happening in paediatric therapies, if that helps?'

'That would be great, thanks.'

'I'll send that through to your email.' She took another sip from her keep cup and looked disappointed that it was empty. 'Hmmm. I'll do that later today. Sorry I couldn't be more helpful, but at least that contact will make me feel like I've done something useful for you. God knows we all want this person caught. Look, I have to dash. Do feel free to get in touch again if you have any other questions. Oh, and all the very best with that,' she said, pointing to my middle.

She headed off in the direction of the stairs and up to the paediatric ward on the first floor. The maternity unit was on the second floor. Perhaps a little visit there would be a good idea, considering I was going to be in there doing the hard yards sometime in the very near future. It might be an opportunity to familiarise myself with the place. My feet started to head in that direction, but then I lurched to a halt, overcome with a wave of Braxton Hicks – and apprehension.

Maybe another time.

CHAPTER 49

Gravity wasn't your friend when you were pregnant. One of my favourite releases from its relentless drag was the delicious sensation of buoyancy that came with swimming. There was something so curative about being immersed in water, its velvet feeling against your skin. If running wasn't an option right now, putting some time in at the pool was pretty good compensation. Moana Pool was close enough that I could zap up the hill in the car and get some laps in during my lunch break. At this time of day the main pool wasn't inundated with children and swim classes, and I often got a lane to myself, thank God. I didn't like sharing. The greatest challenge with swimming had been finding a pair of togs that were small enough for my frame, but big enough to accommodate the basketball and the boobs. In the end I'd settled for some daggy, old-style nana togs and a rash top.

The sunlight pouring in the huge, angled wall of windows dappled across the rippled surface of the water, giving an extraordinarily serene ambience to the space. Swimming was incredibly meditative, much like running, allowing my conscious self to tune out, and my subconscious to do its magic. I was ever hopeful that the kind of epiphany pounding the streets generated would occur in the pool.

The massive fibreglass bulkhead halfway down the pool divided it into twenty-five-metre lengths, doubling the number of lanes available for swimmers, and also making it more pleasant when you were in it for exercise rather than racing. My days of competing in swim meets ended in my early teens, when to progress in the sport you had to commit to 5.30am training starts, several days a week. No one in the family had the dedication required for that, neither the swimmer nor the long-suffering taxi service. Oddly enough there had been no protests or complaints when I gave it up. My swim speed had dropped in recent times due to the fun breathlessness that came with having your internal organs squished upward by an ever-growing baby. Consequently I alternated one lap freestyle with one lap breast-stroke, so I could get my breath back on the breaststroke leg.

I paused for a moment, clinging on to the starting block at the deep end, before setting off on a freestyle leg. As well as counting my strokes before breathing, and the number lap I was on, I counted the number of bandaids and hair ties wafting adrift along the bottom of the pool. It was two of the former and one of the latter today. Great-est of all time had been three and one with a bonus point for one of the bandaids being Dora the Explorer. The curse of wearing goggles was the clarity with which you could see all the crud.

On the breaststroke legs I liked to observe the various forms of humanity that visited the pool. There were the young mums emerg-ing from the changing rooms, trying to keep up with toddlers hellbent on reaching the wave pool and water features. There were the fellow lunch-breaker trainers, although to be fair, they looked a damn sight more serious about it than I did. My favourites were the oldies in their various forms of repair and decrepitude, still getting out there and enjoying a swim, and often a spell in the spa pool after-wards. I fully intended to be banging out the lengths in my eighties, nana togs and all.

Next freestyle leg I swam past the first bandaid, and besides making my left eye twitch at the grossness of it, it triggered a thought I'd had earlier, but couldn't quite put my finger on. Ten metres later, as I spotted the second one, the thought solidified. Wounds. I'd been thinking about Alistair's postmortem report and his observations about the victim's incisions – and they were incisions, as opposed to stab wounds or cuts. They were purposeful.

I paused at the bulkhead before turning around and back into the breaststroke.

There were two issues: the incisions had been made with some-thing extremely sharp, but they hadn't been confident, or tidy. But whoever did this had known enough about pregnant anatomy to do the cutting in two operations, as it were. We had joked about it clearly not being an obstetrician, although even an experienced obstetrician might get the yips when carving open a women down an alleyway in the middle of the night. But what if it was someone else who knew about pregnancy – another health professional? A nurse, or a doctor? Someone who had access to, say, scalpels?

I paused again at the starting block, hanging onto the backstroke bar, catching my breath and trying to see where this train of thought was taking me. I also took a moment to try and unblock one ear that had filled with water and gone weird.

And who would carry a scalpel around, anyway? Nurses, as far as I was aware, didn't tend to carry around the tools of the trade in their handbag or their car. I'd never seen a car first-aid kit that contained anything sharper than a blunt-nosed, kiddie-sized pair of cheap scissors. District nurses, the ones out in the community who visited people in their homes, might, I supposed. Paramedics, if they were on the job? Doctors would have kits if they were making home visits. And midwives – they had to be prepared to go to a birth any old where, any old time.

Still, I found it hard to imagine that anyone in a profession where your one job was to ensure the health and wellbeing of your patient would commit a murder. But then again, there were the Harold Shipmans of the world, or the Angels of Death – nurses who had murdered those who were supposed to be in their care. Nothing could be discounted.

I knew from looking through Aleisha Newman's cell phone texts and phone records that her midwife was Miriam Hardcastle, she of the dramatic rescue, but I didn't have a clue who her GP was. That was something to check when I got back to the office, and perhaps I would take a more thorough look through those phone records. What other health professionals had Aleisha been in contact with in the days, or even weeks, prior to her death? This train of thought didn't sit easy with me. What possible motive could a health professional have? It all kept coming back to that idea of the desperately sick child. What would you do for your child?

Suddenly being in the pool with dead bandaids and God knows what else no longer appealed. All these thoughts really didn't float.

CHAPTER 50

While I was showering off after the swim, another thought had popped into my head, something that had been percolating around the fringes for a while, but which now felt more of a possibility to consider. I know I'd only talked with her this morning, but Dr Harris had made the offer to call back anytime, and I was the kind of gal who always took up an offer. She probably hadn't anticipated a call quite so soon.

I was still in the carpark at the pool, watching some fantails through the windscreen, flitting around the flax bushes.

'Thanks once again for your time. I feel like I must owe you a coffee by now.'

'I'd never turn one down, but honestly, only too happy to help.'

'I've been thinking about how the person who committed this crime could have found out about potential donor matches, if it was to do with saving their own child because they had an illness that required transplantation. I've talked with people about access to medical information – who has it, that kind of thing. But then I got to wondering, what if it was in fact someone who worked in a hospital or clinic setting – could they secretly take samples on their own, from patients, from children?'

'Oof, that's a scary question. Theoretically yes, but in a practical sense, it would be difficult. Children are very rarely left on their own for any length of time. Most of the time they have a parent or family with them, because it can be a scary place and time for kids. If not, there's always staff around. Although, as you said, if it was one of the staff...'

'Yes, sorry to cast suspicion over everyone.'

She chuckled. 'Also, any blood sample would involve needles. Kids generally don't like needles, and they cry, so someone would come running. I mean you could perhaps persuade an older child that this was a normal blood test if they'd had lots of them before, but a littlie or a baby would bellow for sure.'

It did seem a long shot, and also something that would carry a high risk of being caught. Still, for someone who risked committing such a violent act down an alley in the middle of the town, maybe analysing risk wasn't their strong point. The other element to consider was how would you get the sample processed? Fake a lab request? Fake a recipient? Unless you stole an identity or even used that of your sick child. That might work, but there were so many ways it could come back to bite you in the butt. That would all take a bit more mulling over.

'You haven't had any odd reports from parents about noticing puncture marks or anything like that – that they felt their child had been, for want of a better word, tampered with?'

'Gosh, that's a tough question, because some parents come in already really suspicious of hospitals and anything we do, so yeah, I can think of some incidences where they've been adamant something happened without their permission.'

'Where does that get reported? Is there somewhere I can check them?'

'Most of the time their fears are allayed by just talking everything through with them, so it's not reported. There may be something recorded in the patient notes, depending on who was on and how insistent they were. Unless they make a formal complaint, in which case there will be a proper record of it, and it has to be followed up. You could check with the hospital management, I guess.'

Access to that information could be simpler if it was part of a complaints process. I'd have to see.

'Sorry, I'm being called. Got to go. But hopefully that's been of some help. I really would like to think it's nothing to do with any of our staff.'

'So do I. Look, thank you so much for your time, once again, I really appreciate it.'

'No worries.'

I felt like I almost had all of the pieces for this case, but just had to figure out how they slotted together, and of course, who they would reveal in the end. It was like one of those Wasgij puzzles, where they gave you the clues – the view from the other side, or hints from the past – but were too bloody mean to print the solution for you on the box.

CHAPTER 51

Back in the marble edifice that was the police station I set to on Aleisha Newman's phone log. A quick check on her records had shown her general practitioner was Dr Alan Kenilworth at the medical practice in South Dunedin. She didn't have him in her contacts list, but did have the medical centre's phone number, which was the norm. Most of us didn't have a hot line to our GP. If we did, the poor buggers would never get a moment's peace. There hadn't been any calls to or from the medical centre in recent times, so that pretty much ruled that out.

Midwives were another matter – that was a far more specific relationship. Miriam Hardcastle was in Aleisha's contacts, as would be expected. I sure as hell had Naomi locked and loaded in mine. My previous check through the records Otto had shared had only taken in the two weeks prior to her death. This time I went back six weeks, just in case there were any patterns I hadn't noticed.

I could see regular text messages from Miriam, which were mostly appointment reminders. They had increased in the last few weeks; also expected, as I knew my regular check-ups had moved to weekly from around thirty-six weeks. There were also a number of phone calls. Of course, the trouble with phone calls was we had no idea what their purpose was. I could see a couple where Aleisha had rung Miriam, and also some where Miriam had rung her. The only way I could check what they were about was to ring Miriam herself. This was problematic, as if I were considering her a potential suspect, which still felt all wrong, asking her why the call had been made would alert her to my suspicions. Providing, of course, she could even remember the call, or just didn't lie about it. The most recent call had been from Miriam to Aleisha on the afternoon of the day she had died. I was definitely going to have to follow up on that, but it would require a bit more thinking on the best approach.

I noticed that some of the numbers that had previously been logged from non-contacts had now been reverse-searched and the details filled in by Otto. There was still one call from a cell phone in the week prior to her murder that hadn't been identified, which was frustrating. In this instance we couldn't get the skinny.

My eyes scanned further down the list of calls and one of the fill-in names pulled me up short. Naomi Orr. Why on earth would Naomi have rung Aleshia? In all of our conversations she had never mentioned she knew the victim. The call had been placed four weeks prior to her death, so it wasn't a recent interaction. Still, it had me perplexed. The only thing I could think was it related to maternity services. I looked at the date the call was made and scrolled down the text messages that had been sent from Miriam. It was the day after one of Miriam's appointment-reminder texts. In fact, it was made on the morning of the appointment.

Relief midwife? That would make sense.

There was only one way to find out.

And while I was at it I could quietly ask a few questions about Miriam.

I reached for the phone.

CHAPTER 52

At this rate Naomi was going to get heartily sick of hearing from me, but the voice that replied seemed its usual warm self and didn't have any 'bloody hell, not her again' undertones.

'Hi, Sam. What's up? Are things happening?' she asked.

'No, no, all good there. Nothing's moving on the baby front other than lots of Braxton Hicks and her having a few wicked attacks of the hiccoughs.' I did have to admit I found it really amusing when Bubs got the hiccoughs. It was kind of cute.

'Well, I am pleased to hear it, because if it was all systems go the timing would be a bit challenging, with one of my other mothers in labour.'

'Actually, that's one of the things I was wanting to ask you about, and the reason why I'm ringing.' She'd inadvertently provided a perfect segue into the conversation without it getting awkward. 'What's the plan for me if you are caught up with another woman giving birth at the same time? I'm guessing you're not allowed to flit between women and rooms at the hospital and juggle it, are you?'

Actually the thought of having someone other than Naomi help me deliver this kid was bit terrifying. She had just the right kind of calm vibe for me – that knack of allaying my fears. I thought we would be a good team. Paul liked her too and found her equally reassuring. It would be gut-wrenching to not have her there at the last.

'No, it's not like you can say, just hang on there a few minutes, I've got to go see someone else for a bit, back in half an hour.'

'Babies don't have a tendency to wait for a convenient time, preferably in daylight hours?'

'Alas, no.' She laughed. 'With the unpredictability of childbirth we always have a back-up midwife or two in case we need to call on them, and hope they aren't engaged too. I was going to talk with you about this at our next appointment, actually. So for you, the first back-up is a woman called Miriam Hardcastle. She's great, very experienced, and you'd be in safe hands. You'd like her a lot. My second usual back-up is Jackie Evans. She's quite young and a relatively new midwife, but very capable and I have every confidence in her. She's lovely, and all the times I've had to call on her, the women have been really pleased with how it all went.'

'Great, that's a relief to know there's a plan in place. Makes me feel a lot happier about it.'

'Of course, ideally it will be me helping you deliver your little girl, but you never know.'

'So does that work the other way too? If one of the other midwives ends up having two babies arriving at once, you step in and help them out?'

'Yes, we're back-up for each other.'

'Do all of the midwives in the city operate like that?'

'Yeah. We're a pretty small community really. There are not that many of us – not enough to meet demand, to be honest – so there is a certain amount of juggling that goes on to make sure any woman can get the services she needs. But don't get me started on some of the systemic issues around why there aren't enough midwives – our pay and working conditions – we'd be here all day.'

I knew well enough about the shortage and the challenges. The topic came up as a feature on the local news with monotonous regularity. Unfortunately the publicity wasn't doing anything to get the relevant powers to address the root causes of the problem – such as massive underfunding.

'Some of the midwives form, like, a business partnership, collective type of thing. Others, like us, do it more informally. It really depends on everyone's personal circumstances.'

'So you all know each other quite well then?'

'Pretty well. Like I said, it's a small community so we have to support each other.'

Good to know they were a sisterhood. Hopefully she wouldn't see my next questions as betraying that sisterhood.

'There was something else I was wanting to ask you involving the case I'm working on, so it is a little sensitive.'

'Okay, sure, if I can help.'

'It relates to what we were talking about. The woman that was recently murdered. Her midwife was Miriam Hardcastle.'

'Yes, I was aware of that.'

'When I was going through the victim's telephone records, I noticed that you had called her around six weeks ago. You knew the victim? You hadn't mentioned that to me previously. What were the circumstances around the call?'

Too many questions at once. I should have spaced them better. There was a slight pause before she continued.

'Yes, I had worked with the victim, and I didn't mention it to you – couldn't mention it to you – because of patient confidentiality. So sorry I couldn't offer the information before, but now you have specifically asked me, I guess I can talk about it to some extent. It was one of those instances where Miriam had asked me to step in and see the patient for her. Just give me a moment to check my records.'

I could hear her mouse clicking and some computer keyboard noise.

'Here we go. Yes, I saw Aleisha Newman around six weeks ago for her thirty-four-week check-up. We did that down in my clinic space.'

'And everything seemed normal. Aleisha didn't mention any issues to you?'

'No, perfectly normal pregnancy, everything was looking beautifully on track.'

'Did Miriam have another woman go into labour? Was that why you had to fill in for her?'

'No, not this time. She had to take time off at short notice for her daughter. She often has to take time off for Maisie.'

'Oh, is she unwell?'

'Yes. Poor little girl has a rare disease that means she's in and out of hospital, so it's a real juggle and a huge concern for the family.'

'And she's being treated for that?'

'As much as she can be. What she really needs is a stem-cell transplant. It has to be quite specific, apparently, so they're waiting on a donor match to come up.'

'That must be an awful situation to be in. I can't imagine it.'

'I know,' Naomi said. 'It's incredibly tough on them and a huge worry.'

'How long do they have to wait?'

'Well, there's no way of telling. It all comes down to doctors finding the right match. That could be weeks, months, years, or never, or it could be too late, which doesn't bear thinking about.'

Who could live with that kind of a death sentence hanging over their loved one's head? And if it was you, what would you do to prevent it?

Did Miriam Hardcastle do the unthinkable to try and save her child?

CHAPTER 53

My thoughts that this case all came down to the characteristics of the child itself were starting to coalesce into something a lot more solid. My mind played over what Naomi had shared.

Miriam Hardcastle was in a desperate position with her unwell child. If indeed the only chance of a life for her daughter was a stem-cell transplant, then did she take matters into her own hands? The taking of the baby had been brutal, and the woman certainly had some passion. The way she had stormed into the room and come to Lena Cameron's rescue in front of a gobsmacked DI Johns and Smithy demonstrated a ferocity that was both impressive and slightly scary. Had that kind of a temper been unleashed upon Aleisha? She had the medical knowledge to know what to do in a caesarean section, even if she hadn't performed one herself.

She was also in a position to legitimately access patient records, see the test results of Aleisha's amniocentesis, and see if they were a tissue match with her own daughter, or close enough that the treatment had more hope of being successful. In fact, if she had been trying to find a match for whatever her daughter needed, she was in a position to order any blood tests for her patients, and persuade them that they needed an amniocentesis or more detailed investigations. She could have been screening women for years.

The type of stem-cell transplant needed would be dependent on the disease. It would require a warrant to access her daughter's records, I guessed. The only way we could get them without a warrant would be if a life was at immediate risk – the daughter's declining health wouldn't count. I made a note to make sure I talked to a specialist in the field. Hopefully Dr Harris would come through with that recommendation from Starship Hospital, as promised. My head was spinning with the science, and I wasn't even sure if I was getting it right. Was I overthinking this? Possibly, but I felt I needed a lot more detail than the sites I'd seen on the internet could provide.

But Alistair's words rang in my head. He was in there a bit too often. He'd said that if you needed cord blood and a tissue sample, then why wouldn't you just ask? During our chat at the beach Helen Freeman had said someone had asked, but Aleisha had described them as some random person. I would have thought the kind of intimate relationship you built with your midwife would elevate them above that description. I would also have thought that if she had asked, then Aleisha would have at least considered it – and talked with her husband about it – especially if it was to help save the life of the child of someone she knew.

If her daughter had been ill for a while, then had Miriam been checking for matches for some time? Who else had she been midwife for? Another, slightly more sinister, thought went through my head. She would be regularly in the maternity centre at the hospital. As a midwife working in the hospital she would have access to many babies – could potentially have taken samples from them, unbeknown to their parents. I shuddered at that. I was getting a bit ahead of myself there. Did I start looking for those complaints or reports of interference? Where would I even start?

All of this was supposition. There was absolutely no hard evidence of her involvement. I had to think of a plan that would make her give herself away. A way to draw her out. An outrageous idea edged its way into my mind, and the more I thought about it the more plausible it seemed. Could I run it past the team – run it past The Boss? I had to try, because if she hadn't been successful in getting the sample collected from Aleisha, then she could still be searching for that miracle donor. We needed to give her that donor – lure her out.

There was only one way I could think of doing that, and no one was going to like it.

CHAPTER 54

'Sorry, can you run that by me again?' The Boss was looking at me like I was stupid, Smithy was looking at me like I might have a point, and Paul was looking at me like I was totally bat-shit crazy.

'What I'm suggesting is that we plant test results into my medical records – amniocentesis results, any tests that could help identify a potential tissue match for a donor.'

'On your medical records?' The Boss asked.

'Yes.'

'Sam,' Paul said, his voice very tight. 'What you are suggesting is basically using you as bait.'

That was a very dramatic way of putting it.

'Well, I suppose, yes.'

That took a few seconds to drop.

'No fucking way.'

'Out of the question.'

'It might work.'

Paul, The Boss and Smithy, exclaimed in synch.

The Boss raised his hand in a 'stop right there' motion to Paul, then directed his attention to me.

'Although it is an interesting idea, and there is some logic behind it, there is no way that any authority would allow a pregnant officer to take that kind of personal risk.'

'But I wouldn't be at risk. All we have to do is get her to access the records. She is not my lead maternity carer and I have never had a consultation with her, so there is absolutely no reason why she should log into them, unless she was actively searching for potential donors. Our tech people could monitor the logins. The mere act of doing that would be probable cause, enough justification to get her in for questioning and a search warrant for her work and home. We just have to dangle the carrot.'

'It is an idea with merit.' Again he gave the 'don't speak' signal to Paul, who was starting to look like he might pop a vein. 'But if we did this and were going to use anyone as bait, it would definitely not be you.' I had never seen Paul agree with anything The Boss had said so quickly in my life. I felt a pang of guilt that I hadn't discussed this idea with him first before bringing it to the group, but I knew damn well he wouldn't have even let me finish the sentence before shutting it down and reacting exactly like he was right now. 'We could modify Detective Constable Richardson's records, make her appear to be pregnant.'

'That could work,' Smithy said. 'And it would solve the risk problem.'

For me, not Sonia. This was something I was prepared to do because I felt so invested in finding out who had done this to Aleisha Newman and her family. I'd made a promise. I wouldn't expect it of anyone else.

'I'll do it,' Sonia piped up. The Boss had been talking like she wasn't present, as usual. 'It would be a lot safer than using Sam, and if what you said about amniocentesis normally being performed earlier in the pregnancy is right, then it makes sense. It would seem a lot more legitimate if we had me as a newly registered patient now and the results were added to my record at a stage where it would be normal to, rather than adding something in retrospect.'

'That's a good point. But one glaring deficit in this idea is how do we get her – or anyone – to take the bait? How would she even know to go look?'

'Well, I've thought about that,' I said. 'The midwives act as a bit of a collective, filling in as back-up for each other if they have multiple women in labour. My midwife has an arrangement with Miriam and another practitioner where they step in as needed. We could get her to somehow drop a hint.'

'But that would involve disclosing our suspicions and involve a civilian,' The Boss said. It clearly did not sit well with him, but I knew from his expression when I first disclosed my suspicions about

Miriam Hardcastle that he wouldn't be sorry if it was her. She'd humiliated him, and his ego did not take that lightly. The man knew how to hold a grudge. The fact that he was having a level and considered conversation with me about my suspicions and my plan, and was not bawling me out for being ridiculous, spoke volumes.

'Do you trust her?'

'Yes, I do. To date she has been helpful answering my endless stream of questions, and she is discrete. She takes confidentiality very seriously.'

'Paul? What are your impressions?'

Now he was finally allowed to speak he made the most of the opportunity. He leaned forward, counting each point on his fingers as he made them.

'Naomi, our midwife, is good. I haven't had as much to do with her as Sam has, so my impressions are limited, but I'd be comfortable with that.

'As to the harebrained idea of using Sam as bait, for obvious reasons I am dead against that. And you should have mentioned this to me beforehand, Sam.' The look I got from him was a glare of disapproval that would have made my mother proud.

'But, I would support using DC Richardson for that role. We could present her as a woman moving to Dunedin from out of town so that her records were transferred, but with a few added extras, like being pregnant, and with those test results.'

'That would solve a few problems nicely,' Sonia said.

'But that won't work,' I said, reaching out literally and figuratively. 'It's the immediacy of it that's going to make Miriam Hardcastle take the bait, if it is her. Her daughter is very sick right now. Could be dying.' I threw that in for impact. 'Time is not on her side, She doesn't have the luxury of waiting several months to be able to get access to what she needs. We can't plant that information for Sonia and have it play out as a long game. We need someone who is demonstrably pregnant, someone that if she checked in with my midwife would be told, yes, she is due to pop any moment now. It's the only way it can work. We can't pretend Sonia is at full term – it would be hard enough to pretend that she was at half term. Dunedin is like a small town in that regard, everyone knows someone who knows someone, and it would be picked up as a sham pretty quickly.' I worked my way around the room, looking at each of them.

'If it's going to work, it has to be me.'

CHAPTER 55

'Sam, you remember that pinky promise we made?'

My mind jumped back to that afternoon in Kiki Beware with Paul – the laughter, the embarrassment, but also the agreement that because of our personal circumstances and the nature of this case, we'd speak up if we felt uncomfortable about anything, if we were distressed.

'Yeah, I remember.'

He gripped my hand tighter. 'Well I'm telling you right now: firstly, I am so monumentally pissed off with you right now for this whole warped idea, and the fact that you didn't talk with me about it.'

He had every right to be.

'Secondly, no matter how safe you think this harebrained scheme is, it affects more than just you.'

He placed our hands on top of our child. 'This proposal has me fucking terrified.'

CHAPTER 56

'Well there's a voice I haven't heard for a while.'

Pinged in the first sentence. But pinged with sarcasm, which I suppose was an upgrade from being pinged with criticism. Despite that, it was good to hear her.

'Mum, it's been five days.'

'Six, actually.'

She'd been counting? I wasn't sure whether to take that as a good or a bad thing. Either way, a dusting of guilt settled on my mind. But then again, there had been nothing to stop her from picking up the phone and calling me. I mentally swept a little of the grit away.

They always said a strong offence was the best defence. But 'they' hadn't encountered my mother. I went for deflection instead.

'How's everything going down there. How are the kids?' That was usually a guarantee of at least five minutes of Gran-gushing.

'It's school holidays, so they're enjoying the break.' I could hear an immediate lift in the tone of her voice. 'Josh has been with Steve on the farm, helping out. They got him his own mini quad bike, which is a bit dangerous, if you ask me. And I do worry that Sophie is spending too much time inside watching television.' The tone dropped. 'It's not good for her, and she's always on her phone too. She's only ten. She shouldn't even have a phone at that age.'

Considering she thought the sun shone out of Steve and Saint Sheryl's arse, it felt odd to hear Mum finding fault with their parenting. I mean she was the queen of criticism, but it was usually directed at me, not them. Something must be up.

'Everything alright?' I asked. Despite trying to disguise it, even I could hear the tentativeness in my question.

There was quiet from the other end of the phone. Had she heard me?

'Why wouldn't it be?'

She had.

Egg-shell territory.

'You just sounded a bit...' gawd, how did I put this? '...strained. Is it working out okay for you, staying there?'

Tactic change.

I heard the intake of breath and braced myself. But then she then let it out very slowly.

'It's not ideal, but it is what it is.'

It had been a hell of a big adjustment for her, having to move in with Steve and Sheryl after Dad died, and I was pretty sure it wasn't ideal for them either. But those were the conditions and everyone had to make do. A day didn't go by when I didn't miss Dad. We all did. I had to remind myself she'd lost the love of her life in pretty tough circumstances. Again, I felt a stab of guilt when the thought came to mind – rather them than me.

'Anything I can do to help?'

'Well, you could phone more often for a start.' And there we were, back to square one. There wasn't anything I could say to defend that. My right foot was starting to go to sleep, so I shifted my position onto the other butt cheek.

'How are you getting on with the Facebook knitting group?' I asked. Appealing to her mission would hopefully improve the tone of the conversation.

'And when you do ring it's only because you want something.'

Apparently not.

'Mum...' I said. This time it was me who couldn't hide the exasperation.

She must have got the message she might have pushed the aggrieved-parent angle a little too far, and after a little *humph*, answered the question.

'I've had quite a few comments, but mostly along the lines of "they're cute", or "nice yarn", that kind of thing. No one's trumped up with the pattern yet, but there's still time. I'll let you know as soon as there's something interesting. You could comment on the photo, yourself, then you could follow other comments easier. Or at least give me a like.' It wasn't lost on me my mother was asking me for affirmation. I wondered if she realised it. It wasn't something she'd consciously do. The thought did make me smile.

'I shouldn't do that in case someone recognises my name and thinks better of responding.'

'Oh, I suppose,' she said.

'But hey, I really appreciate you trying.' While I seemed to be winning, I thought I'd keep on the positives. 'You'll be pleased to know I finish work tomorrow.'

'I'm relieved to hear it. You really shouldn't have left it so late. I worry about you and the baby in that job. It's not safe.'

If she thought the everyday stuff wasn't safe, she'd have a purple fit if she knew what was being planned.

'You need time to get yourself organised as well as have a rest. And have you sorted that baby room yet?'

I wondered if she and Maggie were secretly in collusion.

'We have started on it – got the cot assembled the other night. But we'll have the baby in with us in the bassinet for a while.' The wicker bassinet had cocooned three generations of my family so far, including Mum and me. It might not have looked the trendiest, and had clearly done some hard service, but the knowledge this wee girl would also be held safe and snug in there was immensely comforting.

'Well, I guess that's something,' she said – again the note of disapproval. 'What about your bag? Have you packed your hospital bag?'

Truth be told I hadn't even thought about the hospital bag. Things had been so frantic with work and the case that it had completely slipped my mind. Could be an idea, though.

'Of course I have, we're all good to go.'

Hopefully one lie to my mother wouldn't make me burn in hell. But sometimes the risk of eternal damnation was worth it to avoid another mini-lecture.

CHAPTER 57

It was done.

Our digi-tech staff, with the cooperation of the relevant health services, had altered my medical notes across the relevant patient information systems.

Naomi, with reluctance, had agreed to find a way to casually mention that I had had amnio further back in my pregnancy. I hadn't told her straight out that it was Miriam that we suspected, but rather that it was someone within the profession, so I'd asked her to drop the hint as widely as she could. I'd explained that she was one of a number of trusted people we were employing to help in the case. I felt bad about the lying, but needs must. I seemed to be doing a bit too much of it lately.

The trap was set, and now all we had to do was wait.

Actually, that was not all we had to do. This was just one facet of the ongoing investigation, and one that could be barking completely up the wrong tree, but in my heart, I knew we were on the right track. The rest of the team were following up on other leads, no matter how tenuous – interviewing people, still sifting through hours of security video footage, and of course dealing with the ever-constant pressure to solve this case being applied by the hierarchy, the media and the community. Half the front page of the *Otago Daily Times* this morning was dedicated to decrying the efforts of the police in solving this case: 'Police at a Loss.' It didn't help matters. We all wanted justice for Aleisha Newman and her family. Contrary to the picture the media was painting, no one was sitting around twiddling their thumbs, except perhaps me.

Being somewhat idle wasn't doing me any favours. My stomach was still churning at the thought of Paul being so upset with me. He'd made an excuse to leave the station, and I hadn't seen or heard from him since. It had been a given that he wouldn't be happy about it when I pitched the idea of me as bait, but I hadn't expected the depth of his displeasure. We were about to embark into this huge, scary new territory of parenthood together, and I had gone ahead and managed to erode his trust in me. Sure, my motivations were noble, and I felt so personally invested in this case, but when I had been thinking through all of the ramifications of pulling this stunt, I had missed what was perhaps the most obvious. I only hoped to God that I hadn't done too much damage.

Maggie had always accused me of being a commitment-phobe, and that I was still holding something of myself back in the relationship. And she'd been right. But witnessing the hurt in Paul's eyes, and realising that I could have inadvertently fucked up our relationship, made me realise how badly I needed us to work. How badly I wanted us to work.

The dread of going home tonight was hanging over my head like a gravid cloud. I knew I was going to have to do some serious damage control, and it was all on me.

CHAPTER 58

Well, here it was, my last day at work, and it all felt very weird. The day had started out as well as could be expected, given the tension in the house. Paul had made a point of making sure that I was feeling okay about this being my grand finale, which of course I was not. He had even packed me a special lunch, which included what he called a celebratory cupcake ... decorated as a pink pig. The fact he must have organised that on the quiet yesterday made me feel even more of a shit for putting him through so much grief.

Now that I was in the office I felt at a bit of a loss. Everyone had buggered off on their tasks, so the place was devoid of life – eerily so. There was no point in starting anything new, so it was going to be a 'tidy up the last of my reports in progress and try to stay out of the way of The Boss' kind of a day. Didn't feel like having my last hurrah on the premises spoiled by his glorious presence.

Of course, the glaring, neon-lit, flashing and tap-dancing thing that marred the occasion, and was the main source of my blahs, was the knowledge that I was leaving here without us having solved the Aleisha Newman case. If I was right about Miriam, then it felt so close, so brutally close. If I was wrong, then ... It wasn't often that I felt like an abject failure, but between the situation at home and the situation at work, today's mood was rapidly sliding down that path. The burden of my promise to Helen and her family weighed heavy on my mind and my heart. It was gut-wrenching that we hadn't definitively cracked it while I was still here. The only consolation was that I was uniquely able to contribute to the investigation from the fringes, if only by being a sounding board for Paul – provided I hadn't pissed him off too much.

I drummed my fingers against the desk top, and looked at the collection of pot plants and trinkets that would have to come home for the next while. God knows where I was going to put them. There was a large empty box sitting under the desk, dragged in for that very purpose, but I couldn't bring myself to fill it until the end of shift. I logged into the computer and pulled up a report on a fraud case that needed finishing. My eyes scanned down and started to glaze over before I'd even reached the bottom of the first page. It was going to be a very long day.

Some of the doldrums was relieved by pressing the controller on the desk and listening to the little whirr of the motor as the surface ascended to standing level, and then descended back to sitting level.

That never grew old.

Footsteps approaching down the corridor gave a glimmer of hope – for some company and of rescue from the tedium of paperwork. *Don't walk past, don't walk past.* It was with great delight and relief that I saw Laurie's head poke around the corner. I punched the air, on the inside.

'Hey Sam,' she said, and looked up and down the room. 'Crikey, where is everyone?'

I shrugged. Didn't want to appear too keen to see someone.

'No worries, you'll do.'

I was very happy to be the 'you'll do' gal.

'What do you need?' I asked. I would pretty much have agreed to any task at this point, short of lifting a piano.

'We've got a few things that need sorting downstairs in the meeting room. If you've got the time I could do with a hand.'

She hadn't even finished the sentence before I was hoisting myself up and heading to the door.

'Happy to – more than happy to.'

She laughed as I breezed on past her.

'Anyone would think you didn't want to be here.'

'Oh, I want to be here,' I said, swinging my arms out, gesturing the whole damn building. 'Just not stuck in there like Nigel No-Mates on my last day.'

'Don't blame you, it's a bit grim.'

We trotted down the stairs and made our way onto the first floor.

'So are you feeling ready for motherhood?' Laurie asked.

'Nope,' I said.

'Ha, well you're not going to have much choice soon, as that kid will be coming, ready or not.' With which she steered me into the meeting room to a greeting of 'Surprise!'

Now I understood where half the populace had disappeared to. A sea of grinning faces welcomed me, and my eyes misted up as I took in the table covered in morning tea treats including a spectacular cake, a pile of brightly wrapped gifts and a bundle of helium balloons straining against their ribbons. Paul came over and gave me a squeeze and a self-conscious smooch on the cheek before Laurie took over the proceedings.

'You know we couldn't let you escape the place without a bit of a fuss, so we all wanted to say best wishes and good luck to you and Paul, but especially to you, because, damn girl, that baby looks huge on you.'

I ran my hands around my girth, and then did a turn to the left, and then a turn to the right, with a little sashay, working it like a runway model, including the pout.

Cheers and applause rippled around the room.

'But seriously, we're going to miss your cheerful presence over the next few months, and we'll especially miss your colourful and extensive vocabulary of ... er, adjectives.'

'Fucking right,' someone piped up from the rear.

'But we won't miss your tendency to obliterate any supplies of chocolate biscuits, and that you never put the lid back properly on the Milo tin in the kitchen.'

'You can't prove that was me,' I said, hands raised.

'I believe there is video evidence. But anyhoo, Sam Shephard, all the best for the future and do make sure you bring that baby in to visit.'

'Here heres' and 'absolutelys' sounded from around the room, promptly followed by a growing clamour of 'Speech, speech.'

The warmth and affection radiating from the sea of grinning faces started to tip my funk on its head. It felt good to be appreciated and acknowledged.

'Well, you know, I'm a girl of few words,' I said. There was a snort from the man to my left. 'So I will keep this short.'

'Just like you,' someone heckled from the back. Otto would pay for that later.

'Thank you to Laurie – I presume it was you – for organising all this.' Laurie was the queen of making sure little events like this happened, thank heavens, because someone had to think to punctuate the grim, day-to-day reality with flashes of joy and fun. She was our social glue. Her curtsey was very endearing.

'And I hope, looking at the morning-tea spread, that Miranda has baked her world-famous ginger crunch.'

There was a whoop and a double thumbs-up from the side.

'Thank God for that. I bags first dibs.'

I turned to Paul then. He was standing there looking serious. 'It takes two to tango, so I'd like to thank Paul for taking the police directive to find new recruits so personally that he decided to breed the next generation. That's dedication for you.' I was relieved to see it elicited a smile.

'Oh, the pleasure was all mine,' he said, to some 'whoars' and lewd comments around the room.

'And before I get all sentimental, and you know I will' – Sonia held up the preparatory box of tissues – 'I just want to say I have loved working with you all.' Which I hand on heart could, because The Boss was conspicuously absent. 'And before you know it I'll be back annoying the shit out of you all again. Please, dig in.'

They didn't need any encouraging and descended upon the table like the eighth plague. I could see a number of people take the grab-and-run approach. There was a lot going on and I appreciated all of them for taking the time, however brief.

I turned to Laurie again and took her by the arm.

'Thanks so much for this,' I said. 'It really means a lot.'

'I know, hon, and it's my pleasure.' And she did know. From day one she'd been witness to my struggles to be welcomed by some noted, and unfortunately senior, people in this place, and that my grudging acceptance had been hard-earned, despite the best efforts of the powers that be.

'Come on and open up some of your pressies.'

She manoeuvred me over towards the pile of gifts. Who didn't love pressies?

'You didn't have to,' I said, 'but I'm glad you did.'

'You haven't seen them yet,' she said, and gave me a wink.

CHAPTER 59

Bubs was showing her appreciation of the excessive quantity of ginger crunch and cake I had consumed by drumming on my stomach with her feet. Well, that's what it felt like. In turn, my stomach was showing its appreciation with some volcanic-grade heartburn.

My smart watch started vibrating merrily, so I reached into my pocket for the phone to see who was calling.

'Hi, Naomi,' I said as I ambled around the room, trying to walk off the heartburn and give Bubs a bit more space.

'Hi, Sam. How are you going?'

'Pretty good, actually. Last day at work, and they just sprung me a surprise farewell morning tea.'

'Nice, that was good of them. I hope there was cake.'

'Oh yes, "was" being the operative word, and I'm paying for it now.'

'Haha, I did warn you about the indigestion. Did they give you presents?'

'Yes, I'm sure the industrial-sized bag of ear plugs is going to come in handy, but I'm not so sure about the poo-scented candle.'

'Trolling you.'

'I reckon, but the wee baby onesie with "Just done nine months inside, my parents are now serving life" was intolerably cute.'

'And apt.'

'Oh, yes, they looked pleased with themselves for that one. Look, I want to say thank you again for how much you've helped me out with this case. And I know you've had your reservations.'

'That's okay, if it helps solve it, then it's a good thing. Hey, the reason I'm ringing is I need to bring next week's appointment forward. I've got another patient who is going to be induced on Monday, so that's going to take up my time. Is there any chance I can catch you for that check-up later today?'

It was a hazard of the job, the unpredictability of women and babies. Pity the little blighters didn't come with a fixed timetable. I fervently hoped this little one decided to make her appearance at a civilised time of the day and without any need for intervention.

'I'm finishing at 3.00pm, so could make 3.30pm, if that works?'

'I'm seeing someone else then, but they live up your way. How about 4.00pm at yours?'

'Yeah, works for me.'

'Great, I'll see you later, then.'

I walked another lap around the room, but by this time the effects of the colossal cup of tea I drank with the cake were making themselves known, so I veered off out in the direction of the loo.

At least the change of appointment would give me some company to look forward to after work.

With Maggie now gone and Paul due late I wasn't looking forward to going home to an empty house.

CHAPTER 60

It was amazing how slowly the clock could go when you were watching it. It was like it did it on purpose. The last reports and paperwork I'd needed to tidy up were done, I'd returned the sundry plates and teaspoons that had accumulated on my desk to the kitchen, set the dishwasher and washed those random bits in the sink. Hell, I'd even resorted to cleaning out the fridge to make the afternoon go by. There were all sorts of alien lifeforms growing in there – the ghosts of lunches past, including one Tupperware container that was so green and bulging that I sacrificed the whole damn thing to the bin. At least now the fridge smelt a bit more appealing and the contents weren't a biohazard.

With half an hour to go I finally found the heart to drag the cardboard carton from under my desk and start filling it with the things that were about to have a six-month hiatus at our house.

This was not how I imagined my last day would be.

My romantic self had thought it would be all ta-tas, kissies and fond farewells as I waltzed out the front door. Granted, there had been a little of that this morning, but since then, it had been pretty much just me, staring at the clock. It was starting to look more and more like I'd be sneaking out the back door, but without the grin.

I started on the 3D puzzle that was fitting everything into the box.

Two ponytail palms – the only office plants I hadn't managed to kill.

Favourite novelty mug, a gift from Maggie: *Don't flatter yourself. I only look up to you because I'm short.* It was one I strategically tried to be holding whenever The Boss was in the room. I don't think he got the message though. I felt a pang of sadness at the thought of Maggie. The house felt so weird without her.

I paused for a moment and breathed through another round of Braxton Hicks.

Proper Dilmah tea bags, because the crap that was provided by work wasn't fit for human consumption.

A packet of ten green-tea bags that Mum had given me because she thought they would be healthier for me. Unopened.

The pile of snacks that hadn't yet been consumed, which included most of a bag of Whittaker's mini chocolate bars, some muesli bars and a half-consumed packet of crackers. On second thoughts I binned the crackers, grabbed the chocolate, and walked over to Sonia's desk to pull open her top drawer and pop them inside. A donation to her cause.

But as I did so, I heard voices coming down the hallway – very animated voices. I shut the drawer and scuttled back to my desk, feeling oddly guilty that I'd almost been caught in the act.

'We'll have to pick up a car.' Smithy walked into the room, closely followed by Paul. They both went straight to the cupboard where we stored everyone's BAS vests and started grabbing them.

'What's happened?' I asked.

'Well, hate to say it, Sam' – whatever it was he was about to say, Smithy didn't look like he hated it, quite the opposite – 'but you were right. We got the call through from tech. Your woman logged in and had a look through your files, went straight to the amniocentesis test results.'

'Miriam Hardcastle?'

'Yes, indeed.'

I looked to Paul, who nodded, 'Yes. She took the bait.'

I felt immensely relieved, but equally saddened and horrified that Aleisha Newman looked to have been killed by someone as trusted as her midwife. And I didn't care what the circumstances were.

'You're off to pick her up? Bring her in for questioning?'

'Yes.'

Sonia appeared in the room, puffing slightly from her rush. 'I got the message. When are we off?' She went digging in the cupboard and pulled out her vest. It looked half the size of the men's ones. I felt a tinge of envy that she was getting to go along for the ride, but it made sense they had ensured there was a woman officer present. That should have been me, but with only thirteen minutes left on the job...

'Right. Good work, Sam. We'll see you soon,' Smithy said.

'Well, actually, no.' I pointed to the clock and shrugged.

'Oh yeah, that's right. Okay, then.' He came over and gave me a hurried, awkward hug. 'All the best,' he said before heading out the door.

Sonia gave me a less awkward hug – 'Don't be a stranger. I'll miss you' – before she followed suit.

Finally Paul stepped up and gave me a hug and a kiss on the forehead. 'Well done. Don't party too hard without me and I'll see you tonight.'

And with that the room was empty, again. Just me and my cardboard box.

I worked hard to swallow the lump in my throat.

'Well, okay then,' I said in their wake. 'I'll see ya later.'

CHAPTER 61

I don't think I'd ever been so pleased to hear a car pull into the driveway, so much so I had to go out and play welcoming committee. After my anticlimactic exit from work you'd think I was craving company or something. I admonished myself for being quite so pathetic.

'Naomi, it's good to see you.'

'Good to see you too. You're looking very expectant there.' She stood next to the car door and indicated my little Honda in front. 'It's okay for me to park here? I won't be in Paul's way?'

'There's just fine. That's my little car. He won't be home for a while yet.'

Torie had come out to greet her too and was busy giving the front tyre a chinny-winny.

She grabbed her bag from the back seat and followed me into the house.

'Did you want a cup of tea?' I offered.

'Thanks, but no. I'm squeezing in one more client after you so I'd better not be too long.' She popped her bag onto the dining-room table and we both took a seat.

'How are things going on the case, now? Any progress that you're able to tell me about?'

That wasn't something I was in a position to disclose to her, but knowing she now had a specific interest after helping us out, I thought the best way to respond and not appear rude or ungrateful was to massage the truth.

'Nothing while I was still there, but I'm done and dusted now. Elvis has left the building.'

'That must feel a bit strange with so much going on.'

'You got that right. But things change, and I guess I've got a big and important new case coming up.'

She smiled and indicated for me to put my arm out to measure my blood pressure. No matter how many times you had it taken, that pressure from the cuff being inflated never got any more comfortable. I felt the bliss of release, but it was short-lived as she pumped it back up again, further this time, threatening to explode my arm before finally releasing it down.

'Hm,' she said, 'your blood pressure is a bit elevated today. It's higher than I'd like. How are you feeling overall? Haven't had any headaches?'

'No, feeling pretty good.'

'How about your feet: any swelling, shoes feeling a bit tight? Do you mind if I have a look?'

I'd ditched the shoes as soon as I'd got home, they weren't as comfortable as they used to be. I obliged by sticking my bare foot out from under the table.

'Your ankles look a bit puffy, but not hugely so.' I took her word for it. 'I like the nails by the way.' They were looking quite tidy for me, in a fetching shade of pastel blue.

'I had to get Paul to paint them because I can't quite reach that far anymore.' He'd enjoyed that task a little too much if you asked me. He was quite fond of feet.

Naomi laughed. 'You're not the first woman who's had to rope in some help. And you're still feeling plenty of movement from baby?'

'Yes, although, surely she must be running out of room in there.'

'It will be getting a bit tight. Now, I've talked with you about pre-eclampsia in the past, and you're at the business end of things where we do need to keep an eye out. So considering your blood pressure is a bit high, if you don't mind I'd like to take a blood and a urine test, just to be sure.'

There was no way I was going to be able to squeeze out a drop of pee. Like most women expecting a guest, I'd made sure I'd gone to the loo first. Not a smart move in retrospect.

'I can do the bloods now for you if you like so you don't have to go out again down to the lab.'

It was handy that she had that skill – she'd taken my bloods earlier in the pregnancy when I'd been due the scheduled ones. Now my shoes were off, I wasn't feeling inclined to go anywhere. Unless, of course, Paul suggested going out to Good Good for a burger or something for dinner. That was a different proposition entirely.

I watched as she popped the colourful tourniquet band around my upper arm, but then as usual turned my head away to examine anything else but what was happening with the needle. This time it was some wax-eyes making the most of the kōwhai flowers in the tree out the window. It was funny that I could handle the sight of someone else's blood, and any level of gore, but seeing my own red stuff being removed – nope.

'Little scratch,' she said, and I winced slightly as the needle slid in.

After a few moments a buzzing sensation started in my head and the edges of my vision began to tunnel in. That wasn't right, I thought as my body started to feel oddly heavy.

Oh, shit.

I swung my head around to see Naomi's mouth forming the words 'I'm sorry,' the sound not reaching through the noise of the bees that now swarming through my brain.

Fuck.

I'd made a huge mistake.

CHAPTER 62

The sound of crashing waves dragged me from what had been a dark and warped sleep. A sleep filled with a swirling blackness, a maelstrom of darkness that solidified and melted into the writhing forms of wraiths and amorphous beings – beings that shrieked and groaned. I was suddenly aware of the prickle of rough carpet under my cheek, the ache in my hips and building pressure in the small of my back. The pressure transforming into a wave that spread around to the front of my belly, gripping like period pains, but period pains on steroids. I realised the groans were coming from me.

My eyes flew open.

'Naomi,' I said out loud as the memory of those last moments of consciousness came flooding back.

Where the hell was I? The wave of pain was starting to ebb, so I hauled myself up onto one elbow. That wave was promptly replaced by a wave of nausea, and before I could even attempt to counter it, I vomited onto the floor.

I flopped back down and tried to take in my surroundings.

The room was dark, and chill, although the goosebumps that spread across my body weren't entirely from the cold. The only light crept in from under a wide door to the front and a smaller door to the side. As my eyes adjusted I could start to make out details – boxes, shelves ... A tang of petrol and cut grass overlay an overall mustiness and dampness. I could make out the shape of a window, but it had been covered over. Apart from the square of carpet where I lay, the floor appeared to be concrete. It was a small garage – and it would have struggled to fit even my car.

The crook of my other arm was feeling distinctly uncomfortable. I flexed the elbow, but that didn't relieve the situation. My eyes took in the cannula stuck in my arm, followed the plastic tubing up to an almost empty IV bag hanging from a makeshift stand.

What the fuck?

Nope.

I didn't care what that was, I wanted it out now. I didn't want a bar of it. Jesus, what if it was something to induce the baby? No matter what the hell happened, there was no fucking way she was going to get her hands on my child.

I pushed myself up to a sitting position, rode out the rush of giddiness and nausea, and set to unlocking the tubing from the end of the port. At least I knew there was nothing going into me now. But that wasn't enough. I started pulling back the tape holding the cannula in place, then once it was freed, took a deep breath and yanked the whole damn thing out of my vein and threw it across the room. Blood immediately started seeping from the site, so I pressed down on it hard, trying to stem the flow.

How could I have gotten it so wrong? When my mind had explored the idea of health professionals, and then narrowed it down to midwives, it had never even occurred to me to consider Naomi. I trusted her. How could I have been so bloody naive? How did I miss the signs?

My mind tried to replay our conversations over the last six months, trying to recall anything that could have set me on the right path, if I'd only noticed. I had vague recollections of her talking about her daughter, that she'd been quite unwell, but I had thought she meant in a here-and-now, acute sense, rather than a long-term sense, and I certainly hadn't thought it was critical.

How long had I been here?

I checked my watch, its bright display pushing back against the gloom. Fuck, it was after nine. I'd been out for that long? That would explain why I felt like I'd been hit by a bus. Surely Paul would know something was wrong by now? He must have tried to ring. I patted my pants pocket for my phone. Of course it wasn't there, that would have been the first thing she took off me.

Bugger.

There had to be a way out of here. I rolled myself onto my hands and knees, and slowly got up to my feet. I made my way to the side door, skirting around the lawn mower, my bare feet protesting against the cold, hard concrete floor. My hand gripped the door handle and turned it.

Locked.

Fuck.

I moved further down to the end of the garage. The double doors were of the old, wooden variety, giving a hint as to the vintage of the building. They sagged on their hinges and didn't look exactly square, so it was no surprise when I tugged at them that they didn't budge.

I was a prisoner.

Holy fuck.

CHAPTER 63

My wrist vibrated with an incoming call. The shock of it jarred me like a startled baby. Once I got control back of my limbs, I checked to see who it was.

Thank Christ, it was Paul.

Naomi might have removed my phone from my pocket, but she hadn't thought about my smart watch. Also, she can't have thought to power off the phone, because to be able to connect up it had to be on and somewhere close. I was in a garage, so there had to be a house nearby. This could be my only chance, I had to answer that call. I'd never done it from my watch before so was a mess of fumbling fingers as I desperately tried to hit the little green phone symbol without accidentally hanging up.

'Paul?'

'Where are you?' he asked. The sound was really crackly, but even with that I could hear the anxiety in his voice. That was the last thing I needed to hear right now. I needed calm Paul. I needed solid Paul. I did not need edging-on-being-freaked-out Paul.

My own panic levels leapt accordingly.

'Are you okay? Is the baby okay?'

'I don't know,' I said.

'What do you mean you don't know?'

'I mean I think I'm okay and the baby's okay, but I have no idea where I am. Last thing I remember was being at home with Naomi while she did our ante-natal check. She did all the usuals then said she was going to take some bloods, so I guess she injected something in rather than drawing blood out, because next thing I knew I woke up here.' My voice cracked a little. 'And I have no idea where here is.'

'You didn't notice her inject you with something?'

'Well fuck, just blame the victim, I wasn't exactly looking at the time. Unlike you, I don't always like to watch needles being stuck in me, sorry.'

'Sorry,' Paul said. 'I'm just thinking out loud, trying to get my head around this.' I knew he was, but I couldn't help the panic snappies.

'It wasn't Miriam. I was wrong.' My voice choked up as I made that admission. It wasn't that often that I was wrong, but in the past the ramifications hadn't been this monumental.

'Hey, look, all of the evidence pointed to her, none of us even re-motely suspected Naomi. Don't beat yourself up. You've got to think, okay. Stay with me now.'

'Okay.'

'Describe where you are.'

'I'm in an old garage, like almost-falling-over old. It's small, the only window is high and has bars on it.' I lumbered up from where I'd been sitting in the far corner, facing the door and moved around the space, talking as I went. 'The doors are locked. I'm locked in.'

'Fuck,' he said. 'What kind of doors?'

'Solid wooden ones, no windows.'

'Did you bang on it, see if anyone came?'

I had considered it, and almost did try the ole hammer-and-scream combo, but given I'd been brought here drugged out of my tree, it didn't feel like the wise thing to do. 'I've been trying not to draw at-tention to myself.'

'Yeah, probably a good call. Is there any way you can barricade yourself in from that side? Keep her out? You can't let her get near you, Sam. You can't let her get near you or the baby.'

'I know.' My hands dropped down and cradled my belly and its precious cargo.

I'd had a good scout around earlier, using the light from my watch to illuminate the way. The shelving was all fixed to the walls, but some cupboards were free standing and looked like they had been recycled from an old kitchen. There were a number of cardboard boxes, as well as drop sheets and an array of old paint cans. An unseaworthy wooden dingy leaned against the back wall, but I didn't know if I could drag that. There was the lawn mower; that could be tipped on its side and wedged with some of the generalised crap in here. I could go for the friction and bulk approach in the absence of weight.

'I'll give it a try.'

'Anything else that can narrow down where you are? What can you hear?'

'I can hear the sea. Quite loud, like crashing waves. I haven't heard any cars.'

'Great, the sea narrows it down. I know this line is pretty dodgy, which means your signal isn't great, so you're probably somewhere remote. Listen, I want you to try something. I've got an idea to figure out where you are.'

Hell, I'd try anything right now.

'Yeah, fire away?'

'I want you to go to the Google Maps app on your phone and see if it comes up with the magic blue dot with your location.'

'I'm not on the phone – she took it. I'm using my watch.'

'Okay, that makes sense. Your watch should have the app too.'

Jesus, of course, why hadn't I thought of that? Just then a dragging wave of pain burned across my belly. I breathed out long and hard, hoping like hell that it was just Braxton Hicks, and that Bubs had not decided that this was the opportune moment to make an early entrance into the world. Given the presence of the IV line, and the circumstances, it was a pretty deluded hope. This baby had to hold off until help arrived.

'You okay?'

'Yeah,' I lied. 'Just trying to get comfortable. Give me a moment.' I looked at the display on the watch and tried swiping to another app. Nothing happened. I realised the only way to check was to end the call.

'Fuck.'

'Fuck?'

'Fuck. Nothing, can't do that without ending the call, and given how dodgy this line is, I don't want to risk that.' The sense of deflation was almost overwhelming. I leaned back against the wall and slid down to a sitting position. He must have heard it in my voice.

'Bugger, I knew it couldn't be that simple, but then, it never is with us, eh?' We both had a little chuckle at that understatement. He knew the power of a laugh. 'We can do a broad trace on the phone if the signal is strong enough. I can't believe they left it turned on. We got lucky there.'

I would take any bit of luck I could get. I just desperately hoped it wouldn't run out.

'Look, Sam, I'm going to try something else, but before I do I have a small confession to make.'

'I don't know that this is the best time for big reveals,' I said. 'In the movies people only say that when they think all hope is gone.'

'Well, this has to do with the giving hope thing, kind of.'

His uncertainly had me wondering what the hell was coming. 'Okay then, confess away.'

'Well, it has to do with your phone.'

'What about my phone?'

'I, um,' he paused, groping for the words before blurting them out. 'I set up my phone so I could track yours.'

'Sorry? What? You've been tracking me with your phone? Are you fucking kidding me?' Why the hell would he do that? Didn't he trust me? Did he think I was having an affair or something stupid? Was he such a control freak he had to know where I was at all times?

'I've never used it, I promise. I've never checked out where you are, I'm not that creepy, stalkery guy, but I set it up ages ago, just as a safety precaution. The job has put you in quite a bit of danger in the past, and it seemed like a simple insurance policy, just in case, one day...'

Well, this was certainly 'one day' and while a part of me was pissed off beyond words, another part of me was screaming with relief.

'When I get out of here you and I are going to have to have a wee chat about boundaries. That is completely unacceptable.'

'I know, I know, and I'm sorry, but this is the exact kind of situation I'd thought of when I did it, well, not the exact kind of situation, but you know what I mean.'

'Well quit fucking backpedalling and arse-covering and try it then.'

'Hang on a tick.'

The wait was agonising. My ears strained for any sound outside the room, any indication she was coming back, but all I could hear was the buzzing in my own head.

'I'm sorry Sam, it didn't work. Your signal must be too weak where you are, but tell you what I'm going to do: we're going to get the team out looking for every possible known property or business that Naomi or her husband have that is coastal and could have the kind of garage you're describing. Sounds like it could be a holiday home. And I'm going to get in the car and drive around, see if my phone picks yours up properly somewhere. I will find you Sam, I promise you that. You barricade yourself in there and you keep yourself, and our baby girl, safe. I'm coming for you.'

I fought back the tidal wave of fear and emotion that threatened to engulf me. I knew he would move heaven and earth, that he would not stop until he found us, but would he get here in time? Would he get here before she came back?

I put my head towards my knees and breathed out hard again, as another wave washed across my belly.

'Paul?' I said, trying not to grit my teeth, keep it relaxed, keep it relaxed, breathe through it. 'You might want to hurry with that.'

'Are they coming back?'

My radar immediately went up, but no, I couldn't detect any footfalls.

'No.'

'What then?'

'I'm in labour.'

'Fuck.'

CHAPTER 64

It had to happen, and even though I knew this moment was coming, the sound of footfalls crunching across a path set my heart racing.

I heard a knock on the door – as if she still needed to be polite – and then the sound of the handle turning. The door didn't budge. I'd managed to find an old wooden chair under some tarpaulins and had wedged that under the handle. I'd also put a wooden crate full of paint tins on top of the seat. Plan C was for me to sit on it and add even more weight.

'Sam?' The handle rattled again. 'Sam, let me in.'

I held my breath, which was totally absurd.

'Sam, I know you're there. You have to let me in.'

'Fuck off.'

'I promise I won't hurt you, just let me in.'

'Is that what you said to Aleisha Newman before you cut her open like a fucking butcher?'

The only sound was the crashing of the waves.

'I trusted you. I thought you were supposed help bring life into the world, not steal it, not destroy it. She did not deserve to die like that.'

'I didn't mean for it to happen that way, you have to believe me. It was an accident.'

'What do you mean, it was an accident? You accidentally gave her a fucking caesarean in the back of an alley, and accidentally forgot to sew her up.'

'It wasn't like that. I just wanted to ask her to reconsider helping us and giving us some cord blood and the sample when she gave birth, that was all we wanted, all we needed. But she wouldn't. Not even when I explained – not even when I told her it wouldn't hurt her or her baby, but it could save our Ruby.'

'So you killed her?' The question ended in a groan as another contraction built and I had to release the breath as it surged across.

'No, that's not what happened.' The response was emphatic. 'How close are they?'

The contractions were too bloody close, but I wasn't about to tell her that.

'Fuck...'

When I could speak again I completed the sentence.

'...off.'

'You need my help, Sam. You can't just stay locked up in there forever.'

'It doesn't need forever, they're on their way, you know. Paul and the police, they're coming for me.' He had to be. Despite not calling back, despite my watch going into low-battery mode and conking out, I knew he'd move heaven and earth to find me. That signal we'd had would be enough. He'd find a way, I knew he would.

'Even if they are, you need me now.'

'Why – so you can butcher me too?'

'Look, Sam, I never meant for that to happen. Like I said, it was an accident. I was trying to get her to understand, to agree to arranging the samples when her baby was born, but she just wouldn't see it, she wouldn't do it. She thought I was insane and told me to go away, and we argued. And in the heat of the moment I pushed her. That's all I did – I pushed her, and not even that hard, but she fell. She tripped and fell backward, and oh my God, the noise when she hit her head, I'll never forget that sound. It was a crack, it was so loud, and I could see straight away she was in serious trouble.'

'Still doesn't explain why you killed her.'

'I didn't mean to kill her. I panicked. She was fitting, having seizures, and I thought she was going to die. I was so sure she was going to die, Sam. And if she died, that baby would die, and I couldn't let that happen. I had to do something.'

'Well, why didn't you just call a fucking ambulance, like any sane person would?'

'It would take too long. They would be too late.'

'Haven't you heard of CP fucking R.' The R sound gave way into another guttural groan as the next round of pain hit me.

'I wasn't thinking. I acted on instinct. All I was trying to do was save the baby. I promise you, that was all I was trying to do.'

'Because that baby had something you wanted.'

She was silent for a while, but when she did speak her voice was thick with the depth of her pain.

'You don't know what it's like to watch your child get sick. You don't know what it's like to hear day after day there's nothing more we can do, until one day they give you a glimmer of hope, some-thing new that might work, a new treatment, only to have it dashed because they can't find a donor. And in the meantime you have to sit and watch her fail, watch that beautiful, happy, smiling girl fade before your eyes. So you start looking yourself. You start looking for that potential match. You do what it takes. And then one day, like a miracle, it's there, that one in a thousand. And it's so close, Sam, so very, very close, but they say no. They say no to saving the life of your child. Can you even begin to imagine how that feels?'

I couldn't. I hadn't even met this little one yet, but I felt the inten-sity of that raw kind of love. What would it be like when you really got to know that little person, that extension of you?

'I hope to God, Sam, that you never have to experience that pain. It kills you.'

'That still doesn't justify what you did.'

'I know. And believe me, I feel like some kind of a monster, and I have to live with that. You know what the most awful thing is? It didn't work. With everything that happened in the moment, I was too late. I didn't get the sample in time. It was all for nothing.'

Aleisha Newman had died for nothing. Well, not entirely nothing. Her daughter was alive, Hope was alive, but for Naomi and her husband it was all for nought.

The next contraction left me buckling. I dropped from leaning over the chair, onto hands and knees, rocking, rocking, trying to rock and breathe the pain away.

It was a while before I could speak, and by now my anger was transforming into a mixture of fear and almost pity for her – for the situation she was in, and the situation she had got herself into.

'Why am I here, Naomi?' I said quietly. 'You know those test results were fake, planted on my records. So why am I here?'

'The amnio results were fake, but I knew from other tests that you were close, so close to being a match. You were almost another one in a thousand, which meant your child, and that blood could be the match we were looking for.' Oh my God, of course. She would have been screening me from the get-go too – and every other woman under her care – hoping for that elusive match. I'd been none the wiser that another test had been added to the list of the routine ones. What was an extra vial in the row of tubes that she filled with my blood? Another thought flitted into my mind: was Michael in on it too? Had he been intercepting results as they went through the lab? Checking the women that weren't under his wife's care? Were they a team? He had to be. They would have had Aleisha's baby in their house – he had to know what was going on. How could they be so bloody good at lying?

Another wave crashed across my uterus. Jesus Christ, not now. This was not the time or the place to make your appearance, baby girl.

'Sam, I just need to get that blood, that blood from the umbilical cord, and a sample. That's all I want. I'm not going to hurt you, I promise. It won't hurt either of you.'

'Why didn't you just bloody ask? You didn't have to do this.'

'If I asked, you'd know. You'd figure out the connection between me and you and her, and then there would be no chance – no chance of saving Ruby.'

'So you kidnapped me? You thought this was the answer? Just take it anyway? You've made it a thousand times worse. You're not going to get away with this, you know that, don't you?'

'Sam, I know, and I don't care anymore. I don't care if I go to jail. I don't care if they lock me up and throw away the key. I just want my girl – my precious baby girl – to have a chance at life. I want her to live more than anything else in the world.'

I could hear her gasps as she broke down on the other side of the door.

'That can only happen with your help. Or else she is going to die. You're her only hope.'

Her hand banging against door.

'Please, Sam, please.'

Hand banging in time with her sobs.

'Please.'

I closed my eyes and took a deep breath.

Jesus, what to do?

There was only one thing I could do, and still live with myself.

A wave of fear and apprehension shook me, but I took another deep breath and dragged the chair from the door.

CHAPTER 65

We stood there staring at each other, the lantern Naomi held illuminating the grief, anguish and uncertainty etched on her face, and no doubt the fear and pain on mine.

'Sam, I'm so sorry, I never...'

Another wave swept my body and the force of it dropped me to my hands and knees, the groan that escaped my mouth as unstoppable as the tide.

She reached forward to me then, and I was in no position to resist. I had no choice but to trust her, to trust that after everything that had happened she would do the right thing, the right thing by me and this baby.

'Okay, Sam, how close? How close are the contractions? You have to let me help you. Don't be afraid, I'm not going to hurt you, I promise.'

Is that what she said to Aleisha Newman?

'They. Don't. Really. Stop,' I managed to get out between breaths, my eyes squeezed shut.

'I'm going to need to take a look and see where you're at. When this contraction eases, we'll get you undressed.' I felt her firm, circular motions rubbing the small of my back, and I focussed on that sensation, followed the movement. Anything to take my mind away from the force of the pain.

It finally eased off enough for me to get back up off my hands. I sat back on my heels, trying to catch my breath, opened my eyes to take in the sight of Naomi, her bag with the sample kit on top, her tentative, almost fearful, expression, and I realised in that moment we both had everything to lose here, and we had to trust each other. I gave her a tight smile and a nod, and let her assist me as I worked to remove my pants – felt the conflict of emotions: terrified and repulsed by what this woman had done, saddened by the awful set of circumstances that had driven her to do it, but grateful and relieved that she was here for me, that I was not going to have to do this alone.

Another wave forced me forward again, onto my hands and knees, the ferocity of it overwhelming my senses, the blood thrumming in my ears so I could barely hear Naomi telling me this baby was coming, and it was coming right now.

Oh, Jesus, everything felt so heavy, the dragging, the tightness, and I had to push, but I was scared to push, because, Christ Almighty, it hurt like fuck, but my body took over, it took the matter entirely out of my hands, and I felt every part of my being bear down, felt that burn, that incredible burning as my baby's head crowned, that impossible searing sensation. Through the wall of my groans I heard Naomi's words, her strong, calm words:

'Sam, I need you to pause now. Stop pushing. I need you to pant for me.'

I followed those words, anchored myself to them as I felt her hands check, adjust.

'Okay, Sam, one more big push, you can do this.'

I took a deep breath and bore down with all of my might, and all of the agony and terror of the last few hours burst out of me in a roar that didn't end until I felt that exquisite release, felt my baby girl freed from my body, felt the glorious liberation from pain.

'I've got her, Sam. She's beautiful. She's safe. You're safe.'

The sound of hiccoughy cries filled my heart with an overwhelming joy and sense of protectiveness, and I sat back down onto my heels and rolled around to see her.

I felt a momentary pang of dread as I watched Naomi clamp the cord, take that precious sample and do what needed to be done, but it became clear that there was no longer any need to be afraid, that for her it was over. With great care, she wrapped my daughter in a cloth and brought her to me.

'Thank you,' she said, tears now streaming down her face. 'Thank you so very much.'

I reached out and took that precious bundle, marvelled at that tiny face, at the grave, dark eyes that looked to mine.

I cradled that little girl to my heart and swore I would never let her go.

EPILOGUE

'Well, she looks like you.'

'She looks like a prune.'

'Like I said, she looks like you.'

I would have thumped him, but right this moment my arms were wrapped around the tiny little bundle sleeping on my chest. The ambulance ride into Dunedin from Shag Point was a twisty and windy one, so Paul sat right beside us and the gurney we were securely strapped into, poised to stop any sudden sideways movement.

'You know, you left it a bit late to arrive, missed the big moment. Should have known you'd do anything to avoid being at the birth. Bloody squeamish males.'

'Ah, you see straight through me.' He reached over again and gently stroked her cheek, a look of wonderment on his face. 'Did my best, but, you know, stuff gets in the way, like kidnappers, murderers, that sort of thing.'

'I'll let you off just this once. You'll have no excuses next time.'

'There'll be a next time?'

'If you play your cards right.'

'I might be getting my nails done that day.'

We shared a smile and went back to our new favourite sport, staring at this tiny creature with a mix of adoration, incredulity and mild terror.

'Don't ever do that again, promise me,' he said.

I could have bit back, saying it was out of my control, I didn't see it coming, but that wasn't what either of us needed right now. I knew what he was trying to say, even if he put it badly.

I just looked at him and shook my head.

'I have never been so scared in my life.'

'Me neither,' I said.

We sat on that for a while.

'How did you find me?'

'We were able to get a rough location from your phone signal, enough to know it was coming from around Shag Point. Then we searched the rates information for every house there until we found Naomi and her husband as the owners. Felt like it took forever.'

'I knew you'd come.'

This time it was my cheek he reached out and caressed.

'Oh, and just so you know, your mum rang me in the middle of everything, said something about knitting, and that it was important she talk with you, but you weren't answering your phone.'

'Ha,' I laughed. 'The old girl came through. What did you tell her?'

'I said I was a bit tied up right now, and that you were out but that I'd get you to give her a ring as soon as you were free.'

'You lied to my mother?'

'It was easier than telling the truth.'

'You're learning.'

The light-hearted banter was a relief after the intensity of everything that had happened, but it was still skirting around the elephant in the ambulance. I knew I had to address it, and it needed to be now if I was to follow through with a promise.

'Paul,' I said. 'The samples.'

He sighed then. 'I've got them here, the ambulance guy has put them in a chilly-bin.'

Naomi had waited quietly for the police to arrive and had given herself up. But in the bustle and madness of the aftermath I had lost track of where the samples had got to.

'Thank you.'

I thought about how I was going to word the next bit.

'Paul, it's not just my call on what happens next. You have to be okay with it too, give your consent.'

He sat there, elbows on knees, looking at the floor, rubbing his hands together.

'After everything that happened, what she did to Aleisha Newman, what she did to you, you let her in? You did that?'

The scene replayed in my head, the extremes of emotions that surged within me, and I couldn't suppress the shudder.

'I put myself in her shoes.'

After a minute, he finally looked back up at me, reached out and put his hand over mine.

'You did the right thing.'

I finally let myself cry.

ACKNOWLEDGEMENTS

This novel felt like it had the gestation period of an elephant – actually it was longer, so immense gratitude to those who carried me along through often difficult and turbulent times.

Huge thanks to my amazing publisher and friend Karen Sullivan for her continued support and faith in my work, and to her incredible team at Orenda Books: West Camel for his thoughtful editing, and Cole Sullivan and Anne Cater for their hard work in promoting my work so it can find its audience.

Craig Sisterson, you are New Zealand writers' greatest cheerleader. Thank you for your unwavering flying of the flag and being my number-one fan. Good on ya, mate.

Thank you to the incredible writing and reading community out there. Your warmth and enthusiasm makes all of the hard work worthwhile. Bless ya!

Support comes from so many places, and I am so grateful for my fabulous work team at the Va'a o Tautai – Centre for Pacific Health at the University of Otago. You guys rock.

In writing crime fiction there are a number of people you call on to make sure you haven't completely stuffed up the facts. My immense thanks to Jan and David Checketts, Dom Flatley and Erolia Rooney for fielding with such good grace and humour my weird questions. All stuff-ups are completely my own.

Sometimes you need help wrangling the software, so thank you to Rachel Amphlett for showing me the ins and outs of Scrivener. I'm getting better at it!

This novel was underpinned by a profound sense of grief. In the course of writing it I lost so many loved ones. It is dedicated to the ones we lost: my mum, Heather, my mother-in-law, Sue, my brother Norman, my brother Vernon and my sister Laura. By its very topic and nature it also brought back to me thoughts for my four babies lost to miscarriage. Completing this work felt like a loving acknowledgement of all of these lives and hope for the future.

Family is so incredibly important, and I give thanks for the continued support and belief of my husband, Glenn, and my two fabulous sons, Riley and Corey. Your gentle trolling and digs at my procrastination kept me on the path ... mostly.

Thanks to the anonymous alleyway poet, whose haiku made me stand and marvel.

And to my writing companion, Louis the cat, whose snoring has been the soundtrack to this work.